THE AUTOBIOGRAPHY OF JENNY X

THE AUTOBIOGRAPHY OF JENNY X

Lisa Dierbeck

Mischief + Mayhem
in association with

OR Books
New York

Published by Mischief + Mayhem
In association with OR Books, New York.

Visit our websites at OR Books: www.orbooks.com and
Mischief+Mayhem www.MischiefandMayhemBooks.com

First printing 2010.

Library of Congress Cataloging in Publication Data:
A catalog record for this book is available from the Library of Congress

British Library Cataloging in Publication Data:
A catalog record for this book is available from the British Library

ISBN Paperback 978-1-935928-20-1
ISBN E-book 978-1-935928-19-5

Typeset by Wordstop

Printed by BookMobile, USA

10 9 8 7 6 5 4 3 2 1

For my mother, Janet Dierbeck

PART ONE:

Dan and Nadia

The Accusation

"Nadia, are you cheating on me?" Dan asked on a Saturday night. Wearing only his wristwatch and his underwear, he perched on the edge of the sofa in their hotel suite. He spoke dispassionately, as if wondering whether Nadia had borrowed his umbrella without asking him.

"What are you talking about?" Nadia plucked at the sash of her robe. In one hand, she clasped a compact, decorated with inlaid mother-of-pearl and onyx. She stared down at the black and white design framing her reflection. Her face was flushed. Inside the small mirror, her mouth had formed an "o."

"You heard what I said. I asked you a question. Are you seeing someone else?"

Listening to his voice, one would never guess that he might be angry or upset. This was a useful skill for delivering bad news to the dying, Nadia supposed. Dan had learned his neutral, uninflected tone in medical school.

"Of course not." She clicked the compact closed.

"Sure about that, Nadia? Or do you need some time to think about it?" He was leaning down, clipping his toenails, his feet planted firmly on the June issue of *American Oncology*. The sound of his stainless steel nail clippers rose in volume, an irregular *snip-snap*...

snap snip, loud and grating. All other noises, she noticed, were gradually disappearing.

Nadia slipped a fingernail between the teeth of her comb. She ran the ball of her index finger along the thin strips of plastic, playing them like strings on a harp. She discerned the faint hum of a musical chord.

"You stood me up," Dan said. "We waited for you for hours. You didn't bother to call me. You never offered an explanation. You just expected me to put up with your vanishing."

"Do we have to go over it and over it?" said Nadia, though they'd never spoken about what had happened. "That was weeks ago." She heard irritability in her voice, self-righteous in her claim to fidelity.

"I was worried about you. I still am."

Nadia considered this, anxiously. Her palms were damp, as they'd been last Sunday afternoon, when she'd tried to help her son with his eighth-grade chemistry take-home exam. The correct answer came to her but she couldn't speak. For some reason, she couldn't articulate the simple, necessary statement, "I'm sorry." She'd been dumb enough to think that that evening had been quietly forgotten. Instead, it seemed, Dan had been studying Nadia, for two months now, like a difficult math equation.

She squeezed a tube of makeup and began to daub drops of glittering white liquid in the hollows of her eyes. *Radiance*, it said, in gold letters, on the side of the tube. The cream promised to eliminate wrinkles and dark circles. One segment of Nadia's mind gave attentive study to her cosmetics' application. The rest of her thoughts fled, in alarm, to Christopher Benedict, the senator's son. He lived in a six-by-nine foot cement cell in Triton, New York, just two hours away from the Canadian border. There were three categories of federal penitentiary, Nadia had learned. Christopher's was "supermax." Though this sounded to Nadia like a brand of feminine protection, it meant that he was confined behind bars twenty-three hours a day, with the highest degree of security and the largest number of guards, in solitary confinement.

Dan reached over to the bedside table and opened a bottle of mineral water. With infuriating poise, he poured himself a glassful. "You frightened us. I almost called the police."

"What about the hours *you* keep? You fall asleep on the couch in your office and don't get home till dawn."

"The only times I've done that," said Dan, gravely, "Have been *medical* emergencies." "Medical," in Dan's mouth, sounded like "The Virgin Mother." It was, for Dan, a holy word.

"You've got a double standard," said Nadia. "Do you know how many times I wake up in the middle of the night wondering where you are?"

"I work in a hospital. What the hell is your excuse?" Even "hell" sounded respectful when it came from Dan. She'd often thought that nothing was real to him except for cancer cells. Dan could probably tolerate a straying wife. What threw him into a rage was the mulishness of other oncologists who resisted his innovations, and other physicians' incompetence. If she were to say, now, Yes, I've had an extramarital affair, he'd probably just take out his laboratory notebook and start taking notes. But Nadia was more complicated than that. She'd deceived him so thoroughly he'd never forgive her for it. It was imperative that he never find out.

"I'm waiting, Nadia. Are you going to tell me?"

Nadia tossed her comb down on the vanity. "It's all so simple for you, isn't it? You talk to me like you're the head of everything, running your department. You want to reduce error and improve efficiency, do you? Well, this is a marriage, not a hospital, and I'm not one of your brown-nosing lab assistants." She stopped. Her comb had ricocheted off the wall, landing in a tray of mints, displacing one. The piece of candy had collided against the ashtray before coming to rest beside a matchbox. It was embossed with the words: "The

Parallel Club * Berlin * London * Moscow * Munich * New York * Paris * Rome."

"You make it difficult at this point," said Dan.

Nadia blinked. Her eyes stung. She reached out for the curtains. Her hands became enmeshed in layers of sheer fabric before she was able to make contact with the window. It got stuck when she pushed it open. She shoved. It wouldn't budge. She brought her forehead close, resting against the cool glass pane. The sidewalk lay smooth and flat below.

Across the street from their hotel, the grounds of the Carnegie Mansion were abloom with roses—lit up by lights, kept behind iron gates. Nadia heard a clarinet playing and the clatter of dishes being cleared away. They'd missed the cocktail hour. The Auction for Mercy was about to begin in the ground-floor ballroom. They'd have to attend; it was expected of them. Dan never would never break down, lose his head, crumble. A driven, competitive man, he'd excelled in three careers at once, as a research scientist, an oncologist and a surgeon. Dan kept calm under pressure. It was this trait of level-headed rationality which had drawn Nadia to him. Dan, people said, was the kind of rocklike man one ought to stand next to in a fire. That was just what Nadia had done when she'd been in trouble once. She'd singled him out for his kindness, his reliability and his sense of perspective. And then she'd pursued Dan tirelessly. But there was something else in him, withdrawn and passive. Nadia had become attuned to it. Now, as she watched him adjust his shirt cuffs, just so, he seemed indifferent.

"It was your birthday. I'd made that reservation months in advance," Dan said, reviewing the events of that terrible day, in April, when Nadia had almost gotten caught. "Nadia, please. All I do is… all I ever do is…try to…"

Nadia sat bolt upright in her chair. In all their years of marriage, she'd only once seen him weep. But the moment passed. It had just lasted an instant.

Dan inserted a cufflink through the buttonhole of his sleeve. He started tucking the tails of his white smocked shirt into his freshly pressed tuxedo pants. "I've spent my life," he said, and didn't conclude the thought.

He had not spent his life trying to make Nadia happy. She'd never been at the center. He expended his best energies on ministering to the ill, the phantoms, wresting them from death, restoring them, nursing them along, playing savior to them. His patients were his damsels in distress. Cancer was his enemy. The drama that absorbed him had left Nadia on the periphery.

Nadia's breathing slowed, and she felt immobile, helpless, like an unconscious body laid out on an operating table. A breeze blew across her face, but she still wasn't getting enough air. She wondered if he could hear her stealthily gasping for breath. She imagined her lungs as a pair of butterfly wings. They seemed not to be functioning.

"I'd really like to understand you, Nadia," said Dan. "Nadia Tatiana Larina." He spoke, slowly, thoughtfully, as if recalling the name of an old college roommate. "Nadia Larina, the woman who forgot her own birthday."

Nadia exhaled through her nostrils, and kept on doing this, concentrating only on the exhalation. She ran a brush through her hair and stole a glance at Dan. She wondered if anything real belonged to her.

Her husband's face gave away nothing. Round-cheeked and olive-skinned, he had the disorderly hair of an orchestra conductor; his thick eyebrows and black beard gave him a ferocious, even sinister appearance. He rarely lost his cool, however, thanks to his training. Dan was a disciplined and honorable man. He kept his equilibrium by holding his feelings in check.

Dan pulled a sock up over the shapely petite calves that had never seemed sturdy enough to support all 200 pounds of him. It was a black dress sock with silver stitching at the toe. The specific appearance of this sock took on an ominous intensity, a hidden significance, in the manner of observations made for the last time. In January, Nadia had ordered ten pairs of these socks. It was the day that Dan and the kids had gone snowboarding in the Catskills while Nadia had holed up in the attic. She'd listened to *Madame Butterfly* while Blondie had snorted at her feet, chewing a rubber toy shaped like a pretzel, holding her paw over it to keep it firmly in place, making it squeak and whistle, lending a comedic syncopated rhythm to Puccini's opera. Nadia could recall every detail of that leisurely Sunday afternoon, which had been unremarkable to her at the time. The gray ribbon of the river had wound past the hill outside her window, while her fountain pen had scratched across the catalogue order form. The space heater that warmed Nadia's legs had hummed in its corner. Blondie had growled, hearing an intruder, a black squirrel that had jumped on the roof from the oak tree and had scrambled towards their chimney. Nadia had glanced up to see the photograph she'd taken of Christopher. It made her hold her breath, as if the senator's son weren't a prison inmate, but a protean being, a shaman who could inhabit the leaves, the squirrel, the sky, the photograph, as he wished, occupying Nadia's thoughts, making a miraculous surprise appearance. A visitation.

She'd been transfixed by the angular face, the arrogant expression, the intent black eyes that took in more than they gave away. When she'd taken that photograph of Christopher, she'd opened the aperture too wide, let the film become overexposed. But she'd caught the glint of mischief in his gaze. As the leader of the Bond Street Aktionists, he'd modeled his group after a band of Viennese artists. Christopher believed in breaking the law.

Dan was using a shoehorn to wedge his foot into his stiff black leather oxford. "Did you know the other physicians at Mercy are under the delusion I'm intelligent? They say it's just a matter of time before I get the prize." He glanced up at her, neutral, with that clear scientific vision that judged nothing, that missed nothing.

Here was a fleeting chance for reconciliation, Nadia's cue to proclaim: "Yes, Dan, you deserve the Nobel Prize in medicine." Every year, Dan's colleagues placed bets on scientists like gamblers at a racetrack. Dan, though hidden away in an unprepossessing hospital, was favored to win. Even on their first date, he'd told her, "Before I'm fifty, I'm going to win a Nobel." Nadia had been shocked by his egotism, but had soon learned that such talk was typical for scientists, whose progress was concrete, dramatic, and measurable. Diseases were eliminated, vaccines invented. People lived, because of Dan's breakthroughs, instead of dying. But Nadia had missed her cue and, instead of praising her husband in the interest of peace, she kept silent.

"I treat patients who haven't got a prayer," he said, dusting off his credentials, as if Nadia needed reminding. "They came to me because they were written off everywhere else. Every other oncologist in the U.S. gives up on these cases as hopeless. Only I..."

"I *know*." She cut him off, impatiently. She didn't like herself for it, but she was jealous of Dan's patients—the time and devotion he lavished upon them. She was envious of Dan's reputation as a pioneer, a maverick who made daring medical advances. It galled Nadia that Dan couldn't confront her honestly tonight without hauling out his accolades, his medals of honor for medical heroism. They had, at some early point in their marriage, begun to engage in a contest. Who was the most significant player in the wider universe? By now, having given up her gig with *National Geographic* to stay close to home for the kids, Nadia had lost. She was a respected photographer, but she wasn't curing anyone of terminal illness. She'd stopped making her annual pilgrimage to the Amazon, so she couldn't credit herself with trying to save the rain forest. Her photos of monkeys and tree frogs no longer appeared on magazine covers.

"I wonder," Dan said, "if we even know each other."

"We've had three kids together." Nadia twisted a strand of her hair and plunged a hairpin through it; the metal scraped her scalp.

"We have." He gazed into her eyes, steady, searching.

"I don't know what you're asking."

"Tell me who he is. The man on your wall. He's everywhere. You plastered his face all over Red Barn."

"Red Barn is private. You promised me that."

"Nadia, you've been painting his portrait since we moved in. Ever since we bought our place in Riverbend."

"*We* didn't buy anything," Nadia snapped, unpleasantly. "*I* bought the house, not you. When I met you…" she began, and then regretted it. How clumsy. She had actually been going to say: When I met you, you had nothing.

"You've got his portrait around so you can look at him. Is he your boyfriend?"

"You're not allowed inside my studio, Dan. That's the rule. You spied on me."

"God only knows what you do in there all day." He was unpacking his suitcase. He took out his leather travel case and his neatly folded undershirts and set them down on the bedspread, digging deeper into the bag. "I hope it's painting, Nadia. Honestly."

She turned her back on him so he couldn't see her face. She made a grab for the notepad on the desk, simply because she needed something to occupy her hands. The thin, raised letters at the top of the paper spelled out, "1050 Fifth Avenue." Senator Benedict had owned a condominium less than ten blocks away from this building. Nadia had been inside the Parallel Club more than once before.

"Nadia." He removed a large padded envelope from his suitcase.

As soon as Nadia saw it, she knew.

Dan crossed the room with a determined gait and placed the package on the vanity in front of her. It was addressed in scrawling green capital letters "TO: JENNY X." In a much neater hand, in crisp black script, someone had written: "c/o Mrs. Nadia Larina Orsini." The upper left hand corner of the package wasn't handwritten, but printed, and the return address was: "U.S. penitentiary, USP Triton, P.O. Box 300, Triton, New York, 18472."

"I've been intercepting these letters for weeks," said Dan.

"You intercepted letters." The words had lost their meaning.

"They're intended for a fugitive with no last name. A woman you've been in contact with."

Nadia bit the inside of her cheeks to keep her face from revealing what she felt.

"When I found the first letter, I marked it 'no such address, please return.' And then, one day, Nadia. One day when I came home early and you weren't there. I opened one."

In the center of the envelope was a mysterious bump. Nadia withdrew her hand, fast, as if the package from prison might explode.

Solitary Confinement

Christopher was waiting outside a narrow, messy office in Unit C. The room was not much bigger than Christopher's cell, and not much better, except it was one notch closer to the Outside. The shrink had an old metal desk in there, a sign that said "Nelson Feith, C.S.W.," and a pair of beat up wooden chairs. He'd hung artwork on his walls, from the art therapy sessions. These pastel-hued watercolors were pieces of shit done by morons. Only a bright yellow cornflower caught Christopher's eye, and he stared at it while Nelson finished talking to Little John, an ordinary-looking man who, forty years earlier, had poisoned his younger sister and both his parents. Famous and feared, Little John had been employed by the Mafia for twenty-eight years as a hit man. Little John was about to get out.

As Little John left Nelson's office, he passed Christopher in the corridor. His leathery old face crinkled. He gave Christopher a wink. Little John, supposedly, had been "rehabilitated."

Christopher thought that was a load of horseshit.

"You splitting, Little John?" said Christopher, casually. One unwritten rule at Triton was never to express jubilation about a man's departure. That would be to admit that the prisoners, trapped here, were abject. No one *said* they wanted to leave Triton. No one, on the other hand, pretended to adore it. So Christopher spoke as if Little

John had just dropped by the penitentiary for a day or two and was now ambling out the door over to the movie theater.

Little John opened his fist, which had been clenched, and showed Christopher something hidden inside it.

"What's that you got?" said Christopher, keeping his voice low. Luis, a guard he was friendly with, was standing two feet away, leaning against the wall, reading a copy of *People*.

"It's for you." Little John smiled benignly. "Hold out your hand and take it."

Years of imprisonment had taught Christopher when to say yes, and when to refuse. He held out both his hands. He had to keep them together because of the chain.

Little John placed a black square object inside Christopher's palm. "It's all in here." He looked deeply into Christopher's eyes. Little John's eyes were olive green, with brown and yellow sparks inside them. They were icy and terrifying.

"Thanks, babe," said Christopher. Never show fear.

Little John, who was five feet tall and came up only to Christopher's shoulder, leaned in close to him. "Stop being such a stubborn ass," he whispered. His breath stank. Everyone's teeth were rotting. Dr. Marlowe, the dentist over at the infirmary, was a wino. He let the men's teeth decay. Then he shot their gums with Novocain and ruthlessly pulled out their bad teeth. Whether or not he'd attended dental school was an open question. His diploma came from an institute of health in Nicaragua. Despite all this, Marlowe's generosity with ether, administered with a free hand in the dentist chair, kept him popular.

Christopher turned away from Little John to avoid the stench of his mouth. "Yeah, well, Little John, take care of yourself out there, hon," said Christopher. He called both guards and prisoners "hon." It made him feel better about himself. He'd called most people "baby" or "babe" or "honey" on the Outside, too. The ability to bestow an endearment: He took this one liberty. "I hear it's weird out there in the world," he told Little John. "So, Old Man, good luck to you."

"You need to learn. To play the U.S. penitentiary game, Christopher," said Little John. "Move for move. Devise the strategy. Are you listening to me, my brother? I'm giving you the best advice I know."

"Okay, sweetheart. Good-bye and thank you."

Little John took off down the hallway, a free man, without even a guard to follow after him.

"That sly fucker," Christopher muttered.

The black box Little John had given him wasn't a box at all. It was a book. When he turned it over he saw it was imprinted with faded white letters that spelled "Holy Bible."

That was one way out. Everybody said so. Attend the daily interfaith study and discussion classes with Brother Bill. Go to Jesus, find religion, get a God. Brother Bill liked the men at Triton. He liked converting them and saving them and praying for them. He had influential friends in the Justice Department. He knew how to work the system. Parole boards desired to hear certain things, and a wise man figured out what those things were. The men who got out had all added the same ten words to their vocabularies.

But Christopher, who'd been at Triton for nearly twenty years, had refused. He'd never committed a crime—not as he defined it—and he would not confess to any wrongdoing.

"A missionary tried to convert me," said Christopher, flinging the toy-sized book onto Nelson's desk. It fell against the base of a steel lamp, its pages fluttering.

"Wow, who could actually read this?" Nelson picked up the Good Book. "This print is microscopic. You'd need a magnifying glass." Nelson was a skinny sixty-year-old in an old sweater and polyester trousers worn to a shine. But his gaze was shrewd. Christopher had known immediately that he was better than the other prison headshrinker, Tom Dunn, had been. Tom Dunn was simple. Nelson was smart. Christopher preferred smart people.

"I'll bet you Little John doesn't ever read the Bible. He pretends," said Christopher. "It seems like he doesn't need the Scriptures anymore, huh? Now that they're setting him free again. Being devout was just a ploy. The perfect prison break plan. He fooled you."

"Well, now that Little John is moving to Montana, he can buy himself his own copy. It was kind of him to pass this edition on to you, don't you think?"

Christopher made a rude noise, blowing air out of his mouth, pressing his tongue against his lips.

"You have every reason to be skeptical," said Nelson. "But sometimes, Christopher, cynicism builds a barrier. Things change in a hurry when you let go of that. Couldn't your pessimism be a defense mechanism?"

"Here we go," said Christopher, maneuvering awkwardly across the room, rattling his ankle chain. The chain was just long enough to let him walk if he took small mincing steps, but he couldn't run. "You don't get the right to pick my brain apart, Nelson. Just because I'm locked up."

"Tell me about the Aktionists," said Nelson, digging inside his file cabinet, where he kept a copy of each inmate's central file. He pulled out a comic book. *Aktion*, it said, in twenty-point type. The cover illustration showed a fat, middle-aged man lying in bed, naked. His S.S. uniform hung on the back of a chair. He had kept his cap on. A girl with cropped blonde hair pointed a rifle at the man's temple. "Senator Benedict is a Nazi Pig," said the crimson words painted on the bedsheet beside him.

Christopher remembered this comic book. He remembered that rifle, an M109 Springfield, semiautomatic. It had been real, and loaded with bullets. He'd drawn his cartoon from life, using the gun, the girl, and the guy (one of his art teachers) as models. Christopher had subscribed to a theory, back then, about art as a transgression, not a painting to be purchased but an "aktion"—a profound visceral experience. He'd followed the Aktion Manifesto until Herr Otto

Muehl, who'd written it, had gone to a jailhouse in Berlin. Otto had screwed things up in general by turning himself in.

"Fuck," said Christopher. "Where'd you find that thing? I did that when I was a *kid.* You investigating me or something?" He reached up to scratch his neck, which itched. A bedbug had bitten him again. He let his hands fall back onto his lap, the steel chain clinking. It was because he'd attacked Edwin Cole, an obnoxious prisoner who'd goaded him, that Christopher's wrists were cuffed and his ankles manacled.

"I'm interested."

"What's the point?" Christopher shrugged.

"When you first got in here, you were serving a sentence for drug trafficking. That was all they had on you. You were supposed to get out in seven years. You keep assaulting folks. So."

"So?"

"So, I'm wondering if you're still leading this extremist political group. From the inside."

"Dude," said Christopher. "The Bond Street Aktionists didn't trigger a national movement or anything. That was smoke and mirrors. It was just some twenty-year-old art student's fantasy."

"Which art student would that be?"

"Duh. Me."

"I'm just curious about your values these days."

Christopher stuck his finger down his throat. His chain jangled. "Gag me, man, Values. It's because you'd use a word like that. That's why I've never wanted to hang around in here and talk to you."

"But you're here today, talking to me, aren't you?" Removing a photograph from his files, he pushed it towards Christopher. It was a black and white glossy, eight inches by ten.

"Oh, the goon squad," said Christopher, sighing. "They can seize my stuff. They can just take away every fucking thing." He looked at the picture for a minute. "That is *my* photograph. I took that with my

Rolleiflex, my own camera. You guys ought to give that real personal shit back to me."

"Who was she?"

"Some girl I went out with. When I used to go out with girls, when I used to live in a house, with other human beings in it. What difference does it make to you?"

Nelson tapped the corner of the photograph against his hairy chin. The sight of this bothered Christopher. He had little that belonged to him, and someone else fondling his stuff incited him. He felt the switch inside him flick on. He imagined wrapping his chain around Nelson's throat and choking him. Naturally, this sweet dream was impossible to realize. He'd need a twelve inch rope to strangle anyone—or, better yet, a three-foot length of fishing line. But he was chained at the wrist and waist. "Don't touch my photo," Christopher said.

Nelson continued to tap the corner of the photograph against his face, bringing it this time to his lips. His eyes never left Christopher's.

It was a test.

"Are you trying, babe, to piss me off?" said Christopher. "Because I have to tell you, darling. It's working."

"You say *babe* and *darling*," said Nelson. "But you mean the opposite."

"That's right. You're a real bright boy, aren't you?"

Nelson handed the photograph over to Christopher, setting it down gently on his knee. The girl in the black and white photo looked up at him.

Christopher's heart did something strange. He'd had one heart attack already, and it had landed him in the infirmary last winter for thirteen weeks. The girl was wearing a thin white dress made transparent in the sun. Her face was wide and her lips were pouted in a kiss. She was wearing false eyelashes and enough eye shadow for a drag queen. A few freckles, peeking out beneath her makeup, were sprinkled across the bridge of her nose.

"Look, I was a radical peace activist," he said. To his embarrassment, a teardrop had formed in the corner of his left eye. He leaned back, as far as he could, looking up at the lighting fixture, a white globe. This electric light, shaped like a sphere, was the closest thing to a full moon that Christopher had seen for the past nineteen years. As he stared at the bulb, his tear rolled backwards along his forehead and into his hairline, tickling him. Nelson would think he'd been perspiring. Sweating was permissible, but not crying.

When he was sitting upright again, Nelson was flipping through his file. This was unnerving, like being dissected.

"I will kill you, Nelson, I will kill you," Christopher told himself, over and over again, a mantra. These four words uttered like a rhyme often helped him. What was keeping Christopher alive, here at Triton, was his methodical revenge plan. Everyone who'd fucked Christopher over would be made to apologize. Everyone who'd let Christopher down would have to grovel and suffer and die. The comic books he'd drawn as an art student had been full of stabbing, blinding, and amputation. He had a vision of blood spurting a vermilion fountain through the air. Violence invigorated him. It was just what he liked to think about when his mind went on vacation, the way some folks daydreamed about sunbathing on a beach.

Nelson closed the file with a rustle. "Most of the prisoners in here did something greedy, mean, ignorant, or lazy, Christopher. These men had no money and no job. They needed cash to support themselves, and they had no skills. They stole what didn't belong to them..."

"If you believe in private property," Christopher interrupted. "I don't. It's bull."

"The felons over in Unit A have committed grand larceny," said Nelson, giving him an odd look. "They're nonviolent, for the most part. There are inmates on the compound, in your unit, who have committed homicide. Your background has nothing in common with theirs. Nothing. Your story, Christopher, is different."

"Fuck my story."

"You had ideals," said Nelson. "And you advocated lawbreaking as a way to incite chaos. Because...?"

"Because? Because I was on smack, babe. Because I was a garbage-head."

Nelson cupped his chin in his hand. He raised his eyebrows. "I've never heard you talk about yourself that way before."

"Get real. You read too many books. You watch too many movies. What are you trying to do? You're going to get me to 'open up' to you and then you'll come to my rescue? Oooh. Nelson. Oooh." He fluttered his eyelashes.

"Open up," said Nelson. "You said that with some sarcasm."

"No shit, Sherlock. Forget it. I thought it would be a nice change of pace to take a walk over here with my friend Luis, and come to sit in your office, and talk to somebody literate for an hour, but this was a mistake. I'd rather go back to my cell. You make me want to chew open the veins on my inner wrists."

"Do you think about that a lot? Because I'm concerned about that. Suicidal ideation. If that applies to you, you let me know."

"I'll be sure to send out a press release. Come on, asshole. You've been in jail, haven't you?"

"What I thought about when I was doing time was how to get my life back."

"Yeah, well, mister normal and healthy. Congratulations."

"Next April, you'll be forty years old."

"Why do you pretend you care about me?"

"You were twenty when you were arrested," said Nelson.

"And?"

"You regret anything you did? Sounds like you do."

"I don't regret crap," Christopher said.

"I'm a fool, you said. Tell me more. You're feeling...what? Angry. Critical?"

"I pity the poor taxpayers of America who are buying your services," said Christopher. "You are my best argument against the U.S. government. I don't have time for this."

Nelson slid Christopher's file back into the cabinet, under the letter "B." It was labeled "Prisoner #1200814B." That figure, 1,200,814, represented a quantity. Men went to prison every day. Nelson said that two million people were incarcerated across the country.

"I see," said Nelson, "that you're in the Hole, in solitary. No time to talk to me. You need to get back to your unit—to do what, exactly?"

"Contemplate my wall, babe. Stare at my ceiling."

"You could have gotten out on good behavior in five years. Your sentence right now is thirty to life, C.B."

Christopher grimaced. "Did I just hear you call me C.B.?" he said. "I'm not C.B., asshole. You call me Benedict, or you call me Christopher. My last name or my first, it's the same. But no cute crap. No initials, no nicknames. Fuck you."

"Thirty years to life, without parole, Christopher Benedict," said Nelson. "I may—and I'm just saying *may*—be able to get that changed for you."

"Why would you?"

"They came down pretty hard on you."

Christopher had slammed a guy's head against the wall, in self-defense. He'd punched out a couple men. These were viewed as serious infractions in the pen, where fresh new crimes were tallied against stale old ones. The night he'd been apprehended, right after the accident in Lucidora, Christopher had had four illegal handguns and the M109 stashed in his warehouse. Though he'd talked of overthrow, he'd needed firearms for survival. Christopher had been a small-time dealer in a corner of South Brooklyn where the guiding principle had been "kill or be killed."

"I believed in guns then and I still do," he told Nelson. "If the government has the exclusive right to bear arms, the people have no power. I love the people—dirty, rapacious, explosive, wild. And I loathe the government."

Christopher didn't need to read the newspapers to know what was going on. They were all living in a military dictatorship; Congress and the courts handed over the reins. Inside and out, men were under twenty-four-hour surveillance. The Feds were wire-tapping. They were listening in on phone conversations, patting down pedestrians, looking for political subversives in public libraries and college classrooms. Since he'd become an inmate, the U.S.A. had been inching towards fascism. By now, for all he knew, it was a police state.

Christopher had defended his business from competitors, a time-honored tradition, same as the Suits would have done. The dealer on the other side of the canal had needed to see he was armed. A gun was a deterrent.

The rest of the time, he'd been making art. He'd studied at Pratt with George Arden, the Czech photographer, and Trisha Yost, the Swiss installation artist. Even a yahoo like Nelson knew who *they* were. Admittedly, Christopher had been something of a junkie and a pill-head. But he'd been a student, too, and in his pursuit of art, he'd been serious. The violence on display in his art work had initially been simulated. They'd needed blood, so they'd opened a bottle of tomato ketchup. It was guerrilla theater. Breaking a few laws meant little to him when, he believed, the State went around conducting global massacres. The Law was a fiction, an invention. For better or worse, it could easily be rearranged.

"Talk to me, Christopher. You've been at the pen longer than anybody else. You have seniority here at Triton."

"Not really," said Christopher. "What about Henry? Henry has been inside for five decades. Around forty-six, forty-seven years. Hasn't he?"

"Henry Godwin. He passed away last week. He died of old age. In his sleep."

Christopher pulled the chain taut on his ankles. He felt the steel links pressing through the fabric of his jumpsuit, digging into a tendon. Pain, he'd once preached, could aid focus. Lose the fear of pain and transcend entrenched mental limits. He'd envisioned a new breed of anarchist who'd shatter the old institutions. Now he stared down at the chain between his feet. Pain had lost its cachet for him; it was nothing more than an irritant. "Yeah. So?"

"You knew about Henry's dying?" said Nelson.

"No, but so what? He was human. He got old."

"I want to help you escape that fate. Henry's fate. Expiring behind bars. I'd like to see you on the Outside. Rehabilitated."

"I can't be rehabilitated. I won't be," said Christopher.

"Why not? What does that mean to you?"

"That I'd admit I did something wrong. Well, honey, I didn't. I'd do it again. If you let me out, I'll pick up where I left off."

"If you make some positive changes, you'd go up before the parole board within three years," said Nelson. "You have my word of honor on that."

"What would I have to do, exactly?"

"Think about what you did. A woman died because of you. The bag of heroin found on her body was stamped with a skeleton. That was the Aktionists' logo."

"What woman? The girl that died was my associate. She was a war veteran."

"That's not what I was told."

"Chick dies after she does what she wants. She lived her life. She made her choices, not me."

"She was young," said Nelson.

"If she didn't come to me for her drugs, she'd buy them someplace else. What happened at Lucidora couldn't be prevented."

"Think about her, that's all I'm suggesting. You like being alone in solitary confinement?"

"No, dude. No. It's boring."

"You try it my way. I can get you a shared cell with a former street poet, a former gang leader, an interesting guy called Angel, in Unit B."

"Unit B? That's not supermax. That's minimum security."

"How long has it been since you've had a blanket and a pillow on your bed? A lid on your toilet? A door to close for privacy, a seat? A book to read? A pizza delivery?"

Christopher said nothing. He'd been denied those things.

"You like to paint?" said Nelson. "You like to write? I can get you art supplies. Pens, paper. Access to them. On a regular basis."

Christopher, hanging his head, stamped his feet. His chain jingled like bells.

"When was the last time you took a walk around the grounds, outside?"

"Why are you doing this?" Christopher said, softly. "You want to fuck my ass, or what?"

"That's the only reason people help each other out in your experience," said Nelson, pondering his pen. He was rolling it, a joint, between his index finger and his thumb.

"In my experience, people don't help each other. Period."

"Come back to Group. Let's try again. Twenty years is too long for what you did. That's what I think."

"You're saying to me: Play the game," said Christopher. "That's the same thing Little John was saying."

"I don't see it as a game, Christopher. Society has certain standards. If you do things right, inside here, at Triton, some important people might take notice. Isn't there anything that intrigues you?"

"Sure, lots of things. I like pussy. Pussy intrigues me."

"Besides that. I mean something I can get for you. Films, documentaries, novels. I'm trying to motivate you."

Christopher let out a laugh. It was a cross between a bark and a howl. "Flowers."

"Flowers?"

"I only get outside an hour a day," said Christopher. He made a gesture towards Nelson's window, which looked out onto the brick wall of the building opposite, Unit E. "I'd like to garden. I used to have a garden in a greenhouse. I raised prize orchids a long time ago, me and my mother. We won third place at some fucking orchid show."

"When was this?"

"I was nine years old. You do the math." He sat quietly for a while. "She cross-pollinated two varieties of orchid, one hardy, the other fragile. She named it Christopher. She named it after me. It was pink."

"That was an affectionate gesture," said Nelson, nodding with his headshrinker's enthusiasm. "But you feel ambivalent."

"Fuck it. I'd just like to grow flowers again. But I'm not talking to you about my mother. You're not putting your reductive harness on me, babe. I'd rather check out in my cell than talk to you about any of that. I am into gardening. Gardening floats my boat. Okay? I'd like to feel the root-ball in my hand. Smell the soil. Water the plants and watch them grow. Stupid shit."

"It's a deal." Nelson stood up and clasped Christopher's hands between both his own.

"Whatever makes you happy, asshole," said Christopher, but on the way back to his unit, he wondered what it was, exactly, that he'd agreed to. He had the distinct impression that something precious had been bought and sold.

Girl's Gone Wild

Christopher's first letter came at Christmas, a shipment from limbo, without any explanation of how he'd tracked Nadia down. By March, she was deluged: a package from prison began arriving every month, then every week, then twice a week. The letters grew longer, the parcels heavier. One morning in April, Nadia woke up determined to put an end to them.

While she was driving to prison, the sun hid behind a veil of clouds, sending a soft lavender light over the road. The old jeep bumped along Interstate 87 and tossed Nadia up and down in her bucket seat. The car seemed to be rocketing forward with a mechanical determination, as if it possessed a strong, independent will of its own. The jeep was delivering her to the U.S. penitentiary at Triton, where Christopher Benedict—the senator's boy—had completed two-thirds of his sentence.

The wind shook the branches of the trees. Twenty miles outside the town limits, Nadia became consumed with anxiety. She had the absurd fear that she wasn't steering the jeep entirely on her own. Something had grabbed hold of the wheel. Something had summoned her.

"Calm down, stupid," she said—not to herself, exactly, but to the part of her that heard a feral call—and put the brakes on. The jeep slowed. Being behind the wheel distressed her; she was out of practice. Nadia seldom drove. She preferred to ride her bicycle. Red Barn was on her own property. To get to work, she just slipped on a pair of boots, grabbed her thermos of coffee, and took a quick hike along the footpath, with Blondie running ahead and barking, eager to harass the woodchuck who lived under the shed. Down a ravine and across a field they went every morning; the studio was set a half mile from the main house Nadia lived in with Dan and their sons. Locked inside a custom-built safe at Red Barn, Nadia's lies were listed on a stack of 500 index cards. She had to study her own lies to keep track of them.

Lie number 321. Nadia had said that she'd once injured her neck in an accident and had developed a phobia, afraid to drive, ever since the collision. Thankfully, Dan was too preoccupied with side effects, white cell counts, blood test results, and treatments to question her. He had the absent-minded-professor syndrome. Dan had swallowed the phobia story, or seemed to.

A loud screech gave Nadia a start. She looked up to see a turkey vulture circling overhead. The jeep swerved to the left before she steadied it. The sky had darkened. The high altitude had left her short of breath. She was driving in the shade thrown by a mountain.

Decelerating down to thirty miles an hour, Nadia tried to register her immediate surroundings—the pile of bricks left outside to deteriorate, the three-wheeled trailer submerged in cattails, the decrepit mobile homes. By mistake, she kept picturing Christopher inside a cinder-block cell, lonely, too alone.

She'd never been inside a prison and didn't know what it would look like. Maybe prison had a fun side, an untold side. Maybe Christopher had charmed the inmates. Maybe he'd enrolled in college-level courses, had rediscovered Shakespeare. Or he'd started performing a Black Mass at the penitentiary as he'd boasted in his interview on *60 Minutes*. Leave it to Christopher to cast a spell. He'd have found a supernatural technique to wreck Nadia's marriage for her. He'd managed, already, to get her to make one magnificent error.

Nadia pushed the button for track two on the jeep's CD player. Track two never failed to calm her down. Whenever her thoughts circled in an irrational direction, she listened to opera. Now, as she steered the jeep past a sign that said "Welcome to Triton!" (as if people came to the prison center of New York State for a leisurely pleasure trip), the melodic strains of Tchaikovsky were supposed to start playing over her speakers. But they didn't. All she heard was a long, drawn out hiss, the scratchy sighs and whispers of obsolete technologies, old recordings. Her son, Jeremy, must have reloaded the CD player when Dan had driven him to swim-team practice the other day. Instead of the dignified Russian grandeur she'd hoped for, Nadia heard a thrumming. The faint drone was broken, jarringly, by the crack of a drum. It took her breath away. She knew this sound: Christopher's drumstick banging out a rhythm, nine clangs on the lid of a garbage can. It was the first bar of a soundtrack that should have been illegal. It appeared on the government's annual list of inappropriate materials.

Alone in her studio in Riverbend, there were times when Nadia took a hammer to certain DVDs and CDs, shattering them. She bundled the silvery slivers up in sheets of newspaper, sealed with tape and tied with string—in neat, dismaying parcels, like shrouds for dead things. Her children's hamster, Frodo, had been disposed of in such a bundle. Nadia often sneaked to the town dump at off-hours to throw out the trash.

Nadia hit the eject button and, with a shaking hand, she tossed the offending CD out the window like a Frisbee. It landed in the branches of a roadside rhododendron plant. It remained there, a flat shiny disc, decorating the foliage along Interstate 87, a leftover silver Christmas ornament. Not a good idea. She weighed whether or not to pull off the road, turn around, and retrieve it. Her kid was going to be pissed at her. Rule one of parenting: Don't destroy any property that has been claimed by your child. If your kids unearth something that belonged to you, they see it as an inheritance; it belongs, they think, to them, too. She'd learned this as a result of a venomous negotiation over a pair of jeans, splattered with paint, ripped, tattered, and safety-pinned, which she'd thrown in the rag bin in the garage. The clean-cut, fresh-scrubbed Jeremy—her middle child—had promptly salvaged them. She'd have to lie to him. She'd say she'd never seen any CD in the jeep.

Rule two of parenting, she was sure, was "Don't lie." Well, too late. It would be no exaggeration to say that Nadia couldn't get out of bed in the morning without prevaricating. And she'd outsmarted all of Them. It was *she*, not he, who'd opened the money-market account with a quarter million dollars in it, while Christopher had been led away in shackles. It was *she*, not he, who owned twenty-two acres of riverfront property along the Delaware River and a six-bedroom Victorian home. It was *she*, not he, who'd launched the career in photography. *Not* Christopher, with his cheekbones. Christopher had become a scandal, a blight on the illustrious Benedict clan, a Who's Who of founding fathers—mayors, governors, poets, industrialists, and philosophers. Though estranged from her family, Nadia had become a woman of consequence.

And yet the prosperous, blissful Nadia was here, in her jeep, hurtling towards him like a psycho. "Jesus!" Nadia told the road. "What am I doing?"

A hawk soared overhead. A groundhog rooted in the shrubbery by the road. The trees raced past. A guy in a red bandanna, seated low on his Harley, his chrome handlebars catching the sunlight, stole up behind her jeep, overtook her, and roared by.

"What are you doing, what are you doing, what are you doing?" Nadia asked.

But the road didn't reply.

She was risking her marriage, and who knew what else.

"You can still change your mind, you lunatic," she told herself.

Nadia steered the jeep down Main Street. Since her last abortive visit, the town of Triton had remained the same. She noticed four vacant storefronts with signs in the windows that said "For Rent." As she drove closer to the federal penitentiary, the houses got uglier and smaller. The paint on the facades began to peel. The gardens that had been planted, on the southern edge of town, were swiftly replaced by narrow yards with cement floors. There were long stretches of run-down buildings. While she was stuck at an interminable traffic light, Nadia studied the few stores that lined the avenue, selling only the most depressing items. Orthopedic shoes were piled high in one store window next to a plastic foot. Toupees, in another storefront, sat atop dingy faceless heads. A third window was cluttered with bedpans, crutches, and canes. Slabs of polished marble in gray, pink, and white had been neatly assembled, in three rows, outside a shop at the edge of town. It took Nadia a moment to realize that the rocks were tombstones.

Signs of human habitation began to dwindle, with fewer buildings and more boarded-up houses. At last, there was nothing at all but naked ground. Slowing to a crawl, Nadia passed a laundromat with a sign that said "Suds Wash." Along one wall was a mural of soap bubbles, each globe animated by a pair of eyes. Outside the laundromat was a folding chair, and on the chair sat a one-legged man.

She steered right, around a corner, and the penitentiary appeared. It huddled, by itself, on the flat land, an imposing construction, sterile and anonymous. The barred windows were mere slits; they belonged on a medieval fortress. The grass was withered here. The front gate radiated gloom; the brick walls, a malignant despondency.

"Hey darlings, I'm in a cage for bad guys," Christopher had written. "I'm in the Hole. Lost my temper, lost my privileges. I'm without a book, a paintbrush, my camera, without even a newspaper or television. Nothing is guaranteed here and even the pen I hold in my hand—to write this to you—can be taken away from me on the slightest pretext. Here, they bury guys like me alive. It's the thought of you, darlings. It's the thought that keeps me going. Have a heart for me. I need friends. Please write."

In the penitentiary parking lot, Nadia donned a pair of designer sunglasses and sat in the jeep for a while with her eyes closed.

You Burn My Book

The love letter was burning inside the kitchen sink. Dan had read only a few pages, randomly, in haste. He'd torn them up, setting them on fire. Now Dan crossed his arms over the shelf of his belly and watched the flames consume the cheap, thin, recycled paper. A charred scrap, its edges orange, sent off a drizzle of soot, shooting embers into the sink, spattering black confetti across the enamel basin. Dan pulled apart the next sheaf of pages and read them, holding an unlit match in his hand. He couldn't think. The words turned into meaningless hieroglyphics. Dire possibilities swarmed around in Dan's head, accosting him, relentless. Eight days had elapsed since the shock of Nadia's birthday party; he'd intercepted this suspect parcel before she could get to it.

The letter was a tome, written by some obsessive who'd carried on for sixty pages. Segments were dated, like diary entries. They were illustrated with pencil drawings—faces, maps, and floor plans—and interspersed with lines of dialogue, like a script. Dan leafed through the manuscript, skimming it. The paper was the color of cardboard and coarse in texture. Each page had two lines running horizontally across it, splitting the rectangular leaf into three smaller rectangles. The letter might have been written on a stack of paper towels taken from a dispenser in a public restroom.

Thumbing through the manuscript from back to front, he came to a title page, where a single sentence was scribbled. It was written in the too-large handwriting of the clinically insane. Like the printing on a poster for a thriller, the letters wiggled.

THE AUTOBIOGRAPHY OF JENNY X

The last page of the letter said: "I spend too many hours thinking about you both, not always in a nice way, I admit." It was written in green lettering that rolled drunkenly up and down on a slant.

> My mind goes in circles, and I start to question everything. I hear a roar come up in my eardrums and I begin to doubt you, along with my other so-called friends. Someone reported me after the accident in Lucidora, didn't they? Now tell the truth. Someone ripped me off. Someone close, one of our own. Why don't you ever write back to me if you're the innocent? Where are all those brownies you offered to bake me the last time we spoke, to say nothing of the regular visits, the loyalty and friendship, the Aktionists promised? If you do not come to see me, to talk to me, I'm not kidding. I'll lose my marbles. I'll be forced to include you on my list of traitors. I've been thinking about it for a long time here and, let's face it, I've nailed down my two prime suspects.

Dan had ignited a bright dancing bonfire in the sink. He fed one more page to the flames. The scribbled sentences were devoured, leaving a trail of smoke. Dan had the sensation that his feet and legs had disappeared from under him. He ran his hands up and down along his flanks, rubbing his lower back, trying to convince himself his body was intact. Nauseated, he vomited into the sink on top of the letter, dousing the paper with his undigested breakfast. Water, the color of fresh raspberries, came up out of him.

The smoke alarm went off.

It took him a few seconds to register what the sound meant; the scream matched his inner state. His temples throbbed as he tried to make sense of it. He could feel his old reptile brain lumbering to life, little-used, coming out of a long hibernation to offer him its slow-witted comprehension of fundamentals.

Danger, Dan, Bad.

That was the extent of it. He heard the prehistoric roar. His arm reached slowly towards a bottle of organic grape juice; his fingers closed around its neck. He took a sip, rinsed the bitterness from his mouth and spat the juice back out. A few drops of grape juice dribbled out of his lips. The screeching continued and still he couldn't respond. Lobotomized, he began to lurch around the kitchen, a big wounded creature looking for the goddamned smoke alarm.

"Oh, shit," he whispered. "Shit, shit." The physical arrangement of his household left him baffled. As a rule, Dan could never find anything—brooms, mops, cleansers, recycle bins. He had no idea where the smoke detector had been installed. It was up on the ceiling someplace, that was all.

"*There* you are," Dan said when he saw a little bright light flashing orange. He clambered on top of the kitchen counter, teetering from right to left, and made a grab for it, stretching out his fingers, reaching for the alarm, a small plastic apparatus screwed in to the ceiling a few inches to the right of the lighting fixture. He lunged forward towards the windowpane. He imagined himself falling, breaking his back, cracking his skull open. Finally he grabbed hold of the flat plastic disc and pulled. He wrenched the alarm out of the ceiling until it dangled by a twisted pair of wires. Its accursed light kept on winking; the mechanism kept up its horrid scream. Stirred by the activity, Blondie pulled back her black lips and bared her teeth at Dan.

"Shhh, Blondie, it's only me," Dan pleaded, his voice breaking. It seemed to him that everything in the house—objects, pets, people—had turned on him. "Good dog. Please don't bark," he told her, but she kept up a low warning rumble. All he'd done was come home early; he might have been a thief, breaking in, for all the sympathy his own dog showed him. Just as Blondie began barking madly, Dan removed the black and copper-colored battery from the fire alarm, silencing it. The sun was slowly sinking into the river by then, turning the clouds a hazy dark gold, and he still had more than twenty pages left to read and burn. He had wasted time puzzling over some of the sentences—the last portion of the letter was written in indecipherable madman's handwriting—and examining a few strange little illustrations, drawn so faintly, he couldn't make them out. He did not know what time to expect Nadia. Her peregrinations were her own business, or had been, until now.

He'd left Mercy at the uncharacteristic hour of 3:00 P.M. In the wake of the birthday party disaster, Dan thought it wise to become the sort of husband who was vigilant and unpredictable. He'd arrived at Bridge Street, in Riverbend, at ten minutes before four. Dan had found himself hip-deep in the crusty week-old snow, staring down at the metal mailbox marked ORSINI on the road outside his house. He opened the mailbox and looked in. A brown paper package rested inside, tilted at a diagonal, leaning against the tin wall. He considered leaving it there for Nadia to deal with. Mail belonged to Nadia's domain. Dan had nothing to do with letters, catalogues, or bills. At the hospital, he received supplies, tissue samples, reports, articles, studies, letters from doctors around the world, letters from patients thanking him for saving their skins, and subscriptions to medical journals. At home, he received nothing of importance.

Occasionally, a few envelopes appeared on his desk, just as dinner appeared at night. Nadia reheated his meals in the microwave, serving him at the single place-setting on the dining room table, where he ate off antique Russian plates edged in gold. His family had dinner without him, at seven. The smooth running of the household was conducted out of sight, by a team of Elves: Nadia, a driver she occasionally hired to chauffer her around, the two babysitters, a lawn-mower, a pool man, a tutor, two housecleaners, a floor-sander, a plumber, a painter, a wallpaper-hanger, and a pair of handymen. Dan had never met any of these other people, had only heard about them from Nadia, and he paid them no attention. They had created clutter when they renovated the upstairs bathroom—the hammers lying on the floor, the broken plaster in the corner. When the Elves redecorated the living room, he ignored it. The order was restored after a few weeks and the mess went away. He barely noticed the new furniture, the new appliances, the new bathroom fixtures. Fresh soaps gathered themselves in a glass bowl in Dan's bathroom. Clean cool smooth cotton sheets and thick soft blankets arranged themselves on the bed for him. Wool sweaters materialized on the shelves of his closet in November and, like the icicles that melted on the front porch, the wool sweaters vanished in the spring. This was the normal way of things.

Unless they came to his department at the hospital, letters and envelopes had no significance. Mail didn't ever cause cancer. It didn't ever contract cancer. It couldn't ever cure cancer. Mail, therefore, was of no use to him.

The package was addressed, in large letters "TO JENNY X," followed by "c/o Nadia Orsini." The first line—"Jenny X"—had been written in a lopsided script, in smudged green felt-tipped ink. Written in small even letters beneath that was Nadia's name, their street address, their town and their zip code.

Maybe there was an innocent explanation. Perhaps Jenny X was among the Elves. She might have been a babysitter or a housekeeper who was an illegal immigrant. This was Dan's best hypothesis, yet he didn't quite believe it.

The wind blew a fistful of snow off the lower bough of the Douglas fir, sprinkling stinging flakes onto Dan's cheeks. His car stood idling behind him as, tentatively, he squeezed the package. He shook it. He squeezed once more, harder. He read the name over again.

Jenny was a plain name, like a Sara or a Jane, but "X" suggested darker qualities. While he examined the return address in the upper left-hand corner, a quivering sensation began in his elbows. He had seen patients react this way when informed of bad test results. They got the shakes. Some rallied; others went to pieces.

Tamping down his panic, Dan buttoned the package inside his coat. He got back in the car and parked it, but instead of going in to his house through the garage door, as usual, he turned around and walked outside. Forlorn, Dan stood in the snow looking up at the windows.

"Anybody there?" Dan called. His voice reverberated in the clearing. The house might have belonged to someone else, to any other family, to any man. A branch creaked by the shed near the woodpile.

"Hello, I'm here!" He turned towards the Delaware River. "It's me! I'm home!" The wind moaned through the thick cluster of trees on the hill behind the house. He wondered, suddenly, if those old shacks were ever illegally inhabited. A vagrant could easily crawl into one in the winter, to get out of the cold.

"Here Blondie!" Dan called to the dog. "Good girl, Blondie!"

He heard a whimpering from behind the door, and the scratching of claws. Apprehensive, he trudged through the snow and up the front steps. The Elves hadn't been here. No one had shoveled.

Inside the house, almost two hours after discovering the package in the mailbox, Dan was holding another lit match against what was left of the love letter to Jenny X. The pages had been numbered one to sixty; he had another twenty pages to destroy. He'd just set them alight when, through the kitchen window, he saw a jeep appear at the foot of the hill. He knew that car. It belonged to them. The back of his neck prickled. Only now did it come to him that, when he'd parked his Saab earlier that afternoon, the jeep had been inexplicably missing from the garage. The jeep was moving closer, up the road, as steady and resolute as a beetle crawling towards its destination. But Jeremy didn't have his license yet. And Nadia didn't drive.

"Crap," Dan said to Blondie, who lay on the floor by her water dish, watching him. The dog scrambled to her feet and whined.

This was not the first time that Dan had intercepted a brown paper package. Similar packages had arrived when they'd first moved in. There'd been no name indicated on the return address, only a prisoner's I.D. number. He'd sent them back to a post office box at the federal penitentiary, having assumed that the packages had been intended for the house's former owner. He'd simply marked them Return to Sender and, for whatever reason, had never mentioned them to Nadia. It had required some self-control, on Dan's part, not to open them.

By now, the jeep was halfway up the hill. Dan could not imagine who was in that car. Nadia had a terror of driving.

Dan grabbed the telephone off the hook and dialed Nadia's cell phone.

"Hello?"

"Nadia, it's me," said Dan, too loudly.

"Who is this?"

"Don't you remember me?" he joked, dismayed. He reached for the refrigerator door and opened it so hard that it swung back on its hinges, hit the wall behind it, and slammed shut again. "This is your husband," he said, quietly. "My name's Orsini. Dan."

Nadia chuckled softly. "Dan, we have a terrible connection. I couldn't hear you just now."

Dan had succeeded in opening the refrigerator. He stared at the food on the clean plastic shelves, green peppers and celery in clear containers; strawberries in sealed bowls. "I'm glad I caught you."

"Can I call you right back? You're at the office?" said Nadia.

"No, I'm not at the hospital. I'm home."

There was a long pause. "You're home now?" Her voice sounded higher, less secure.

"Yes. I came home." He couldn't think what to say to his wife to explain his presence in the house in the middle of a weekday afternoon. It was as if he'd broken some unspoken custody agreement. The place was hers by daylight.

"Is something wrong?" she said, her car nosing along the road that led directly to their driveway.

"No. Not at all."

"Sure?"

"I just wanted to be close to you." As he said it he realized it was true.

Another long pause suggested that this wasn't what Nadia expected of him. He couldn't remember the last time he'd said such a thing. Maybe never.

"I just wanted to be nearer to you, Nadia," he said, again, his voice deepening, remembering something—a spontaneous act of love in the woods from nine or ten years ago. Lifting her T-shirt and flashing her breasts in the dusk, Nadia had unzipped his fly on a warm spring day and had blown him, tranquilly, on the hillside. Never repeated, it had been her whim to have sex out in the open country that morning. As she'd pulled her shirt off, as she'd fallen to her knees, removing the clip that kept her long hair up in a bun, he'd perceived another side of her, for a few minutes, and never again. While they'd embraced, half-naked, a jogger had passed on the road below. Dan had told her, "We can be seen." Nadia had looked up at him with a fiendish little smile and had said, "That's the point. I know."

"Dan, I'll be there in two seconds," said Nadia on the telephone, speaking in a strained, forced tone. "Believe it or not, I'm in the jeep. I'm driving."

He saw her blinkers flashing. In another moment, she would turn left and she'd be home. "Driving? I don't understand. How could you? You don't drive. You can't. It isn't possible."

"I taught myself to drive again," she said, laughing. "I've been practicing secretly. I wanted to surprise you."

Dan didn't reply. He'd opened the kitchen window and was waving his hand around, trying to clear the smoke.

"I'm doing pretty well, actually, Dan." She sounded like a former patient, or a distant relative he rarely spoke to.

"Will you be going over to your studio?"

"I was planning to, but since you're there, I'll come home," said Nadia as her jeep slowed, preparing for the turn.

"Please wait," said Dan, while the letter smoldered. "One minute. Are you near the grocery store?"

"Dan, I passed the shopping mall fifteen minutes ago." She sounded annoyed. "You said you wanted to see me. I'm right down the road."

"Ah well, forget it, then, you've done enough driving today," he told her, keeping his voice gentle and low. "Just come home to me." The charred paper had formed into a sodden paste when he'd turned the faucet on. All that remained of the letter from prison was a glop like blackened swamp scum. He began pouring the soy milk down the drain, emptying the container, washing everything away. He turned on the garbage disposal. The prisoner's writing was ground to bits.

"Why, what do we need?" said Nadia.

"We're out of soy milk," said Dan, offhand. "Soy's on the cancer-fighting regime."

"Come on, Dan," she exclaimed. "Eight ounces of missed soy milk, or whatever it is. Is that going to kill us?"

"Not immediately."

"Fine. Let me turn around," Nadia grumbled. "I'll see you in a half an hour."

Blondie, as if sensing his treachery to her mistress, sniffed Dan's feet and growled at him.

He had bought some extra time. Rinsing away the last burned scraps of the letter from prison, Dan took his wallet out of his suit jacket. He looked at the wedding photograph he kept inside it. Nadia, on the day he'd married her, in her tailored white skirt and jacket, a zaftig, large-breasted bride with a wasp-waist and big, wide hips. She'd worn a double strand of heirloom pearls around her neck and, on her head, a veiled pillbox hat. The old-fashioned, antiquated outfit was severe and proper, suited more to an elderly person than a ripening young woman in her early twenties. Her dark eyes looked apprehensive as she clutched her bouquet of white roses to her chest. Her kid gloves fit so snugly around her plump hands that the seam of her left glove had begun, at the base of her thumb, to split. The gloves had a fussy row of buttons and a miniature bow at the wrist. They had lodged themselves in his mind, a false note. He remembered wondering if the gloves belonged to her.

A Gated Community

"Yes, hello, I'd like to see one of the prisoners, if I may," Nadia said to the intercom. She was standing inside an empty hallway; the walls and floors were made of concrete. Two steel doors barred her entrance. She'd gotten past the security check in the lobby, where a taciturn guard had sent Nadia's gloves, shoulder bag and sheepskin coat through a metal detector. She didn't have a weapon, but she did have drugs on her. The guard had removed the amber plastic vial from her bag. Reading the label, he'd said, "This is your prescription, right, miss? Don't share these with anybody else," as if, for old time's sake, Nadia might try to slip the senator's son a tranquilizer.

"Hello, can someone help me?" said Nadia, now, in the same poised, authoritative voice she'd use with her clients. She brought her mouth closer to the oval speaker, pressing the button marked "talk" with her thumb. Nadia's thumbnail, like the rest of her fingernails, was coated with "bronze icon" nail polish. She'd stopped at the salon in Narrowsburg that morning to have her hair and nails done. Not that she was aiming to please. No. She'd moved beyond any need to make a good impression on Christopher. Way, way beyond that.

What she wanted was to make him sick with longing.

A storm of static issued from the metal grill. "Who is it?" said a voice, distorted.

"I'm here to visit someone who's incarcerated," Nadia shouted.

"May I come in please?" Heart racing, she began to fumble with her handbag, foraging in its capacious leather depths, identifying the contents by touch. Here was her Pentaflex camera; a canister of undeveloped film; a zoom lens for close-ups; a cell phone; a set of office keys on a Mexican Day of the Dead skull key-ring; and a quilted change purse her daughter Simone had made in the fourth grade. Clutching her compact, she checked her reflection in the mirror. The pretty, ageless face was not quite hers. It had been injected and plumped. She'd hired experts.

The instant Christopher saw her, he'd regret her. He'd probably go right back into his cinder-block cell, pull his sheets off the bed, tie a noose around his neck, and hang himself.

She pushed against the door, but it didn't move. No buzzer had sounded. She'd been waiting in the hallway for more than five minutes. It was just as difficult to get inside the prison, apparently, as it must be to get out of it.

Christopher was in there somewhere, locked up, living in deprivation. He'd fallen from a great height. The penitentiary must have been a rude awakening.

When Nadia had first encountered Christopher, he'd been lounging around a seventeen-room penthouse apartment with views of Central Park. He'd been dressed in pink silk pajamas and a fedora, unshaven, silver hoops flashing from his earlobes, black eyeliner smeared around his eyes, "666" tattooed on the back of his left hand, hair stiffened to the consistency of straw with an admixture of sugar water and shoe polish. He'd been spooning ice cream from a cut-crystal bowl, sipping whisky neat from a miniature airline bottle, already a tad smacked out at ten o'clock in the morning.

Christopher Benedict in his prime.

"Hello, hello! Is anyone there?" Nadia shouted in the empty corridor. If she hurried to see Christopher and drive back, her absence wouldn't be noticed. It was only noon. Dan rarely left the hospital before nine o'clock at night. Her sons would be at rehearsal until at least eight, so she had eight hours left. Still, Nadia couldn't afford to wait around all day for a chat with a convicted felon.

Nadia knocked, three more times, on the scarred steel door. It was covered with graffiti that had been left behind by other visitors. Much of it was cryptic, indecipherable. A fair amount of it must have been written long ago, by Aktionist supporters. "Aktion now," said one message, written lengthwise, along the door's hinges. "Free C.B.," someone else had scratched out at eye level, in long spidery letters cut deep into the metal with a penknife. "Christo rules," said a third, and a fourth one said, "C.B. I miss yu."

Nadia ran her fingertips over the words. Her pulse skittered erratically. Pulling out her key chain, she began to write on the prison door with the point of her studio key. She etched: "C.B. is garbage." It was an adolescent thing for a woman of her age to do. It gave her a jolt. A perverse feeling of ecstasy bloomed in her chest as she retraced the insult. Garbage. But, frustratingly enough, no matter how hard Nadia pressed down, her letters were only barely legible. To do graffiti properly, she'd need a sharp blade. Next time she'd make her mark on this door. She'd bring tools and a can of spray paint. What was she talking about? There would be no next time.

She could not loaf around here in an empty hallway, hoping to see Christopher. She'd wait no longer than ten minutes. Well, okay, fifteen. She'd give herself fifteen minutes and that was *it*. Already, she was having second thoughts. She leaned down and tugged at her pantyhose, remembering how Christopher had always noticed minor defects like stubble on calves, wrinkles in stockings, or bitten fingernails. She had lost sixty pounds since they'd last seen each other. Nadia examined herself through his eyes, now, appraising her legs, her figure, and her shoes. It dawned on her that she was grotesquely overdressed. A diamond bracelet sparkled on her wrist; a diamond gleamed from the gold chain below her collarbone; she wore a diamond chip on each earlobe. Before she'd left her house that morning, she'd put on enough precious gemstones to stock a jewelry store. While Christopher had languished in his cell, Nadia had flourished in the splendor of a real home. Her house had a gabled roof and an English garden. It had a swimming pool underneath a portico.

"Can I help you?" boomed a new voice, crackling through the speakers.

"Yes, I'm here to see an inmate."

A buzzer sounded. This time, when Nadia pushed against the steel door she heard a click, and the door opened. She approached a guard seated inside a booth. "Good morning," she said, her voice wavering as it still did, as a matter of course, in the presence of men wearing gun holsters, caps, and uniforms.

"I'd like to visit Christopher Benedict."

The guard ignored her.

"He's the son of Grant Benedict, the former senator," Nadia added and began to blush.

The guard had woolly gray hair cut close to his head, bloodshot eyes, and wet lips. His bulbous nose resembled a root vegetable. It was the color of radicchio, striated purple and white; he wore a sour expression on his fleshy face. Though his lips moved rapidly, as if he were whispering to himself, he wasn't speaking to Nadia. He was, she gathered, talking on a telephone through a headset, and she saw a telltale wire winding up his left arm like a creeper, disappearing into his ear. The sliding doors on the window between Nadia and the guard were shut; she couldn't hear what he was saying. He'd failed to notice her.

Nadia turned her back on the guard and studied the room. The four rows of plastic orange chairs, attached to one another by metal rods, were bolted to a grimy floor. She caught a faint odor of sweat and cigarette smoke. Brown curtains were drawn over three stained windows. She saw herself, just then, as if from above, and was gripped by the paranoid conviction that her movements were being documented. There may have been a video camera on the ceiling, she thought. It was such a compelling feeling that she glanced up. Sure enough, there was a camera in the corner. Well, they were allowed to do that. It was, after all, a correctional facility. In a room out of her view, men would see her, chronicle her movements and keep watch.

While the guard opened and closed the drawers of his desk, she fiddled with her cell phone, checking to see if anyone had called. The light blinked, signaling that someone had sent her a text message. It was from Jeremy.

"Mom, like surprise parties?" he'd written in his barely comprehensible shorthand (*srprz ptz*). He'd sent her this message three hours earlier, at 9:03 A.M., it said, but she'd turned off her phone while she'd been on the road. Nadia never abbreviated her text messages. She always composed full sentences complete with commas and other punctuation, as best she could. It was hard enough for her to read and comprehend the English language without the missing letters. She sat in one of the plastic prison chairs next to a sign that said "NO food NO radio NO alcohol" and crossed her legs at the ankles. She held her phone with a feigned composure as she wrote back to her son laboriously. Nadia had severe dyslexia, a limitation she worked hard to mask. Her spelling and grammar were abysmal.

"Dear Jeremy, I hat sirprizes. Love, Mom," she wrote.

Before she hit "send," Nadia hesitated, reviewing her sentence. Several times, she'd spelled her own children's names wrong, and they'd teased her mercilessly for weeks. They had no idea how lacerating their remarks had been, that she'd cried herself to sleep. The kids were hardy souls who didn't, for instance, hide in the bathroom to avoid an intimidating Ivy League dinner guest. Because of the cocoon she'd built for them, her children had never felt shame. Shame, in their household, belonged to Nadia alone.

When she was sure that her message was okay, she pressed the green button. "Message sent," the screen read.

Jeremy must have had his phone on, in class—which he and the other eleventh graders had been pointedly forbidden to do. A chirp sounded within instants to tell Nadia that he'd written back to her.

"Warning 1 4 u."

Huh? Great. This took her some time to translate. It appeared that her husband, sons, and daughter would be throwing her a 'surprise' party, that coming summer, in July. Terrific. Nadia disliked being reminded of the birthday. She abhorred surprises of any sort. She found surprises terrifying. But she could hardly divulge her fear to Jeremy. He was a relatively well-adjusted child of comfort, a boy who'd never carried a switchblade in his back pocket or gone to bed in an unheated room in an SRO dressed in a hat, gloves and a winter coat. Nothing menacing or unpleasant came into contact with her children. Nothing scratchy or synthetic touched their skins. She spent thousands of dollars on their school wardrobes, decking them out in softest cashmeres, merino wool, and calfskin. Some people could pay a month's rent with the money Jeremy spent on a single pair of jeans.

"Dear Jeremy," she wrote. "Draw me a birtday card and I'll be heppey. I hat partease. I am too shi. Love, Mom."

As Nadia returned her phone to her bag, she chipped the bronze metallic nail polish on her flawlessly manicured fingernail. "Shit," she whispered, tapping on the glass, still waiting for the guard to turn his attention to her. It had been essential to her plan, that fingernail. She needed to prove that she didn't bite her nails the way she'd done at Saint Lucy's School.

Nadia opened her compact and took another surreptitious peek in the mirror. She no longer looked composed. She wasn't sure if she had anything to show off. She wasn't sure if she was attractive, successful, and adored. As a rule, happily married women probably didn't sneak off to see men who were serving thirty-year prison sentences.

The sign over the door said EXIT. Good advice. She'd accept this as a useful command. But as she began to step away, something rattled. Turning back, she saw that the guard was looking at her, finally, and that he'd slid open the transparent door inside his booth. He motioned a welcome to Nadia.

Her hands reached down to smooth the fabric of her outfit. She'd worn a fitted jacket—perhaps a touch too tight—with a crepe dress, somewhat flimsy for this bitterly cold, windy April day. Her fingers fidgeted with the pearl buttons at her bodice. She discovered that a button at her breastbone had, of its own volition, popped open. She pulled at the collar of her dress lest her cleavage be exposed. She buttoned her jacket, then unbuttoned it, then rebuttoned it again.

"I'll be right with you," said the guard.

The clock on the wall behind the guard's desk counted out another minute. Screened behind his bulletproof shield, he was filling out a form. In the most irritating slow motion, he opened an ink pad, took out a rubber stamp and carefully stamped the first sheet of paper, and the second, and the third, raising his metal contraption each time, and plunging it down again—bang! He was making a concerted effort to line up the stamp so that it would print evenly. He sorted through a rack of forms to the left side of his desk. He removed a sheet from the top rack and scribbled something illegible in the center of the page. Only now did he turn to Nadia, his gourd-like head swiveling on a thick neck.

"Name," he said.

"Um, Christopher Benedict."

"I need a name, lady," he said, raising his eyes to look at her coldly.

"*My* name?"

"That's what I asked you."

"I'm not... What do you need my name for?" she stammered.

"It's the procedure, ma'am. I need an I.D. from you, driver's license or a valid passport. Identification with a photograph and date of birth."

"Oh. Well. I'm just an old friend," she said, breathlessly, stepping back, atremble, as if it were she, not Christopher, who was a convicted felon. But here she was, reaching for her wallet, about to hand the guard her driver's license with a wretched fatalism. She stopped herself, leaving her wallet to poke out of her purse.

"I went to school with Christopher Benedict, you see," she said, her hand on her driver's license, covering it, punctuating this tidbit of unsolicited personal information with a nervous giggle. "We were classmates. At a graduate program in the fine arts. At Yale." Oh, sure, that would win her points with the prison guard.

He gave her a quizzical smile. "You're not the inmate's wife, are you?"

"No!" she said.

"Are you his sister? Or his mother?"

"Neither."

"Is your name on the Approved Visiting List?" he asked her.

She shook her head, no.

"Has a Special Visit Request Form been submitted to the Inmate's Unit Team?"

"I don't think so," said Nadia.

"Lady, here's how it works," he said, interlacing his fingers, folding his meaty hands on his desk. "No visit takes place at this correctional facility without completing the Special Visit Request form. The application can't be made by you, ma'am. It must be made by the inmate in question, and it must be registered with us a minimum of four weeks in advance. The proposed visitor is then submitted for approval by the Warden and the Camp Administrator. The Unit Manager will notify the Captain, the Operation Lieutenant, the Control Center, and the Visiting Room Officer that your name has been added to the Approved Visiting List. Assuming you *do* receive approval, the next opening is Thursday the fourteenth of May at eleven."

"I beg your pardon. Could you repeat that? I missed something."

"Let me make it real simple for you," he said. "No walk-ins."

"So I fill out the form? I don't understand."

The guard sighed. He looked up, as if seeking help from heaven. "These are the regulations." His eyes moved to Nadia's diamond bracelet winking against her freckled wrist, and back up to her face. "Regulations," he repeated. "Some things you can do. Some things you can't. Rules. Ever heard of them?"

"Of course I have," she breathed.

He might as well have said it aloud: "Drop dead, you cosseted bitch." Nastiness sparked in the guard's pitiless eyes, in the set of his mouth, in the bellicose way he sat there on his swivel chair, chest out, ready to fight.

"Look." He tapped the point of his pencil on a vast appointment book, almost the size of his desk. "I've got you down for eleven o'clock on May fourteenth. Think you can hold out for your little boyfriend until then, lady?"

Other women had been here, doing this, taking illicit voyages to this backwater town, drawn by the unseemly presence of isolated men in maximum security. Later in the day, when he took his thirty-minute break, he'd describe her, laughingly, to another guard. He'd make a punch line of her.

"I won't be back."

"Suit yourself, ma'am," he said. "I can't do anything about it." He crossed the date off the list with a squeak of his felt-tipped pen.

Leaden casts encased her legs as she walked away. The fretful energy that had lifted her up had deflated. She felt as heavy as she'd been before she'd lost the sixty pounds, all that unsightly weight. Now what she had to look forward to were four hours of monotony. She wound her way back, back down the same dusky corridor she'd just come from, back through the security check in the entrance hall, where she raised her arms while the first guard screened her again with his metal detector. He poked, once more, at the contents of Nadia's bag with his hairy, stubby fingers.

"You're clear." He gave Nadia a nod that seemed to say: You didn't get what you wanted when you came here today.

She had hoped to bribe, bully, and beg Christopher, to make him stop. Every letter she received from him had the corrosive potential of lye. If Dan were ever to read the things Christopher had written to her, she could lose her husband and her children.

But her visit had a sentimental purpose, too. In Red Barn, in Riverbend, Nadia had marked today's date on her calendar with a drawing of confetti. She'd come here to celebrate his birthday with him. Maybe he'd stop writing if she were kinder to him.

"Come find me," he'd written. "I'd give anything to see you. Bring me some of your brownies, make me happy for a minute."

She had wanted to bring Christopher her brownies. Like it or not, she was indebted to him.

Here at the Zoo

Outside, Nadia ate one of Christopher's brownies and sank down onto a wooden bench. It was scabbed, missing a slat. She threw a crumb of chocolate at a robin, which pecked it to pieces, and she stared morosely at the prison yard. Barbed wire lined the top of the fence, crowned by bristling metal spikes. It was difficult to imagine a sadder place. Across the field, in a tree house of sorts, on a platform that rose above the bare white birch trees, a uniformed guard patrolled, pacing slowly as he moved from one side of the structure to the other. He had a machine gun strapped across his chest. She could see the holster on his shoulder, his arm cradling the gun.

Guys were led here, and one day they were allowed back out, or they got old and died inside. They lived within these walls, like the flocks of birds Nadia had photographed at the aviary. Curtailed, contained, the tropical parrots had flapped their multicolored wings and had flown forty feet forward before veering right and flying forty feet back again.

The federal penitentiary stood—a monument to the sins of men. She stared up at the barricades, the cement and steel structures. She could no longer see the man up on the watchtower. She sensed a lull and imagined the guard was taking a break. Idly, she ran her hands along the chipped splintered wood of her bench. Her fingers fell into a groove where letters had been cut into the wood. AKTION.

Wandering around, Nadia drew closer to the prison yard. No one seemed to pay much attention as she ventured forward, walking past a loose, low barricade of rusted chicken wire. Here, she found, she could look through the fence. She saw a broad square of concrete the size of a football field and, on the far side of the yard, a lonely patch of green. It was then that she noticed the gaunt, graying man dressed in a jumpsuit. Something compelled Nadia to look at him.

The prisoner in the yard was too far away; she couldn't see his features clearly. As he walked, his movements were slow and faltering. He appeared to be wearing a pair of glasses, too large for his face, as enormous as goggles. His lenses glinted in the sun. He turned gradually towards Nadia—on the alert. Now he was looking directly at her.

Nadia stopped breathing.

The man in the jumpsuit didn't move. He froze. In one hand he held a bundle of twigs, in the other, a rake. At his feet was a black plastic bag full of branches and leaves.

The man standing in a threadbare field could be Christopher. Nadia stared at the prisoner through the diamond-shaped spaces in the fence. She leaned up against the barricading wall. Its rough stucco surface dug into the palm of her hand.

It was like going to a nature preserve to see a wild creature, the last of its kind, the last Siberian tiger or the last pygmy hippopotamus. As she watched the man on the other side of the gate—*was* it Christopher?—cross the prison yard, rake in hand, disturbing images began to run through Nadia's mind.

Christopher's once-kingly posture was gone. This man hung his head. Christopher's beauty was tarnished. This man was ravaged. But he moved with a weary animal grace as he pushed his rake over the soil, a man grown strong, accustomed to manual labor. He leaned down to pick something up—a weed or dead leaf—and threw it inside his garbage bag. They must have given him a job to do while he served out his sentence. Christopher, Manhattan royalty, had been reduced to this. He'd become the prison gardener, though there wasn't much garden here to tend, only a thin strip of greenery surviving on the outskirts of the prison compound. It contained a few scrubby bushes and plants. Christopher was raking around a shrub in the distance. She could hardly see him—not the specific details of his face, nor the color of his eyes. Still, every cell and nerve ending told Nadia: That's him. Now he was a ruined man, imprisoned, shipwrecked. Was this what Nadia had wanted? Did Christopher deserve this? A small sound came out of her while she stood outside the penitentiary, staring at the sinewy figure that had to be Christopher. She answered, yes.

The man in the jumpsuit raised up his hand and began to wave at Nadia, gesticulating frantically.

All aflutter, Nadia waved back.

"No! No! Get away!" He began to run towards her.

In confusion, she looked up and saw the sign, in bright yellow lettering on a black background, impossible to miss: "Danger! Electric Fence. 10,000 Volts. Keep Back."

She dropped her hands to her sides and, as the man in the jumpsuit hurried over, in a quick loping gait, Nadia turned away. As she tried to move, her heel caught, sinking into the mud. For a second, she was trapped, until her stiletto released her. Kicking up a clump of dirt and grass, Nadia ran. She turned a corner and careened towards the gate.

In the parking lot, she rolled herself up into a ball on the front seat. She rested her head on the steering wheel, covering her face with her hands.

Get a Clue

Christopher rushed toward the dark-haired woman on the other side of the fence. An armed guard shouted at her from a hundred feet above, his voice echoing like distant gunfire. The woman stumbled and was gone. Christopher was looking through the wire at no one. The tree and the bench went blurry. For an instant, he persuaded himself that it was Jenny, here, now, against all odds, his letters had reached her. But, as he stared out at the empty space, he admitted that it couldn't be so; there'd been no physical resemblance. Hardly anyone visited Christopher; she'd never come to see him.

The guard was out of sight now, inside the watchtower, and Christopher had the prison yard to himself. He squatted down on his haunches and ripped out a handful of weeds, stuffing the clump of roots and dirt into his sack as the weather turned and the air grew chill. "It hurts," he whispered, while the first snowflakes sprinkled themselves over his face and hands. "It hurts," he repeated. This was what Nelson had instructed the men in Group to say. It wasn't easy, for some reason. He hated making the confession. Whatever magic was supposed to accompany it wasn't working. A woman had gawked at him as if he were a one-man freak show. An instant later, she'd run away, scared of him. Monstrous Christopher.

In her haste to escape, the woman who wasn't Jenny had dropped her wallet on the ground. The wallet sat there now, collecting drops of snow, a black rectangle that had come to rest on a horizontal field between the vertical lines. Dry parched earth and browning grass. Glancing in the direction of the guards, Christopher pretended to be digging up weeds. His heart thumped. He was fairly certain that the guards couldn't see the wallet, but he couldn't be sure. He never weeded over here by the fence, fearing that some trigger-happy guard would shoot him, accusing him later of trying to escape. He only had a moment or two before Watchtower Man got on his walkie-talkie and reported Christopher to the other thugs, his cronies.

The woman had left behind, not only this wallet, but a footprint. The toe of her shoe must have been pointed, like a witch's boot, because he could see the imprint it had made. Near the triangular shape was a hole, the size of a dime, and deep, as if it had been dug out of the dirt with a knife. That was where the woman's high heel had gone down into the earth, practically tripping her. She must, he surmised, have been wearing stilettos. A single daylily grew nearby, its long stem whipping in the wind, its stamens flicking every time a snowflake hit.

Christopher composed the shot for the lens of a camera he no longer possessed. He framed the tableau with his hands, the way an instructor of his had once taught him to do. Still life with flower and shoeprint. As the snowfall gained speed, particles of icy white dust began to cover his artistic composition. A petal peeled away from the stem and spiraled down to the ground, like a Netherlandish vanitas he'd studied in art history as a boy.

Christopher shielded his eyes and scanned the horizon. The guard up in the watchtower was staring at the sun, shoulders squared, jaw thrust outwards. Guards, he reminded himself, were just poor slobs doing their poor slob jobs. They didn't give a shit, nor did they especially want to shoot a guy's head off. What would seriously alarm that guard: a prisoner pole-vaulting over the fence.

Christopher turned around to take a look at the second day guard, a Sioux named Lincoln Mountain. Nearly seven feet tall, he leaned on a cane, blocking the Unit B exit like a boulder. Lincoln appeared to be straight but he wasn't. He'd sold off his painkillers last spring after knee surgery. He had a teenage son, in juvenile detention someplace, facing charges.

The sun had passed over the top of the watchtower. It was early afternoon, and still Christopher lingered by the fence. He raked the earth. He pulled up nonexistent weeds. He reached into his gardener's apron and pretended to plant seeds. None of the guards seemed to want to bother with him. It was just that past winter that Christopher had finally been allowed to leave the maximum security unit, transferred to a minimum security cell in Unit B. The guards in Unit B were slackers. They were overweight and out of shape, junk-food eaters noshing on fast-food apple turnovers. Lincoln was all right. Like most everyone, he could be purchased. Power, money, sex: It was just a process of elimination. Christopher would get to work on him.

At his peak, when he'd had things people wanted, it would have taken him an hour. Now he traded on his status as a statesman's son, on spectral networks and imaginary resources. He had the wallet in hand with the last "Lights out."

Domestic Surveillance

Standing outside Red Barn, Dan listened to the doorbell as it chimed, three times, from inside Nadia's photography studio. He wore his best suit, a double-breasted pinstripe, and he carried a beribboned box in his coat pocket. It was Nadia's birthday, the second of April: He was paying his obeisance to her. Dan had left the office at midday—a rarity—to take her out to lunch at the Windmill. He'd booked a romantic corner table, with a scenic view of Phantom Falls churning against the rocks hundreds of feet below the bluff. The Windmill had won a new star in this year's Michelin guide; Dan had had to make the reservation months ahead. He was pleased with himself for remembering. Nadia had reached a dangerous age, he'd been warned by a colleague, and the birthday must be treated like all perils: as a special occasion.

"Anybody there!" he shouted, having arrived early to park his Saab in the empty lot reserved for her clients. "Nadia, it's me!"

Dan peered in at the window. It was dark inside the front room. She'd taped a sign on the glass that said "Resolution Photography, hours of business, Monday to Friday 10–6." No one was here. Annoyed, Dan banged on the door with the heel of his hand. He had married a Russian-American princess who hadn't even bothered to show up for work. Nice. If Dan had simply wandered away from Mercy Medical Center on a whim, his patients would perish. People depended on him. The stakes for Nadia were lower: snapping photos of newly baptized babies; bridesmaids in their regalia; brides and grooms in their finery. Puttering around with her cameras and paintbrushes, she behaved like a dilettante.

Dan's knuckles rapped hard against the studio window. He looked back toward the main house, but the shutters were closed. Lavishly renovated, Nadia's picturesque barn sat on a hilltop in a meadow. Wildflowers were sprinkled over the new spring grass, their orange blossoms dusted with a light coating of strange April snow. He could hear the river burbling on the other side of the embankment and, from the bushes nearby, a songbird warbled in a duet with a cawing blue jay. Nadia worked here, in this earthly paradise. For just an instant, Dan pictured a patient's cadaverous face—the bluish skin, the discoloration around her mouth where she had been hooked up to an oxygen machine. He was filled with bitterness toward his wife. He despised Nadia for being effortlessly and unthinkingly alive, heedless of those who fought for it.

His fury passed in a matter of seconds, leaving him confused. More than one physician at Mercy had accused Dan of identifying too closely with his patients. His colleagues said Dan was "overinvested" in his cases. Yes, but the patients of those other doctors died, while Dan's sickly women were healed by his fanatical dedication to every detail of their treatment.

Bathed in sunlight, Nadia's garden was sheltered by a row of saplings. Her flower beds were bordered with white rocks arranged in neat, shapely circles. Inside a shallow stone basin that rested on the flagstones, a goldfinch drank from water layered with a thin sheet of ice. When the bird flew off, Dan lifted a small terra-cotta pot, filled with chives, which sat to the right of the front door. He removed the spare key to Red Barn from the clay saucer where Nadia kept it. He went inside, took off his shoes and put his feet up, but he couldn't relax. He drummed against the arm of his chair with his fingertips, checking his watch constantly. Nadia was five, then fifteen, then twenty minutes late. After half an hour passed, Dan sprang up to roam around the studio. He inspected a photograph that hung on the wall behind the cash register, a self-portrait Nadia had taken using a timer. A pop song from an oldies radio station insinuated itself, now, into Dan's thoughts.

"Why don't you listen to my advice? Never make a pretty woman your wife."

He gazed at his wife's photograph, searching her face for signs that she'd been unfaithful to him. The suspicion had taken up residence in his mind. He felt it put down roots, begin to grow and spread. Doctors' wives got bored. This was conventional wisdom; everybody said so. If Nadia had wanted to reserve weekday mornings for an adulterous liaison, she easily could have done it. He had his hands full, running his department at Mercy. Dan was far too frazzled to monitor her behavior.

Dan's shoes pounded on the plank floorboards as he traversed the front room, jangling his keys. Nadia, he mused, had him enslaved. Dan had toiled to build a protective bubble for her, an oasis in which she grew organic vegetables, dried fresh flowers in a handmade wicker basket, kayaked along the Delaware in the late afternoons, and, in the mornings, swam laps in the swimming pool.

When they'd met, Nadia had been a graduate student in the fine arts program at Yale. Yale University in New Haven, Connecticut… even today, that rarified and exclusive place bewitched him. Nadia, too, was refined. An aspiring artist from a wellborn family, she'd enticed him. Her possessions had not been acquired at Macy's, for an affordable monthly fee, as Dan's family's had. She owned solid cherry wood chairs and a matching table; monogrammed forks and spoons; and a small Renaissance oil painting, possibly an old master, a Jan van Eyck. Colors muted from six-hundred-year-old candle smoke, it depicted an hourglass, a wilting lily, a skull, a moth, a wedge of cheese, and a peach. That single painting, steeped in obscure Dutch symbolism, could bankroll an entire wing at Mercy, Dan supposed.

All that, passed down to her through generations of Larinas, had been of a piece with Nadia herself.

The Orsinis, unlike the Larinas, had been peasants. Dan had a seamstress and a grocer for parents; his ancestors had been Sardinian shepherds. Nadia had wanted him despite his acne and his second-hand suits; her aristocratic lineage was apparent in her hauteur, in her porcelain complexion. Her face was classically proportioned. He'd seen Nadia's duplicate in a museum courtyard, on an ancient Roman sculpture made of smoothest marble. There was majesty in the high, sweeping arch of her brows and, in her great sad eyes, a disquieting depth.

The grandfather clock in Red Barn had struck. Dan's thoughts turned to the first time he'd ever seen Nadia on the Yale campus. Nadia that first day in the library, like an apparition. An elegant young woman, heavy but shapely, full-figured, even stacked, sashaying along, sauntering past the microbiology periodicals. Dan had found himself noticing her, absorbed by her looks—her gait, her textures, her materials. Her high-heeled sandals were made of patent leather; her black dress of linen. Admiration caught at him. He perceived her then through a scrim, a prism of notions, phrases he'd overheard long before, at his father's social club, at their church in Staten Island. Gem. Chic. Sleeveless. Sheath. Genuine. Twenty-four carat. Class A. Pearl. Her movements had created a soft breeze, fluttering the pages of Dan's textbook, and he'd sniffed the air, inhaling her piquant perfume. She'd worn sunglasses, like a starlet. As she strolled along, she swung the handle of her portfolio. A stillness followed her passage. The other science geeks in the Yale Reading Room pushed their lab reports aside and exchanged appreciative glances. Like a Ph.D. in chemistry, a lucrative patent, a high-paying job at a drug company—the woman who had walked by them spoke to a collective ambition.

Though he'd never been able to enroll in Yale—he'd applied and hadn't been admitted—Dan had soaked up the atmosphere in the lecture hall. For two semesters, he'd audited an advanced class on cellular biology. He'd spent long afternoons at the Merck Science Library at Yale. Dan-the-grind, Dan-the-striver, researching and studying. When he spotted Nadia that day, he'd abandoned a mound of scientific journals to forage through the stacks, hunting, hoping for a second glimpse of the Yalie in her little black dress. At length, he'd discovered her, reclining on the floor, leaning against the wall by a pile of books. Her long legs had been stretched out before her, crossed at the ankles, like a passenger in a first class airplane seat. Concealed behind the library bookshelves, Dan had watched her, lured by her curves, struck by the sophisticated gold bracelet and the understated strand of pearls, as she gathered her long hair in one hand, lifting it up off her neck. He had looked at her for a long time, planning out his best line of attack.

Now, sitting in Red Barn, Dan waited. He wondered what it was, precisely, that he'd been smitten with that day. Nadia, her pedigree, her surroundings, her eventual attention to him, all these had blended together invitingly, ensnaring him. He folded himself into her leather armchair, looking out the window and across the field. He pondered the house that belonged to him and Nadia. Yellow and white, it resembled the desserts Simone baked at her fancy French patisserie. "Nadia and I are happy and we have a happy family," Dan told himself, though the truth was that days elapsed during which he never saw his family. Nadia remained elusive. She kept some part of herself distant. He'd noticed her wistfulness, or was it despair, as she sat in the den with an open book on her knees, when she thought no one was watching. It was this part of Nadia that Dan most wanted.

One o'clock came and went, and the coveted restaurant reservation was lost. Nadia never arrived. After ninety minutes, Dan climbed the ladder upstairs to the second floor. Here, within sight of their home, but autonomous and out of Dan's reach, Nadia painted.

The alcove she used as a painting studio was open. There was no door or wall, only a simple rustic loft that had once held hay, and the semicircular barn window looking out across the meadow and the open space. Flecks of dust spun gently in the sunlight. Below was the photography studio, where the former stalls for horses and cows had been converted into a darkroom, a kitchenette, a bathroom, and a warren of supply closets. Dan wasn't welcome in this place. It smelled richly of turpentine and oil paint. It looked like some mythological painter's garret, with its spare high table, angled back, and its collection of brushes sorted by size in four old coffee cans. The canvas Nadia had been working on was covered by a red tablecloth. He lifted the corner of the cloth, which cloaked her easel, and found an unfinished portrait.

The man in the painting had a fox's face, shaped like a triangle, wide at the forehead and pointed at the chin, with a forest animal's close-set black eyes. He had a sly, fey quality about him. His skin was stretched tight over his prominent facial bones. The long straight hair belonged to a shampoo commercial. His lips were thin but well-defined, and his mouth was long, curving sharply upwards at the extreme outer corners, like a lizard. His naked body was simian, the muscles taut. Two tins of paint sat on the easel's shelf, one marked "clown white," and the other "rosebud." Next to these, on an index card, Nadia had written a note, complete with her misspellings. "Bild up base of white and roze underneeth," it said. "Deevine skin. Supranatural male beauty. Glow."

Where his genitals should have been, the painting was defaced.

Have Your Cake

Nadia had forgotten him.

Behind a locked door at Mercy Medical Center, Dan curled up on his own examining table, drawing the patients' striped blue "dressing room" curtain closed for privacy. His homey office felt forbidding to him now, cold and charmless. His peripheral vision registered the speckled linoleum floor, the box of latex gloves, the echocardiograph, and the scale's dull glint of stainless steel. The metal examining table, hard against his hipbone and ribs, was terrifically uncomfortable. Through the window, he saw a swirl of snow in the hills. It was four o'clock on the afternoon of Nadia's birthday. Although it was already April, a blizzard was blowing in. He held his cell phone to his ear, listening.

"Everything set?" Jeremy said.

"I think we have to call the party off," Dan said, rolling onto his back. The ceiling lamp was cracked.

"What?" Jeremy said, loudly and dramatically. "No. Fucking. Way."

"Jeremy." Dan grabbed a tongue-depressor from the dispenser.

"Sorry, Dad. I mean, absolutely no way. I tricked Mom by warning her, and she said no surprises, so now she'll go ape-shit."

"Do we need to have another talk about the swearing? Don't do it at school. I don't do it at work." Dan grasped the tongue depressor in both hands, hanging on to it like a handlebar. He refused to tell his son what had happened. He was incapable of saying that Nadia had disappeared. Dan had been torturing himself for hours with the thought: She won't come back. He'd been left drained and listless by the shrieking fear inside his mind.

"I'm not at school, we're at home," Jeremy was saying. "Simone's here getting ready to play hostess."

"Let me talk to her." Dan's voice wavered at the thought of, eventually, having no choice but to disclose the situation to his oldest child, his daughter. He didn't want his kids to hear him weep. With a snap, he broke the tongue depressor apart, splitting the cheap thin wood in two.

"Dad wants to talk to you, Simone," said Jeremy.

"Do I look like I can talk right now, fuckhead?" came his daughter's deep, throaty voice. It reminded him, occasionally, of *The Exorcist*. Though Dan remembered her as a little armful of newborn infant, Simone was suddenly grown—a surly pastry chef with green hair and multiple piercings. Simone rescued stray dogs. Just last year, she'd led protests against Dan's laboratory until they stopped testing chemicals on lab rats. Never mind that the rats were being cured of cancer. Simone advocated garbage-picking. For three months, she refused to buy food or clothing, scavenging industrial-sized dumpsters at the mall.

Once upon a time, Simone had been a delightful infant. A sweet-smelling baby girl who'd slumbered peacefully, content to nestle in the crook of Dan's arm. In his mind, Baby Simone continued to live just as she'd been, napping in her daisy-patterned jumper, her bluish eyeballs moving under her wafer-thin eyelids, shielded by her floppy terrycloth sunhat. Within a year, however, she'd become unruly. He'd given her a bottle one day, and she'd kicked her legs and rolled her eyes up in her head, her face the color of his grandmother's Sardinian spaghetti sauce, screaming. She'd done badly in school—not a little badly, but mega-badly, as in C-'s and D's and reports with comments such as "Simone is disruptive and uncooperative. She may prefer to explore a new environment," which was the D'eusseau Academy's way of saying they were close to kicking her out of school. Dan had gone from indignation to concern to defeat. Now, instead of wanting her to attend a university and become a doctor or a lawyer, he wanted only to avoid calamity.

He wanted Simone not to get pregnant until she had finished dating losers. He wanted her not to be financially dependent upon Dan forever. He wanted her not to get attacked in one of those roughneck bars she used to frequent. And so forth.

"Simone can't talk, Dad, she's doing this elaborate frosting," said Jeremy. "You have no idea. This cake has four tiers."

"Five, douche-bag. Can't you count?" cried Simone.

"I hate it when she sounds like a low-class poot," Dan said. Poot was the Orsini family code word for slut, a shortened form of the Italian *putana*. It suggested a girl who threw herself around aggressively and wore short skirts with bosom-baring shirts—all of which, in certain phases of her adolescence, Simone had done.

"You sound like a poot again, Simone," Jeremy helpfully informed her.

"Can you see what I'm doing, dick-face?" said Simone, her voice loud and clear now, as if she'd made a special effort to scream into the telephone.

"Dad, we have to stop breaking her balls. In effect," said Jeremy.

"Agreed," said Dan. He hurled the splintered remains of his tongue depressors across the room, scattering them around the wastebasket. He had, by now, cracked all of them in half. Dan lifted the caps of the plastic container in search of something else to break. But aside from a few cotton gauze bandages concealed in their sterile paper packages, the jar was empty.

"Tell Simone I can't wait to see the birthday cake, and I applaud her skill and her craft," said Dan, climbing down off his examining table.

"Dad applauds you," said Jeremy.

"Smart move, Dad, you just saved yourself a fortune in psychiatry bills," Simone yelled.

While they talked, Dan stared at himself in the mirror. He stuck his tongue out at his reflection, opened his mouth—silently screaming at himself. He grabbed a fistful of his wiry hair and tugged as hard as he could. He could hardly stand to conduct this familial conversation. His eyes watered. Nadia was missing. He had to delay his children's pain—even for just five minutes longer. He would keep the truth to himself as long as he could. It felt as if a life were at stake. When Nadia's desertion came out, the foundation of the family would crumble.

"Dad, my clever sister is putting the final touches on what may well be the most amazing birthday cake ever made in American history," Jeremy said in a stage whisper. "It's a masterpiece. It's covered with reels of film. These reels of film are looped like garlands. It looks like black lace. Ladies and gentlemen, it's an insane little cake."

"Well, let's postpone the big bash and enjoy the cake at a small family gathering instead," said Dan, blinking at his office: his desk, his file cabinets, his bright yellow wall with Nadia's framed aerial photograph of the Amazon River slicing through a swathe of rainforest.

"Agreed?" Dan said. "Just us. No visitors. Just Orsinis."

"No good, Dad," said Jeremy. "What kind of blow-out fortieth birthday party is that?

"We can't do it, Jeremy. Our guests would have trouble getting home in the snowstorm," said Dan. "Call them, please, and we'll reschedule the party for another time."

"I can't call them all now," said Jeremy. "Dad's getting cold feet. Dad's bailing," he informed his siblings.

"It wasn't that many people. Twenty?" said Dan.

"Twenty-six RSVP's, not including us. But we invited some of our friends too. Let's just have the surprise party like we planned, Dad, please. If you leave now, you'll be home by five."

"I'd much prefer to have it be just us, just family, a simple dinner," said Dan, wondering when he would break down and begin to cry.

"Aren't you supposed to leave there before the storm hits anyway?" asked Jeremy.

Dan took the head off a clay figurine that a patient, now cancer-free, had made for him. It was an angel. Her head had broken off. He'd repaired it with rubber cement, but now it had come apart again.

"I can't find your mother, Jeremy," he said.

"Can't find her? Isn't she at the studio, working? Dad lost mom," he reported.

"Well, no. She didn't show up at lunch."

"Mom stood you up?"

"Basically."

"Mom's cheating on Dad, we think," said Jeremy.

"I didn't say that."

"Amendment: Mom's not cheating on Dad."

"Our father should stick to treating his patients," said Simone, who must have grabbed the phone for a moment. "A surprise party is way beyond his capabilities. Logistics are not our father's fucking area."

There was a scuffle, a thud, and then Simone's voice asserted itself anew, harsh and tough. "What the fuck, Dad?" He and Nadia had raised this tough-talking hellion. Simone was a changeling.

"I'm worried about your mother. She's officially missing."

"Yeah, well, that's because you didn't listen. You didn't listen to me. Because you think you're smarter than everybody," said Simone.

"No fighting today, Sisi." The boys had called her Sisi when they were babies.

"No fighting, no swearing, no cigarettes, no alcohol, no refined flour, no white sugar, no red meat," said Simone. "You know what happened here? You drove Mom crazy by being a control freak."

"I'm sorry, I'm so sorry," said Dan, overcome. Something in his life was going very wrong.

Simone heard his distress. She skated over it with her blasé cruelty. "Our father is having a nervous breakdown," she said, flatly. "He thinks Mom may have left."

"Maybe she's..." Jeremy said.

Their voices fell to whispering.

"Could be. He neglects her," said Simone. "And you two boys treat her like shit."

"We don't. Do we?" said Jeremy.

"You act like she's the housekeeper, the kitchen maid," Simone said. "You never put a dish in the dishwater. You never lift a finger. Dad doesn't either, not the king of the cancer empire. He has to work sixteen-hour days. He doesn't have time for her. Now maybe she wised up and went away with whatshisname."

"Who is whatshisname?" said Dan, pulse accelerating.

"That hot carpenter that hangs around sniffing after her," said Simone. "Max Dial, Max Drake, or something."

What else didn't Dan know? And how had his family turned out like this, so inconsiderate? Dan had noticed the callousness of his children before, combined with a dead-on reportorial accuracy, especially in Simone. As kids, they'd all done comic impressions, mimicking their classmates and their parents, skewering them ruthlessly and collapsing in laughter. Dan's children had a mean streak.

Dan moved the mouthpiece away from his chin so they wouldn't hear him sniffling. He had a box of tissues on his desk. They were for his patients, not for him. They were for the sick, who came to him in pairs, two by two, accompanied most always by a mother, a son, a daughter, a husband. Twenty times a day he confronted it: the faces of women in mortal fear, the stricken warriors who listened, dry-eyed, women diagnosed with ovarian cancer, looking him in the eye and responding to the news, the numbers: thirty percent survival rate; seven in ten will die. We can treat it, we can fight it, we can remove the diseased organ. One young woman lying in her hospital bed had clutched his hand and had said, looking up at him, "Don't let me go." How could he explain? Who survived and who flatlined wasn't up to Dan, but his patients didn't believe him.

Now Dan took a tissue himself. When he withdrew it from his face, it was soaked. Dan had zoned out on the phone. He heard his son shouting at him, "Dad, hello, hello."

Dan recovered. "I'll be home soon. I guess we'll go ahead with it."

"So, what's the scheme?" asked Simone. "Caroline Delaney is bringing Mom, they're coming to our place, and then we have the party. Right?" Caroline Delaney, a landscape architect, was their next-door neighbor.

"Simone," said Dan. "I do love you and accept you as you are. I know that you're hardworking, gifted. If I've ever been less than supportive..."

"Dad, we both know that you weren't 'less than supportive.' You busted my chops. You were brutal," said Simone.

"I apologize. Parents don't know everything, Sisi. We just try."

"Are you calling a moratorium on ball-breaking?" said Simone.

"Um, well. No."

There were new muffled noises over the telephone. "Just hurry up and come over, Dad, I'm sure she'll be here eventually," said Jeremy. "Mom has no friends. Where could she go?"

"Your mother has plenty of friends."

"Not really, Dad. Half the people we invited, she doesn't even know. She's pathologically shy. She's afraid of people. Haven't you noticed?"

"The word pathological is not a joke."

"But *Mom* says that. She says: Shyness is my pathology."

"She never says that."

"She says it. All the time," said Jeremy.

"I'll be there in forty minutes or so," Dan said.

His wife talked of "pathology," and painted portraits of naked men? Muscular young carpenters wanted to take her to bed? Nadia drifted farther and farther away from him. Dan didn't want to go home. Here at Mercy Medical, he knew just what to do—how to alleviate suffering, how to provide nutrition, how to combat debilitating side effects like the iron deficiencies that left his patients weak and depressed. He knew how to remove polluted tissue with a scalpel, how to protect healthy organs, how to suture flesh so that it would heal without infection, lingering soreness, or visible scars. He knew how to bathe an organ with a precisely measured dosage. He knew how to kill bad cells and nurture good ones.

But Dan Orsini didn't know fuck-all about the woman he was married to.

Stormy Weather

Dan took off his lab coat and put on his brown herringbone jacket, changing out of his loafers and into his sneakers. He left his office and strolled down the hallway, half-heartedly preparing to leave the hospital. The clean white vinyl shades, usually kept closed, were rolled up in the hallway windows, suffusing the entire fourth floor of Mercy with intense bright sunlight. There was an apocalyptic feeling to Mercy, just then. It was too quiet, as if all the patients had given up, en masse, and had swallowed strychnine.

Up and down the fourth floor, at the oncology and G.I. nursing stations, a skeleton crew of hospital employees had gathered in groups of twos and threes, listening to their radios and watching their portable television sets. Dan was supposed to have left a long time ago. The corridors echoed with the inauspicious sound of piano chords announcing "emergency" news broadcasts. These began with a clamorous musical introduction like the thunderous hooves of approaching horses.

"This is WORU," said a local newscaster's resonant baritone. "And I'm Jason Griffen. A storm warning is in effect across the region."

A few staffers in green scrubs and white uniforms attended to their paperwork, pens scratching while they bent towards the clock-radios on their desks or their portable transistors. Dan's head nurse, Veronica O'Conner, sat at the reception desk outside the infusion suite, aggressively punching numbers into the telephone keypad, one by one, with the ferocity of someone killing ants with her bare hands. She was canceling patients.

Dan watched O'Conner through the open door. The unwelcome thought crossed his mind that he should have married *her*. With his cell phone in hand, he was calling Nadia for the hundredth time. "You've reached Nadia Orsini of Resolution Photo," said a recording. "I can't get to the phone right now, but your call is important to me." She sounded mechanical, rote. A lump formed in his throat. He was keeping the worst ideas he had at bay, leaving them as half-formed, mute intimations of an encroaching loss that stalked him.

O'Conner's gestures, as she went about her business in the Infusion Suite, had a crisp, competent quality that soothed him. Watching her, he pressed the redial button on his cell phone. Storm clouds gathered outside his window.

"Doctor Orsini!" shouted O'Conner. "What's the matter with you?"

Startled, he dropped the phone. "Nothing, O'Conner," he said. He'd been fretting. He had been imagining Nadia at leisure, strolling past the shops on Pine Avenue, or maybe lying on the floor of some motel room, or maybe dead. A life ended more easily than most people appreciated. Dan often thought his family was in imminent danger. He'd been known to take their pulses while they slept.

Scowling, O'Conner put her hands on her hips and broke out of the reception area, which was shut off from the rest of the office. She approached his doorway and peered in. "What the hell are you doing, Doctor? Do you see what time it is?" O'Conner pointed to the clock on the wall. Her fingernails were long and impractical; each squared-off nail ended with a wide, even, white stripe. O'Conner looked at him meaningfully. She gestured at the window. A thickening fog enshrouded the east wing and west wing of Mercy Medical Center, a benign white brick structure which sat low in the valley. "Do you see what I see?" she said. It was 4:08 P.M.

"A little foggy today," Dan murmured.

"Doctor Orsini, what's in that obstinate head of yours? What are you doing, if I may ask?"

"I'm just doing my job, O'Conner. What are *you* doing?"

"I'm paying attention to the weather report, Doctor. A blizzard is predicted, and the visibility on those roads is getting dangerously low. The Lord is in charge of what happens in the sky, Doctor Orsini. Not you. Get out of here! It's time to go!" She was top-heavy, with narrow boyish hips and long legs. She'd been working for him for years; they'd traded tips on which pharmaceutical companies to invest in; they'd watched the final innings of the World Series in the staff room. Both were fans of the Mets. Beyond that, O'Conner existed for him only as a highly skilled colleague at the hospital. He knew simply that she was organized and efficient. She was O'Conner, to him, not Veronica.

"I've been having trouble finding my wife," Dan said, catching O'Conner's eye.

O'Conner tugged at the chain around her neck and looked thoughtfully at her employee badge.

"She's just not answering me, O'Conner," Dan said, softly. "I don't know what to think."

"How long have you been trying?"

"Since noon, around."

"Call her now." She slid a patient's chart back into an accordion folder, as if she would force Nadia to obey. She didn't look at Dan, and she made an expression, pursing her lips, that he didn't like. O'Conner's fourth or fifth husband had cheated on her. Doting on anyone who was tethered to an IV, bestowing candies and blessings upon the ill, O'Conner always thought the worst of healthy people.

"Quit thinking what you're thinking," he said.

"Doctor, I didn't say anything."

He tried again. Nadia wasn't answering.

"I'd think," O'Conner offered, "that she would have heard about the storm coming. I'd think that she'd call *here*. I'd think she might be worried about you."

"She's probably off on a photo shoot someplace. Every now and then, she takes a bus trip up to the mountains, hours away. Up there in the woods, she may have spotted a moose or a bobcat, or some other wild animal. Her wildlife photos have been printed by the Audubon Society and in *National Geographic*," Dan said, defending Nadia.

"Oh, really? When was this?"

Nadia's color photographs—of marmosets and Brazilian howler monkeys—had been printed on the cover of *National Geographic* five or six years after he'd married her. The trips to the Amazon had been arduous and, if she'd taken the staff job the magazine had offered her, she'd have had to travel three months each year. She had elected to start her own photography studio instead. Neither of them had ever said so directly, but her career was dead. She was talented, but she was no longer viewed as a serious photographer. Mostly, these days, she took pictures of newborn infants, brides-to-be getting their portraits taken, and brides and grooms at weddings. The local gallery indulged her with a show every other year, but that was because Dan and the Mercy trustees were chummy with the owner. Dan and his boss haunted the gallery on weekends, buying whatever paintings and sculptures caught their fancy. It was good for business for the proprietor to exhibit Nadia's photos. What was most disconcerting was that Nadia painted, every day, storing her finished canvases up in the loft at Red Barn, never unveiling them, never selling them, never showing them to anyone. Only her photos were made public. Her painting was done, ritualistically, in secrecy.

"She'd sit in a swamp for hours, covered with mosquitoes, to wait for an otter to show up," was all Dan said. "She'd build this thing they use, in wildlife photography, called a blind? It's camouflaged with sticks and leaves and you'd wait there, and the animals and birds can't see you, and you'd hide. She'd do anything to get the shot.

Anything she needs to do. Mostly wildlife photographers have to wait around a lot." He'd heard Nadia talk like that, but that had been years ago. Now she usually stayed indoors to shoot, preferring the easily controlled lighting system of her studio. Her photographs of birds, which had been made into greeting cards by a friend's company, were exquisite. They showed paired toucans grooming each other's feathers and hummingbirds probing for nectar with their thin beaks, while their open wings thrummed like fairies'. But they weren't taken in "nature" at all. They were obtained at the aviary, the easy way.

"If *I* were married to *you*, I'd forget the photos and start thinking about my husband," O'Conner said, with a blunt, complimentary air that stirred the air with possibility.

"She's a remarkable mother," said Dan, feeling obliged to speak well of Nadia. "The boys are growing up, O'Conner. In all the years we've been married, Nadia has never done anything like this before."

"Like what? Refuse to return your calls?"

"Don't be an alarmist, please. I hate to think what would happen if you took that kind of attitude with the patients. You always tell *them* to think positive," Dan said.

"An observant individual like yourself ought to..."

"Ought to what?" said Dan, startled by an intuition that hadn't resolved itself.

"Trust your instincts, that's all I'm saying. She's a woman, isn't she?"

Suddenly, he was angry. "What's that supposed to mean?"

"I say what I think, Doctor, as I've always done. That's why you hired me."

"Well, you're the expert," he said, snidely. "You've been married now, what? Four times. Haven't you? Or was it five?"

"I stopped counting."

"Nadia's caught up taking photos in the mountains someplace."

"Sure she is."

O'Conner's evaluation of Nadia felt irrevocable. Dan, who had been fiddling with an old New Year's Eve decoration—a dusty paper accordion, covered with glitter, which hung from the front desk—removed it from its string and crumpled it into a ball. "Knock if off, or I'll sack you," he said, wanting to restore their easy camaraderie.

"That'll be the day."

"My wife's a professional artist, that's all I'm saying. She has a degree in fine arts from Yale, which happens to be a top-ranking school." A bell went off in his mind.

"Ah, Yale. I may have heard of it," said O'Conner, dryly.

"Art's important to my wife," he insisted, not sure of his own argument. "She's as dedicated to her work as I am to mine."

O'Conner gave a horrible, dismissive little shrug.

"I'm beginning to be sorry that I ever brought it up." He slapped a file down on the desk, with the feeling that he'd revealed too much, that he'd given something to O'Conner which he should have kept.

She glowered at him, reached into the pocket of her lab coat, and presented him with an official-looking sheet of paper. It was an interdepartmental memo that he'd managed to ignore: "Storm Alert. Mercy Medical Center will close promptly at 2:00 P.M. due to hazardous driving conditions."

"Do you want to come back here in an ambulance?" O'Conner said. "Go home."

"What about you?" Dan helped himself to the colorfully wrapped candies she kept in a wooden bowl.

She swatted his hand. "Those are for my patients, not for you." The patients were Dan's, in reality, but she always called them "mine." "Anyway, you could stand to lose a few," she continued. "Your heart is working overtime. That extra weight on your belly isn't good for you."

"Look who's talking."

"Are you saying I'm fat, Doctor?"

He raised his eyebrows. She had tripped him towards something.

She sighed. "That's it. Next week, you and I, we go on Weight Watchers. What's the point of preventing cancer if we both drop dead from strokes?"

"I'd definitely do Weight Watchers with you!" said Dan, attaching himself to the idea with a fury, as if she'd suggested they spend the weekend on a Caribbean island. "Oh, O'Conner. Let's."

"Fine. What I need you to do right now is..." She showed him the door.

"I'll go when you go," he offered.

"Doctor, here is the situation. I live six blocks away. I'm walking to my house on Old Mill Street. You, on the other hand, have a forty-five-minute drive ahead of you. Your car slides off a cliff, how do you think I'll feel?"

"Probably, since you can't live without me, you'd kill yourself."

"Wrong. Orsini, I'd throw a party. Get out of my hair. You exasperate me."

He watched her waltz back to her desk, noting the high, undulating rump beneath her lab coat. She propelled herself along, her clipboard in hand, her legs sturdy, the muscles clearly outlined through the fine mesh of her white stockings. When she was out of sight, Dan started to go back to work, reviewing the test results that had come in that morning.

"What," O'Conner yelled from the outer office, "Would happen to your patients? It's no joke. I'm not just worried about *your* butt. Who will help those people? They're in bad shape as it is."

"Not all of them," Dan said, peering in at her from behind his door, doing a rapid calculation of statistical probability. A quarter of his patients, the most fragile ones, would meet their demise without him. He had to gain acceptance for his new treatment model. No other doctor knew what Dan knew.

Even as he left the building and descended the front steps, Dan considered turning back and taking Veronica O'Conner further into his confidence. He longed to tell her the miserable thing that had happened when he'd tried to track down Nadia's former classmates. He'd thought it would entertain Nadia to see faces, at her surprise party, from the different periods in her life. Nadia was estranged from her family, and the invitation list had seemed so sparse. He didn't know where to find her friends. She had to have over a hundred acquaintances in Riverbend and the neighboring towns, people who must have liked her, worked with her, had coffee or lunch with her. He assumed there must be a file full of names, addresses, and telephone numbers somewhere. It had taken him some time to locate it. He'd borrowed her address book, on the sly, removing it from the desk drawer he'd finally found it in. He'd called more than three dozen phone numbers in that book, dialing them between appointments during the course of a busy week, grabbing a spare moment to plan Nadia's party. When he'd come to the last page of the address book, Dan had had the sense that very few of the people he'd spoken to knew Nadia well. They were clients, for the most part, whose children she'd photographed, whose weddings she'd attended with her camera in hand. Her candid shots of social gatherings were, Dan thought, a cut above the average. Her prints had a lush hothouse palette which didn't reflect what was actually in front of the camera. Rich greens and pinks, eye-popping reds and yellows in strong contrasting hues could make even a suburban garden look like a tropical jungle. Lately, Nadia had begun to use a new technique. She photographed in black and white, later hand-tinting her prints, painting directly on them with a brush to summon an otherworldly beauty. This method—from black and white to paint—struck Dan as deceptive. It had recently occurred to him that her retouched photographs were deceitful.

Now Dan had come across a virulent strain, in Nadia, of duplicity. He'd contacted the Yale alumni office for a list of students in her graduating class, thinking he'd send out a batch of printed invitations to her friends from graduate school. The fine arts program was a small one, so the thirty students who'd matriculated that year would most certainly have known Nadia. When he'd called the alumni director, the woman had asked Dan for the year in which Nadia had completed her studies, for her year of birth, and for her maiden name. Yale had no listing for anyone named Nadia Larina.

The Birthday Party

A pack of strangers milled in and out of the Orsinis' kitchen, in and out of the living room, in and out of the family room. Empty wineglasses, rims smeared with lipstick traces and ringed red from the Merlot, had collected on the polished dining table. Poppy seeds and pumpernickel flatbreads had been ground into the antique Persian carpet. Crumbs covered a wing-back armchair. A silver serving tray containing half-eaten appetizers rested on the floor. Blondie had stolen it and had dragged it between her jaws to her dog basket in the corner, where she had devoured a dozen spinach pies. Plastic multicolored pick-up sticks, black and white dominos, and red and blue poker chips spilled out from an overturned toy chest in the family room. Underneath the cheese straws left uneaten on the couch lay a full deck of playing cards, in disarray. Two sisters who went to school with his son Will had abandoned a competitive game of blackjack. The cards were fanned out across the three pounds of roasted almonds which were strewn over the Nepalese cashmere blanket. Curled pieces of emulsion-coated paper were littered everywhere.

Twenty guests had shown up, despite the snow, more or less on time. After a while, Simone had started making jokes about *Waiting for Godot*. Bored, glum, the guests had begun to rebel, eating all the desserts they could get their hands on. Simone served them her apricot tarts. She served them her almond biscotti and her butter cookies. She hid Nadia's birthday cake underneath a crate of apples, saving it from the famished horde, in case of mutiny.

The guests opened their party favors within an hour. Inside their goody bags, they found the miniature photo albums Simone had bought for everyone, and the pocket-sized red cameras loaded with self-developing film. They'd spent ten minutes taking blurred photographs of one another, each one no bigger than a thumbnail, before losing interest. Outside in the yard, the boys had begun to dismantle the wilted paper party decorations, soaking wet, falling apart. Snow plummeted from the skies in a direct line, descending quickly, as if each flake had been flung down, hard, from the heavens. The snowfall was collecting rapidly in the garden, mushrooming into great powdery drifts and mounds. They flickered like crystals, reflecting the holiday lights the boys had strung up in the bare branches of the trees.

Dan had been trying to reach Nadia for the past six and a half hours. As soon as it was nine o'clock, he'd decided, he'd call the police. At ten o'clock, he'd call the hospitals.

Someone had paid Brad-the-snowplow-guy to dig everybody out. The guests began to depart soon after he'd finished shoveling Dan's driveway. They left at 8:38 in a single wave, bundling into ski parkas, shouting good-byes, leaving in twos and threes, citing obligations, mumbling about their kids' trigonometry homework. It was an unfortunate instinct in the human beast, this tendency to desert. He'd seen it at Mercy, the close friends whose frequent, regular visits to the hospital mysteriously dwindled just as a patient weakened. But Nadia's guests couldn't be expected to stick around all night. Dan had never met most of these people before, though he recognized some of the faces from the photographs on display at the front desk at Red Barn. Dan could tell they thought his marriage to Nadia was a shambles, or that she'd turn up in an emergency room. He'd noticed them staring at him inquisitively, wondering what inept sort of husband he was.

"Anybody home?" Nadia's voice called out from the front door at three minutes past nine, as Dan finally pressed his internal panic button, just when every last guest had gone home. He was in the kitchen, holding the telephone receiver, looking at the emergency phone numbers posted on the bulletin board. He'd been preparing himself to call the local police precinct to report Nadia as missing.

"Surprise!" Jeremy, Will, and Simone shouted.

When Dan walked in to the living room, Nadia looked baffled.

"What is this?" she said to him.

"Your birthday, Mom. Happy fortieth," said Jeremy. "Sly dogs are we, huh, Mom?"

Nadia clapped her hand to her mouth. She said something to herself, but it was muffled.

"I tried to give you a heads up, Mom," said Jeremy. He turned to his brother and sister. "She hates surprises, so I dropped her a hint." He shrugged in apology.

Dan watched Nadia's face. She stared straight ahead, the features immobile, the eyes moving ceaselessly, searching their expressions for clues. She was rehearsing her lines, she was performing. "Thanks a lot, guys," she said, peevishly.

"We had people over but they left," said Will, crunching a carrot lathered in a creamy fatty dip. (Heavy cream was a primary ingredient in Simone's recipes, a flagrant denunciation of what she called the "killjoy" carcinogen-free antioxidant-rich diet plan Dan had imposed upon his family.)

"How did you manage to get home?" Dan said. "The roads aren't safe." He stuffed his hands into the front pockets of his jeans, clenching his fingers into fists.

Nadia avoided his eyes as she took in the party's aftermath—the dirty dishes, the crumbled crackers, the wheel of Brie left to ooze in the heat, melting on a plate. "Get home?" she said, looking around nervously. "Well, uh, I called the car service. They drove me back. Long wait. Storm. It took a while."

She was dressed for a special occasion, in a form-fitting outfit and high heels. She'd evidently paid someone to have her hair lightened. She was so nervous, Dan saw, she could barely speak. He pressed his advantage. "You couldn't have been waiting for a car service all day. Where have you been all this time?"

"Oh, nowhere. I drove up north, not far, a few miles, into the foothills of the mountains."

"Did you?" said Dan. "How nice. I expect to see the pictures."

She blushed crimson. "What pictures?"

"You go up to the mountains to take photographs," said Dan, speaking each word slowly. "No doubt you were chasing after winter wildlife? A pack of wolves. Or maybe a young coyote."

"I, um."

He almost felt sorry for her.

"You must have been waiting for that wolf for a long time. You were out in the cold for the past seven hours," said Dan. "You should be treated for exposure and frostbite. Let me take a look at you."

"I wasn't waiting that long."

"Why don't we all take a walk over to Mom's darkroom at Red Barn, and she can put her film in the pan," said Dan. "Mom likes to develop her film right away, don't you Nadia? I can't wait to see the prints of this animal. Let's go. Nadia, give me your camera."

"No!" said Nadia, who seemed to be changing into another person right before his eyes. "No. I didn't take any photographs."

"No kidding," said Dan.

"I went to see an old friend who runs a spa," she said, breathlessly. "I soaked in a boiling hot Jacuzzi. They have this lounge where you lie on beach chairs around a shallow indoor pool filled with floating candles, listening to music. I had a massage, and it did me in. I fell fast asleep. I had no idea you'd planned anything. I… I forgot it was my birthday."

"What friend is this? I invited all your friends here," said Dan.

"What friend?" Nadia repeated, in an obvious attempt to stall for time. "His name is Dylan. I'm sure I've mentioned him to you. He's a tattoo artist and he owns a health club. A chain of them."

"A friend, no doubt, from Yale," said Dan, perilously. Never had he heard of the Tattoo Boy before. He could see his marriage like a costly piece of bric-a-brac, made of hand-blown glass, balanced on the edge of the bookshelf. Crash.

"Open your presents, Mom," Jeremy said, and Dan noted, from the way Will had hurried to the stereo to turn the music up, and the way Simone had rushed to the kitchen to get the birthday cake, that his kids had taken it all in. They'd soaked up everything. He might as well have carried a sign: Nadia and Dan, your mom and dad, are rupturing.

In Simone marched, bearing on a plate a five-tiered cake. A tiny camera, made of slivers of chocolate, was the crowning touch. The lower levels were embellished with forty short black birthday candles. Arranged in concentric circles, they were designed to look like film canisters. The icing was garnished with what looked like black and brown lace but was in fact reels of film made of frosting.

Dan watched Nadia. She looked terrified.

Everyone waited for Nadia to smile and blow the candles out. She just stood there.

"I don't understand how you could do this," Nadia said, her mouth making a shape Dan had never seen before.

"Mom, it's just a cake," Jeremy said, with a trace of hysteria.

"Where did you get it?" she said, her expression unaccountably antagonistic. "How?"

"I made it, Mom," said Simone, sensibly. "I make cakes. Remember? I'm a baker. It's what I do."

"Why?" said Nadia, looking frantically into their eyes.

"This is a birthday cake," said Will, pushing his rimless glasses down on the bridge of his nose. "What are you freaked out for?"

"You took my film," said Nadia in a croaking whisper. "That's the original. You found my film and you… You broke into my safe. You looked at it. Didn't you? You're horrible, all of you. How could you? You disgust me. You. You're vile."

"What safe?" said Dan.

Jeremy and Will exchanged a glance.

"Mom," Simone said, slowly. "This is a cake that I made for you at the bakery with Lucille, the other pastry chef. It's made of butter, flour, sugar, and eggs. C-A-K-E, cake. Okay?"

This was the worst thing to say. It reminded Nadia of her poor spelling, her bad grammar, the things that made her different from them. Dan pitied her as her face contorted. She seemed to be standing alone in a desert, wracked with grief. She was no longer with him. Something had swooped down and abducted her. But it only lasted an instant. She held her head high and, though shaken, regained her composure.

Simone, too, was studying her mother carefully. She took Nadia by the hand and led her towards the frilly white confection. "I didn't use real film, Mom. Are you nuts? I wouldn't mess up any film you'd developed. No one's trying to invade your privacy. None of us would ever hurt you. You have our respect." But these were strange things for a daughter to say to a mother on her birthday. Simone spoke down to Nadia, the way a social worker might calm a patient on the ninth floor of Mercy Medical, where the head cases were admitted for episodes of psychosis.

Dan saw Nadia put herself back on, the invisible veil that she must have worn over her face, a costume that he'd never apprehended, a veneer separating him from her. Now, at last, like an actress remembering which play she was appearing in, she smiled.

"Thanks guys," she said. "Thanks so much. It's been a long day and I had too much scotch at lunch. I'm disoriented."

Another silence ensued.

"Since when do you drink scotch?" said Dan.

"Just today. Turning forty," said Nadia. She touched her hair.

"I thought," said Dan, moving closer to her, looming over her, "that you'd forgotten your own birthday."

Her hands flew up in front of her face and for a ghastly moment, Dan thought that she expected him to hit her.

"Scotch with your old friend, poolside, at the spa," said Dan. But the Furies had gone. He felt a growing concern for this other person, the one crouching behind Nadia. The air in the house seemed to shift. Someone gentle and shy had entered the room, someone he had never met. She was a large-eyed, timorous creature, skittish, uncertain, like an approaching doe. Dan understood everything, just then, but he knew nothing. He'd only caught a glimpse. She was gone.

"Come on, it's a party, Dad," said Simone, diplomatically, clearly trying to prevent her parents from launching an epic argument. "Let's have a nice time. You never pay any attention to what Mom does all day. Let's celebrate. Don't start getting jealous now."

"Of course I care about your mother and her... activities," said Dan. He scanned Nadia's face for the Other Woman, the one who must have been beaten. He was sure he'd seen her cringing, shrinking from a shadow, protecting her face from a ghostly male hand that she'd imagined raised against her, set to attack. Rigid, she'd held her arms up, crossed at the wrists, making a screen for her face like a prizefighter warding off a blow. Some bastard had pummeled his wife? Some bastard had mistreated her, had scarred her. In their bed, late at night, lying on his back, holding her hand, Dan had run his finger along that deep scar she had on her palm. He'd touched it, quietly, without saying anything, asking her about it only with his fingertip. Nadia's scar ran from the base of her index finger to the heel of her hand.

"How did this happen?" he'd said, once, holding her close, pressing the scar tissue. She'd shaken her head, no, closing her hand, taking her hand back, hugging herself.

"I have a blood brother," she'd said. That was all.

And Dan, accustomed to his patients and their reticence, to staying within the bounds, within the permissible limits of scientific questioning, hadn't pushed her for information.

Now Nadia hurried into the kitchen. Dan heard her opening and closing cabinet doors randomly, banging them, futilely. She didn't seem to know what she was doing in there. She was trying, Dan thought, to collect her thoughts, to prepare more lies for him.

"I'm starving," Nadia said, striding casually in to the dining room with an empty glass from the kitchen. She'd made a special trip to get it, while a dozen clean glasses had already been lined up on the dining table.

"Let's open the champagne, Dad," said Will, unsmiling, somber behind his eyeglasses. He was fourteen years old and he spoke and behaved like a middle-aged man.

"Your mother doesn't drink," said Dan. "Except on her birthday, and she's already hit the bottle today. Heavily."

"These are delicious," Nadia said, bright and chirpy, crunching an appetizer that was the size and shape of a ping pong ball. "Did you make these, Tootsiepie?"

Simone was always 'Tootsiepie,' babied, given pet names. Simone was indulged, provided with extra pocket money and a new leather coat, a new car, a new refrigerator and stove, new furniture, a new haircut at the salon, a new pair of boots, a new apartment of her own.

"I did make them, Mom," Simone said. "I catered the whole party, using you guys as my guinea pigs. I might start my own catering company. Even the Newland Coopers liked my cooking. If I started my own business, instead of working at the restaurant... Maybe they'd invest." The Newland Coopers were a prominent Pennsylvania clan. They'd been manufacturing luxury leather goods since the 1800s.

"Magnificent," said Nadia. "What a fantastic idea, your own

company, of course you should and you will. No wonder the Newland Coopers were awed by you. You're my star. Dan, try some of these amazing... what? What are they?"

"They're little cheese soufflés," said Simone.

"Have some, Dan." Nadia's dark sparkling eyes looked at him beseechingly. She was saying: I know you're angry at me, but the kids put up all these decorations and made food and cake, let's not fight now.

"Complication" was the term Dan used, at Mercy, for the unintended consequence of a medical procedure. Dan, with difficulty, put the complication with Nadia aside. Whatever else had taken place, she was healthy and alive.

"What's all this?" Nadia cried, with showy exuberance, her hands fumbling with the bright metallic gift wrap, a stack of packages, tied with ribbons. She opened a card, tearing the envelope raggedly with her fingertips. "From Caroline. Was Caroline here?"

"Quite a few people were here," said Dan. "Around twenty of them."

She looked up sharply. "You're joking."

"We invited a few of your friends," Simone said.

Without meaning to do it, Dan revisited the injury, again. He said: "Including your classmates from Yale. I tried to invite them, in any case."

"Oh, college administrations are as bad as government agencies, aren't they?" Nadia looked hopefully from one face to the next. "Yale. Ah. They're such a bureaucracy. The red tape at that place used to aggravate me." Nadia frowned, shaking her head dismissively. She drained her glass and poured herself more champagne. Her hand shook ever so slightly, like a patient showing early signs of Parkinson's disease. Some of the bubbling liquid spilled on the sleeve of her jacket. She daubed at it with a cocktail napkin and pushed her sleeves up. "Let's see, what did Caroline get me?" Prattling on, Nadia held the gift out, displaying it.

He saw a vein in her forehead twitch spasmodically. Secret thoughts flickered in her eyes.

Dan dropped the Yale topic because of the way his children were looking at him. Whatever it was that their mother had done, they didn't want to know about it. She had returned to them from someplace dangerous.

Nadia thanked everyone like a movie star accepting an Academy Award, her behavior too carefully choreographed, too staged. She began pleading exhaustion, and fled upstairs with her swift, sure footsteps. She went right to sleep. Dan lay beside her slumbering body, on the opposite side of the mattress. He rolled on to his side to keep Nadia, in her white silk nightgown, within his sight at all times. He couldn't sleep. Every few minutes, he opened his eyes. Yes, she was still there beside him. Yes, she was all right. He could see the moon and the branch of the oak tree through the window. This view from the bedroom window had been a symbol, to him, of what he'd attained. He was Doctor Dan Orsini, The Provider. He had made a beautiful family, started a thriving medical practice, acquired a big comfortable home, built an indoor swimming pool, and bought a Saab. But now that moon was enigmatic. Dan kept watch over his wife that night. He thought: She may be taken from me. Nadia needed guarding.

Best Revenge

Only faint threads of light filtered in through the grated six-by-six-inch window in Christopher's cell. He was turning the pages of a tattered paperback novel. As soon as Angel began to snore in the bunk beneath him, Christopher withdrew the wallet, silently, from his armpit. The leather, damp from his perspiration, felt soft and supple. It was lambskin of exceptional quality. The size and shape of an envelope, like an evening purse, the wallet had a snap closure in the center. The surface was decorated with stylized flowers. These were rougher, bumpier patches of leather attached to the smoother lambskin like encrustations. Even in the dimming light, he could see the flowers were the colors of Easter eggs—orange, lemon, raspberry. Against the black background, the effect was oddly jarring. Christopher closed his eyes, breathed in the perfumed scent of the leather mixed with the residue of other smells from inside a woman's handbag—the perfume, the lipstick, the cosmetics, the makeup brush full of face powder, the ink from a magazine, the sweat from her hand, the metal keys, the oils from the strands of hair caught inside a hairbrush. Female smells whispered to him. He stuck his hand in his jumpsuit and pulled on himself, but he couldn't get hard. Jail had left him limp. Only weirder things got him going, and he tried to avoid thinking about his revenge fantasies. Now that he was participating in Group, now that he was writing it all down, nothing was his own. His very thoughts were being monitored.

What could be more tragic than a ruined dick? It made him want to scream. He gave one last squeeze to the cold bump of skin in his hand, throttling it. He wanted to tear it off and throw it at the wall, really. It had become a hindrance, a burden. Useless piece of shit. Just one more thing to add to his new list, written for Group, of regrets. It felt like a raw chicken breast, floppy boneless white meat.

"Oh, fuck it," sighed Christopher, giving up in frustration. He put his hands behind his head and began to imagine what sort of woman the wallet must belong to.

Nothing ever had flowers on it, not around here. He missed them terribly, the flounces and the frills, the panties and the heels. Femininity had congealed into one fragrant jumble in his mind, a fashion runway, a feather boa, a pair of lips, eyelashes, a crotch, all pleasantly combined, his old Garden of Eden, his lost paradise. This was why he'd signed up to be the penitentiary gardener when Nelson had rewarded him for good behavior. Now he could be near living things that were delicate and pink. It was the only effective way, at Triton, to get Outside. One hour of strenuous exercise in the yard daily, that was what the men of his old unit had been allotted.

The colorful leather flowers on the wallet were girlish, jaunty, sassy, flirty, frivolous, saucy. Adjectives, a list of them, Nelson said to always start out by taking pen in hand and making a list, a shopping list, a wish list, a shit list, a list of feelings, a list of actions, a list of the women loved and lost, a list of the grievances suffered, a list of harms done.

The flowers didn't correspond to Christopher's impression of the sleekly dressed, uptight, nervous woman who'd paced the prison grounds that afternoon. That lady had been buttoned-down and businesslike, while the wallet was whimsical. The owner of the wallet, he imagined, was the endearing sort of young woman who'd wear plastic cat's-eye spectacles. She'd like satin lingerie in crazy neon colors, black nail polish, and rhinestone hair clips. Best of all, she'd give blowjobs to guys she'd never met before, climbing good-naturedly into their cars.

He held the wallet while the dream girl sprang to life.

Slim, padded, the wallet's design brought to mind his days as a child seated in a private room at the Parallel Club, that shrine to wealth and power on upper Fifth Avenue. He'd held a black leather menu that felt just like this against his fingertips. The waiter had handed Christopher the menu with a flourish, and he'd said, "Morning, Mac." It was the waiter's game to call Christopher "Mac," and to have him look at the menu. This was strictly a formality, because every Sunday Christopher had ordered the same thing: flapjacks. He'd held his menu upright against the white linen tablecloth, and he'd knocked down his water glass, the wet stain spreading over the banquette cushion, the ice cubes falling into his lap, making a mess on his chair, the floor, his pants. He hadn't done it intentionally but his parents thought he had. It was as if an invisible poltergeist were out to sabotage him. That year, Sunday after Sunday, Christopher had spilled the water every time they took him to the Parallel Club. At last, his presence had been banned.

Like those menus of his childhood, the lost wallet had a spine down its back and two leaves on either side, two flaps that opened up like a book. In his cell, so many years after his last visit to the Parallel Club, Christopher slipped a curious, optimistic finger into one of the wallet's pockets. No bills, no money. An investigation of the other pocket revealed, in the corner of the flap, a collection of receipts. He had to take these over to the window to read, climbing quietly down the metal bed frame of the bunk bed, creaking softly, keeping his back to Angel, and listening for his breathing to be sure he was asleep.

The first receipt was from Salon de Quartier on New Wharf Avenue in a town called Narrowsburg. The receipt had been filled in, by hand, and dated. It had been a long time since Christopher had seen a road map, and his knowledge of geography had begun to fade, along with everything he knew about the outside world. Still, he was sure Narrowsburg, on the Delaware, was many hours away from Triton. The mystery woman had spent nearly three hundred dollars to have her hair colored, cut, and styled and to get a manicure and a pedicure.

Christopher whistled under his breath. Three hundred dollars to get herself fixed up. That very morning. On her way to Triton. Oddly enough, this thought uplifted him and even his flaccid dick gave a happy little throb. Some chick went to the hairdresser before she went to jail. How expansive. His Mystery Date could be a lawyer, on her way to a meeting with some murderer on death row, needing to look gorgeous so she could... What? Go to the governor and plead for a stay of execution? She had to be a nut-job. Miss Mystery Date was a mad housewife, getting her jollies from guys behind bars. She liked serial killers, she liked the Ted Bundies. She was pen pals with some madman in the unit. She exchanged letters with the damned. She might be a prisoner's imaginary girlfriend. He'd seen it happen. Inmates, even the worst of them, had their fans.

His dick went back to sleep. Nothing for Christopher here. He searched around in the wallet, sighing. The second receipt was dated back in December. It came from a restaurant in Milford called Le Refuge. It seemed Little Miss Mystery was a snob. She had a hankering for establishments with French names: a petite bourgeois affectation. She had spent another $1,442.00 at the French restaurant, though he couldn't tell from the waiter's scrawl how many people had dined with her. One thousand four hundred forty two dollars, crap. She had plenty of money, this lady who wore high heels, a suit and pearls to the penitentiary. She was loose-fisted with her cash, spreading it around. He'd been like that, himself, as a young man with money. As he held the scrap of paper in his hand, it dawned on him that the date of this meal had been Christmas Eve. He knew of a circle of people who refused to cook during the holidays. They were a self-important, affluent group. His mother and father had been among them.

The third receipt was from a camera supply shop in Poughkeepsie. She'd dropped close to four thousand dollars, a few days ago, on a tripod and a vintage Super 8 film projector, the kind he'd had as a kid in art school. Mystery Chick was a photographer, either a serious amateur or a professional camerawoman. His dick responded to this with a single, startled twitch. He brought the wallet to his face. He pressed it against his cheek as a feverish child might grab his babysitter's cool hand. A hope had started to spring up in him, but he'd been disappointed too often, and he tried to stop the wish from taking shape. He couldn't resist digging into the wallet now, searching for new clues. Each leather compartment had a pocket sewn into the lining. She'd left bits of paper in the left one, pushed down at the bottom. He withdrew a homemade card, cut from heavy paper, with a note written in childish, looping penmanship embellished with drawings of bats, rats, and spiders.

"Happi Moather's Day," it said, "Frum S."

At the River's Edge

Unable to sit still, Dan was outside the hospital, pacing the riverbank that ran alongside Mercy Medical Center. He marched in circles through the hospital grounds, tossing his stethoscope over one shoulder like a neck scarf. His unbuttoned lab coat fluttered around his legs; a breeze brushed his cheek. Orange, purple, and yellow tulips blossomed riotously, in the formal gardens, by the hundreds. The bright colors assailed Dan's eyes. Off he raced. The wind off the river smelled of faraway places. It urged him onwards, pressing him to run for it.

Dan wasn't himself of late. In the last three weeks, since Nadia's surprise party, two of his favorite patients had launched written complaints against him. He'd mixed up their files, confusing a benign calcification in the left mammary with an invasive ovarian malignancy. To his shock, he'd recommended the wrong procedure for each. He'd advised the seriously ill patient to opt for a lumpectomy, when what was urgently required was a radical hysterectomy. It had been his patients who discovered the error, not Dan. He'd never once slipped up like this in his eighteen years at Mercy. Suddenly, his personal preoccupations threatened to envelop his medical practice. Unless he took care of the problem with Nadia quickly and efficiently, his patients were at risk. His career might be irreversibly damaged. Anything could happen. If Dan didn't get it together, he might kill someone by accident.

Lost in thought, he stopped to stare at the river. How restful it looked. All around the hospital, people appeared to be enjoying themselves. Their lazy pleasure grated on Dan. He wanted to charge madly across the lawn, wild-eyed, screaming out to warn them: The end is near! Not the end of days, perhaps, but the end of a life with Nadia. For hours, he'd been deliberating the unthinkable. His indecision had made an exile of him, alone, cut off, even here at his own hospital.

Yet these others lounged, contentedly, underneath the shade of trees, lying on top of their spring raincoats, spreading out over the grass to peruse newspapers and chat on cell phones. Hospital employees dressed in sea green scrubs or snowy lab coats, while the patients wore pajamas, slippers, and sunglasses. Rolling along in their wheelchairs, they sported their white plaster casts and sterile gauze bandages with a defiant panache, as if flaunting fashionable accessories. Like maimed tourists, they clustered on the lawn, eating sandwiches in Styrofoam take-out boxes. Several pairs of patients were playing chess, brows furrowed in concentration as they bowed over the gray and black checkerboards built into the old stone tabletops. Some patients were accompanied by shiny wheeled machines which towered above them. Needles were attached to the backs of their hands with tape. Plastic tubing stretched from their arms, gleaming in the sun like spider's silk.

From across the lawn, all of this seemed fantastically remote. What Dan had guessed about Nadia frightened him; it never left his mind. She'd been false. He needed to take an action but something prevented him.

Dan hummed and whispered to himself like a babbling schizophrenic. He moved rapidly past the staff parking lot. He took short, even steps with his brown lace-up Oxfords, carving out a pattern of figure eights, crunching on the gravel. His hands were in constant motion, thrust deep in the front pockets of his lab coat. One hand was balled up into a fist, picking at his cuticles, cracking his knuckles. The other hand pinched at the delivery notice he'd found in their Bridge Street mailbox. A second package for Nadia had arrived at the P.O. box in Riverbend.

Dan's frenzied thoughts spun outwards in all directions. A Beatles song was stuck inside his head. He didn't know the name of it, recalling only snatches. It sounded to Dan like the prelude to a murder. The haunting minor key presaged menace.

"I told you before," Dan sang in staccato, stressing each syllable. "You can't do *that*." Keeping rhythm with his fleet footsteps, he punched his hipbones repeatedly with his fists.

A pair of squirrels, digging up dirt in the tulip beds, froze at Dan's approach, tails twitching.

"I told you before," Dan sang, striding towards them, watching the two rodents crouch low to the ground. They made a bolt towards the bushes, abandoning their prey—a peanut in its shell—next to a row of grape hyacinths.

"You can't do *that*!" he shouted aloud. What a reprehensible little song! It foretold the tale of Dan and Nadia, predicting that Dan would marry a two-faced user. He'd sleep beside her, basking in her warmth. He'd become her childbirth coach up on the second floor, inhaling and exhaling with her, holding a stopwatch to time her contractions in the Mercy obstetrics wing. As each child was expelled into the bright lights of the delivery room, he'd severed the umbilical cord.

But Nadia could do *that* to him.

One week after Nadia's surprise party, Dan had come upon the convict's letter to Jenny X. Though he didn't grasp what any of it meant, his belief in Nadia had nearly shattered. If she couldn't explain herself—the hours left unaccounted for on her birthday, the prisoner's package—he was prepared to exit.

Four different times, in the quiet of the living room, Dan had resolved to confront Nadia directly. Four different times, he had turned to her, taken her hand in his, opened his mouth—and failed. Instead of demanding the facts, he'd offered to make her a cup of tea. It had been surreal to sit beside her and sip hot green tea from her gilt-trimmed china, while silently debating whether or not to demand a divorce. He practiced what he would say, but it sounded too deranged. "Excuse me, dear, but are you involved with any criminals, by the way? No? Oh, good. Then we're okay."

As he retraced his steps by the benches along the river, Dan's fingers crumpled the slip of paper. He'd re-read it a dozen times.

"Delivery attempted to: Mrs. Orsini . I.D. required. Please present this receipt to the Central Station to collect package." At the end of the form, the postman had filled in a blank in blue pen. He'd written: Oversized package. Postage due. Undeliverable.

Dan intended to intercept this second package. This time, instead of burning it, he'd preserve the handwritten pages that spilled out of the padded envelope. To learn what Nadia was, he must keep calm, poring over every word. The letter from prison would dictate her fate, like an oracle.

He sat down on the bench. He crossed his left leg over the right one. He rested his ankle on his knee. His right foot had started shaking again, of its own accord, a nervous habit he'd developed—and conquered—during medical school. The shaking foot was back again.

"Damn you," said Dan, as the foot continued to wiggle. He grappled with his ankle, grasping it between both hands, wrestling the appendage into submission. "Stop it," he hissed at his shoe. If anyone had seen him, they'd think he was a madman.

"Earth to Orsini," said a woman's voice.

Glancing up, Dan saw O'Conner standing behind his bench.

"I asked you if you wanted the chicken salad or the chef's salad, Orsini. Is your hearing impaired?" she said, sardonically. "I'll have to set up an appointment for you, for a hearing test."

"Oh, hello O'Conner," said Dan, startled. "Uh, I'll take the chicken."

"This is very nice," O'Conner said, in a tone of perplexity, handing him a cardboard tray and looking around the riverbank, with its blossoming flower beds. "It was uncharacteristically considerate of you, Orsini, to invite me."

"Nice day," Dan said, weakly. He had asked O'Conner to meet him here for a reason.

"You're welcome."

"Oh?" said Dan. "Right. Thanks for lunch."

"You owe me eight bucks." She eyed him with curiosity.

Dan patted his pockets. "I..."

"You don't have any cash on you. Tell me something I don't know."

"I owe you one," said Dan, opening the various containers on his tray—juice, water, fruit salad.

"One, huh?" said O'Conner. "More like one a week. My expenditures on your lunch come to roughly $500 a year. But, you see, Doctor, I reimburse myself from petty cash. So who's counting?"

Dan closed the containers again. He wasn't hungry. "I'm a rotten boss, aren't I?" he said. "I hear what you're saying. You're saying I take everything you do for me for granted."

"I've learned over the years. Never ask a question that you don't want answered."

Dan tore open a cellophane packet of breadsticks. His thoughts drifted away: to Nadia in pearls and a sleeveless dress with a low-cut back that formed a V at the base of her spine. She'd strutted through the double-doors of the Yale library, clopping in her high-heeled sandals, turning the students' heads when she sailed past them. She had cut quite a memorable figure as she strode across the reading room, her hair in a glamorous upsweep, her eyes hidden by her sunglasses, her tasteful, knee-length dress hinting at the hourglass of her shape. The dress had been slit along one leg, giving Dan a tantalizing peek of inner thigh.

Shaking off the memory, Dan dumped his breadsticks on the tray, scattering sesame seeds over the ground. A sparrow obligingly pecked at them. He sensed that O'Conner was staring at him. He speared a cube of chicken and spun the fork around, ever so slowly, leaning down to inspect his food. "Do you think this chicken is organic?" he asked, narrowing his eyes. "I hope Mercy isn't feeding our patients poultry that's stuffed with antibiotics. Are they? My last study showed that high dosages are a factor..." He didn't complete his thought.

O'Conner knew all about Dan's antibiotic study, of course. She disapproved of his obsession with chemical-free food. His emphasis on diet tended, she said, to place too heavy a burden on the patients. They had enough to worry about as it was. They should eat whatever they wanted to, O'Conner insisted.

"Antibiotics," she said, dismissively. She didn't deign to answer him.

Dan, rejecting his chicken, nibbled cautiously at his salad. "This romaine is slathered in pesticide," he said.

"No doubt," said O'Conner, chewing noisily.

He picked up an oatmeal cookie and held it up for general viewing. "Butter, animal fat, trans-fats," he said. "Are they deliberately poisoning people, there in the cafeteria, so they'll get ill? I can't understand it." He dropped the cookie back onto its plate.

O'Conner leaned across him, reaching into his tray. "If you're not eating that cookie, I will. May I?" Between mouthfuls, she said, "What can I do for you, Orsini? You said you needed my help."

"Hey, O'Conner, give me a bite." He broke off a corner of cookie, his thumb grazing her hand. Her female skin, with its extra layer of fat and surfeit of estrogen, was seductively smooth. Underneath the epidermis, her bones were as slender as Eskimo ivory carvings. Her fingers reminded him of his own corporeality. All women's hands felt heartbreakingly delicate to Dan.

O'Conner took her hand away from him.

Dan popped the bit of cookie into his mouth, tasting the forbidden sweetness of refined sugar. He scrutinized the shore opposite, fixing his gaze upon the little town of Cold Brook. Beside a cinema's marquee and the flags of a car dealership, he saw the arc of a Ferris wheel tracing its gradual descent.

"Can I ask you to do me a monster of a favor?" He pulled out the yellow slip of paper from his lab coat and handed it to O'Conner, together with Nadia's passport. He'd ransacked her studio early that morning, planning to return the passport after nightfall. "I'll understand if you can't do this. No hard feelings."

O'Conner squinted at the yellow paper. "I don't have my reading glasses. This is from the post office?"

"It is. It's for Nadia, and I want to open it before she does. They'd give it to you, if you say you're Mrs. Orsini. They won't give it to me. Obviously, I'm not my wife. They'll see that right away at the post office. I'm a man."

O'Conner groaned. "You're asking me to steal someone's mail. That's illegal, Orsini. Highly."

"It would mean a lot to me."

O'Conner flipped through the old, brittle pages of the passport. "How farsighted *are* you? I don't look anything like your wife."

"The passport's out of date," he murmured, taking hold of her elbow and squeezing. Again, he noted the sumptuous smoothness of her skin, so like Nadia's. "It's an old photo. No one will notice."

Bracing himself for an inquisition, he watched O'Conner turn the pages. They had been stamped, twenty-two years earlier, in Athens, Istanbul, and Tangier, although Nadia had never once mentioned traveling.

"Nadia Tatiana Larina," O'Conner said, reading the maiden name aloud. Something about the passport looked faintly wrong to Dan. He did not know what he'd do if O'Conner were to confirm this impression.

"What exactly do I get out of all this?" asked O'Conner, giving him a sharp look.

"I'll take you out for a drink," said Dan. She hadn't questioned the passport, he saw, with relief. His malaise played pranks with him: The passport was perfectly legal. If there was anything suspect about the quality of the paper, the government seal, or the ink, the eagle-eyed O'Conner would have caught it.

But she just pointed her index finger at the sky, moving it around in a slow circle, like a drunk at a party. "A drink with you. Whoopie, Doctor," she said.

"Thanks, O'Conner. I owe you."

"You sure do," she said. "What you ought to do is double my salary and give me a promotion."

He and his colleague sat quietly, side by side. Dan closed his eyes and tried to meditate with the sun warming his face. "Nothing in the world can hurt you," he told himself, a phrase he'd read in a dying patient's Buddhist prayer book. "There is nothing. You are the one drop of water, splashing, separated only for a single moment before returning to the stream, rushing, eternal."

He didn't believe a word of it.

"That's enough for me, O'Conner," he said, impatiently, opening his eyes and standing up.

"Ultraviolet rays," O'Conner agreed, and they made their way back into the building. As they entered the gloomy stairwell, the relentless internal patter began anew: "I told you before: You can't do that," over and over.

The Visitor

"Did someone come for me?" asked Christopher. As he spoke, he could see the guard named Luis making secret hand signals behind Christopher's back. Luis, with whom Christopher was cordial, shrugged emphatically, opening his arms wide. The gesture said, clearly, "I don't know what to do. Christopher Benedict is going mad."

Fred indicated with a nod that the signal had been received. Fred was against him, too, now. Fred agreed.

"You're not supposed to be over here, Benedict," Fred said to Christopher. Fred was known to all as a fuckhead. His office, at the end of the hall, was lined with cabinets marked "A-E," "F-K," "L-R," and "S-Z." These cabinets were traps for paper dolls. The square metal boxes slid in, and they slid out again, to display or conceal personal information. The files contained records of every man's crime, every man's confession, every man's love letter and short story, every man's protest of innocence. They wrote it all down, the guys who pretended to be on your side in Group. They kept notes on prisoners' thoughts and dreams, the novels they read, the tales they told, the pictures they drew, the phone calls they made, the books they wrote.

Christopher had to be careful.

"Mr. Benedict became very upset just now, Fred," said Luis. "Never had any other visitor before, just his best friend, just one guy who comes around once or twice a year. He thought he saw his woman out back, on a bench, while he was doing the planting this morning. Not the first time that she's been here sitting there, watching him, Mr. Benedict thinks. I said he could come in here with me and talk to you about it." Luis had been a guard at Triton for all the years that Christopher had been a prisoner. Once large and muscular, Luis had slowly shrunk, turning into a little old man, ready for retirement. He had skin the color of the teak easel that Christopher had done his first paintings on, in his parents' penthouse, when he was a boy. Luis's long sorrowful face was handsome, ageless, and covered with dark brown moles. With his trousers sharply creased and belted high on his waist, he managed to look stylish, every day, as if he weren't watching over a building full of criminals, but was on his way out to an evening of ballroom dancing. He was unfailingly polite to Christopher.

"I've never had another visitor," Christopher repeated to Fred and Luis. "Please, man."

"A lady came in," Fred said, opening a file drawer, continuing to do his paperwork. "She came yesterday."

"For me?" asked Christopher.

"She asked."

"And you fucking sent her *away*? That was my visitor, you fuck. Are you crazy?"

"Visiting days are four times a year, Benedict. This is news?" Fred gathered up a stack of papers and tamped them down against the desk to straighten them.

"The List! The Form! Everything is a list and a form with you people. Oh, fuck, Fred," said Christopher. "Please. You're a real pal, aren't you? Like everyone else in the world, you had to go and skewer me." A blood-spattered painting appeared inside his mind. He'd seen it before, many times: the bone-chilling mental snapshot taken in Lucidora. It was a high contrast portrait of himself this time, in black and white. It was a photograph of his body with a hole through the temple, a tunnel clear through to the other side, an underground escape route. Brain matter and blood were seeping out from his head, leaving a dark amorphous shape to expand, slowly, over the white tile bathroom floor, like an oil spill.

Men perished at Triton. Years earlier, only a few months after he'd begun his sentence, a prisoner had jumped a guard and had committed suicide in a shower stall, shooting himself in the center of his forehead with the handgun he'd snatched. People went nuts Inside. It was easy to get angry at yourself, at the guards, at nothing, at the impenetrable wall that separates a man from sunlight.

"You're coming up for parole, Mr. Benedict," Luis reminded Christopher gently.

"You fuckers. You scumbags," Christopher whispered.

"Don't do it. Think about it," said Luis and, reaching up to him, put a large hand on Christopher's shoulder. "Come on. She'll be back for you. She wanted to see you and she will. On the first Tuesday in May. Don't you worry yourself so much about it."

"She won't," said Christopher, bitterly. "She'll never come here again. Not even my own brothers call me. Not even…" He had to stop speaking. "My mother."

"Now, Mr. Benedict, be calm," said Luis.

"I'm not calm, man. How can I be calm? I am shit."

"You're not shit, Mr. Benedict. Mr. Benedict isn't shit, right, Fred?"

Fred didn't reply. Fred was honest. He hated Christopher, not in an active way—Christopher wasn't important enough to be bothered with—and he didn't cover up his disdain.

"It never helps me out, you know, when I start feeling sorry for myself," said Luis, a mystical smile coming over him. "My wife Maria died," he said, still smiling kindly, "When a truck backed into her and knocked her down. I pitied myself too." He patted him again.

"You can get another wife," said Christopher, enraged at every human being who was lucky enough to be on the Outside.

"Oh, I can't. I never would be able to marry again. My Maria took my whole heart with her, Mr. Benedict. Everyone has a load to carry on their shoulders here in this world. You're not the only one to bear it, that's all I'm saying."

Christopher pulled away, shaking the old man off him.

"Shhh," said Luis, as if Christopher were a wild bull, a frightened, wound-up animal. "Mr. Benedict."

"I'd like to kill both of you," said Christopher.

"You come up next month, now, don't you?" asked Luis, his voice sonorous and deep, undisturbed by Christopher's threat. But on the other side of the office, Fred's hand had moved to touch the holster. He cupped his hand around the handle of his gun, looking Christopher in the eye. They could shoot prisoners in self-defense. It had happened twice, just in the last three years alone. No one ever got in trouble for it. The prisoners were always wrong, and the guards were always right.

"Mr. Benedict," said Luis. "Remember that you're just about to come up in a few weeks. For parole."

"What was her name? The girl that came here to see me. Didn't she tell you?"

Fred hesitated, hand on his gun. Then he let go of it and picked up his clipboard instead. "No," he said, giving Christopher a look. "She didn't want to leave a name."

"It was *her*," Christopher told them, turning first to Luis, then to Fred. "Jenny X from the Bond Street Aktionists. My Jenny. She came to see me."

Luis nodded. "It sure might have been your lady," he said. "Sure thing."

"Don't you talk down to *me*," said Christopher. "Don't you know me? Don't you recognize who I am?"

Luis stopped nodding. Something happened to his eyes, as if two invisible shutters had been wide open for Christopher and now, quite suddenly, had slammed closed.

"I remember Jenny X," said Christopher. "She had the devil in her. I recognized the devil in the way she moved."

Luis and Fred exchanged a look.

"It was her, you two stupid assholes," said Christopher. "It was my girl Jenny who came here for me."

"She'll be back to see you, Benedict," said Fred, glancing up at the clock. "You have a half hour left to finish up outside in the yard."

"She was wild Jenny," said Christopher. "We formed a group, see. Me and Jenny X, we started a global peace movement."

"Sure you did," said Luis. "Come on back to the yard. Bible study starts at four o'clock, you know."

Christopher bit his lower lip with his front teeth, hard.

"If you do all right and walk the line, you can see that woman in three months' time," Luis told him. "Three months is nothing, after what you've been through. We are talking about ninety days here. Chill out, please."

"Poor sucker," he heard Fred say to Luis, while two other guards took Christopher by the arms, grabbing him hard enough to leave a bruise. Blue at the center, violet at the rim, it manifested like a starburst. It left a trail of lavender asterisks, no bigger than pinpricks, trickling down in a broken line towards the vein on his inner wrist.

I'm Only Sleeping

As he lay in bed on Saturday morning, Dan heard the heavy footsteps of his sons clattering up and down the stairs like a herd of stampeding bison. The front door shut with a slam. It opened again, swinging back on its hinges and hitting against the outer wall with a bang. A leaping untamed antelope ascended the staircase, taking two or three steps at a time, from the sound of it. A bedroom door was flung open. Objects were thrown around inside Jeremy's room.

"You little shit! Did you take my iPad?" Jeremy shouted.

"Watch the language!" shouted Nadia's voice from far away, outside on the lawn.

Jolted out of a dream, Dan was alert now.

Two thumps and a whooshing sound meant the shutters and the window had been thrown open. "You inconsiderate miscreant, where the F-word is my iPad?" Jeremy yelled out the window.

"Jeremy! Keep it down!" Nadia shouted at the top of her lungs.

Dan gazed up at the canopy above their bed. He was not awake enough to be colonized by his panic, but in a few more moments, he knew he would be. Yawning, waiting for that omnipresent waking terror to overcome him, he wondered how he'd come to live in a state like this: one in which a boy of Jeremy's age needed such expensive computer gadgetry just to get inside a neighbor's car and go to the mall to see a movie on a Saturday. He reached for the alarm clock and stared at it. It was eleven o'clock in the morning. When he was Jeremy's age, he would have been on Long Island picking apples with his father. He would have been working steadily, with a break for lunch, from 7:00 A.M. on through the afternoon. He'd spent his Saturday mornings driving to the orchard in his father's truck, loading it with bushels of fruit and bins of lettuce, spinach, and cauliflower to be sold in the Orsini produce cart. He'd had a night job at the Stony Brook Diagnostics Center, washing out test tubes and organizing microscope slides containing human tissue samples. He'd spent Sundays doing his homework. The lowest grade he'd ever received was an A–, unlike any of his children.

Now the door to the master bedroom opened with a creak. "Dad, you're not awake, are you?" said Jeremy.

"No, I'm not," said Dan.

"You haven't seen my iPad, have you?"

"No, I haven't."

"Want to come with us?"

"I can't come with you, Jeremy. I'm sleeping."

"Want to hit the batting cage this afternoon?" Dan and the boys had Saturday outings.

"Yes, sure."

The door clicked shut. The young antelope's hooves clattered down the stairs for a final time, Caroline revved up the engine of her silver Mercedes in the driveway, loud bad music blared out of the car speakers, someone yelled "Not Metallica," and the music changed to a piano concerto, someone else yelled "Fuck no!" and the music changed again, and the Saturday morning expedition team drove off down Bridge Street and over the river to the mall. Dan was fully conscious. He wouldn't be able to fall back asleep. His pulse had quickened; his anxiety had been raging in the wake of Christopher's second letter. He wished he'd gone with his family, as a distraction, but lately it had become difficult to be in the same room with Nadia.

He covered his face with the soft pillow. As soon as he had the house to himself, he'd start in again. Spying on his wife. It had become a compulsion, a mission.

Twenty minutes later, unbuttered whole-grain bagel in hand, he was trudging through the meadow to Nadia's studio, bleary but intent, wearing only his pajamas and a sweater. He entered her studio, leaving the lights off, and warily cased each room, half-expecting to encounter another man. He began looking for Nadia's address book. He searched for it in her desk, where he'd originally found it, but to no avail. She'd moved its hiding spot. This in itself was damning. There must be something inside the little book which she was eager to keep concealed. He ran the flat of his hand along the bottom of her table, the underside of her couch, her armchair and her footstool. The key to her storage cabinets was taped underneath a shelf in the kitchenette. He detached it carefully. He rooted the address book out, finally, in her hanging files, where she kept her financial records. It lay tucked between a stack of bills marked "paid." The torn cover, if he wasn't mistaken, looked more battered than before.

It showed a reproduction of a painting of Venus, riding her seashell on the waves, her long blonde hair festooned around her naked figure. Nadia—or someone else—had carefully glued the picture back together. Four rubber bands kept the binding secure. Dan riffled through the volume, page by page, searching for a clue to Nadia. The tenth page was blank except for one entry for a Mr. and Mrs. Nathanial Henderson. In the margin by the address Nadia had written "D.B.—clients." Other pages made reference to this unidentified person, using the same notation. Nadia had written in pencil, lightly, as if prepared to erase it. "D.B.—client" appeared above the name "Zellinger, Ralph." Here, she'd added a reminder to herself: "Mention D.B. & Yale."

On the inner back cover, defying any attempt at correct alphabetization, she'd written "D.B.," again, followed by a street address. The location was in New York State. Dan had seen the name of that town before. It had been stamped on the packages to Jenny X. Blackwood Hills, New York, was the postmark.

Later that afternoon, avoiding his family, Dan drove to the cemetery in Scranton. He stopped in the flower shop and bought an assorted bouquet. It came inside a green plastic cone, sharp as a stake, to pierce the earth. In the cemetery, as a finch warbled musically from a nearby tree, he bent down to leave fresh flowers by the headstone that marked Belinda Daniels's grave.

He looked at the simple tombstone. It was the numbers that he saw, not the words. The birth date. The life span. Brief, in this patient's case. It was almost five years now since Belinda Daniels had died. She was the one that he'd revisited in his thoughts, checking to see if he could have improved the odds for her, if he'd missed something in her treatment regime. At sixteen, her rapid metabolism had spread disease faster than his medicines could retard the living organism that had invaded her organs. It had quickly washed Belinda away, in one forceful tidal wave, flooding her system with mutating cells until she collapsed on a staircase between the third and fourth floors at Mercy. She'd been gone by the time she'd been transported downstairs to the E.R., leaving nothing behind but a thin form beneath a sheet, the breasts still new. It was this girl, Belinda Daniels, who had taken Dan's hand in hers—her fingers already growing cold, her circulation already slowing. She was the one, lying in her hospital bed, who had looked up at Dan, her eyes enlarged in her shrunken face, her bone structure exquisitely fine, her skin radiant, ethereal. The illness, paradoxically, made these women ravishing, made even a plain patient pretty. She had said to him, "You won't let me die now, Dr. Orsini, will you?"

"You'll be all right," he had lied. He had told himself: She'll live through the week, or at least the night. So I'm not misleading her. She will not die right this moment. It was the only time he'd been afraid to tell a patient the prognosis. He carried it, still, the weight she'd handed him that night at Mercy, asking him to save her when it wasn't his fault and he couldn't help. Dan wasn't a superstitious man, and he didn't know why he'd come here to the cemetery to ask a dead person what to do.

Dan rose early that Monday, before the sun had risen, while his family was still asleep. He showered and dressed in the downstairs bathroom to avoid waking anyone else up. He skipped his morning cup of green tea and his all-bran and soymilk breakfast. He gave a bone to Blondie and left the house. He didn't drive to Mercy Medical.

In a coffee shop in town, Dan called O'Conner to say he wouldn't be able to come in to work.

"What's wrong, Doctor?" said O'Conner.

"Upset stomach."

There was a pause. O'Conner's silence told him she was skeptical. "Is everything all right, Dan?"

"I'll be fine, thanks, Veronica."

"It's a lot of cancellations," she said. "First the storm, and the time you took off last week. There are twelve patients expecting to see you."

"I'll be in first thing tomorrow. I count on you. You'll handle things." He hung up, inexcusably infuriated. It hadn't fully hit before: Sisters of Mercy Medical Center owned him. He had sacrificed his nights and his weekends for the hospital. He stumbled around his house on Saturday mornings like a zombie; he never took his wife out; he was exhausted, half asleep; he sat in sports stadiums watching his boys play basketball, barely keeping score. Meanwhile, the hospital engulfed him. He didn't want to be Dan and Veronica. He wanted to remain O'Conner and Orsini. He had a vague premonition of unpleasant, mechanistic forces hounding him, closing in.

In Milford, he turned off at Pine Street and parked in front of a diner that he'd never been inside. He sat on a red swivel stool at the counter and ordered a jelly donut. This mass of dough, sugar and fat wasn't part of the Orsini nutrition plan, his cancer-fighting diet, which consisted of green tea, tofu, kale, legumes, and blueberries. He ate his jelly donut with a knife and fork, slowly.

Anyone looking at him would have thought he was indolent. But Dan was occupied. He was reassessing his first impressions of Nadia.

The night Nadia had strolled in to the Lantern Tavern in New Haven, where Dan tended bar on weekends, he'd almost fainted with fear of her, that special fear that is exaltation. "Oh, I go to Yale," she had let slip. What had she said, precisely? Her enrollment at an Ivy League school had been high on Dan's list of Nadia's enchantments. It was a bedazzling accessory, like her casual name-dropping: Cole Porter and Zelda Fitzgerald had been guests at her great-grandparents' dinner parties.

He'd thought about Nadia, the arty girl from Yale, incessantly. As soon as the bar had emptied out, he'd tried to write up his lab notes, only to find himself full of Nadia, instead. It had been his practice then to take a Ritalin so he could keep up his grades and hold down a job, dispensing with sleep. Wired, jittery, drinking his black coffee and popping his pills, he'd pictured her while he sat in the empty bar with his chemistry textbooks spread out in front of him. He'd imagined waking up in his own bed, in the dormitory at Colerite Community College, with that lovely face beside his on the pillow.

He'd been awfully impressed with himself for having the nerve to ask Nadia Larina out. He recalled the thrill of victory he'd felt when she'd linked her soft arm through his, as they'd ambled around Saybrook, a quaint town located midway between their two colleges. The village square had been all green lawn and white colonial houses clustered around the church with its cross, crisply outlined against the sky, atop a steeple. He'd been proud to walk with her, showing her off, wearing her like a charm, in the days before he'd earned his medical degree. Before Nadia came along, other beautiful women had rejected him, nicking his pride. His conquest of Nadia Tatiana

Larina was proof of his basic operating theorem: Though Dan had been attending an undistinguished two-year community college, he esteemed himself as exceptionally brilliant. He would outperform the children of privilege. His confidence in himself never wavered once he had Nadia at his side.

At night, in his dormitory room, Nadia had clung to him with ardor, and with a moving gratitude, as if she were Ophelia on the verge of drowning, and Dan her hero. He'd accepted what she told him, never prying, never extracting the personal history she demurely withheld. She had mentioned her family of displaced White Russians who'd fled to the English countryside after the October Revolution. Much diminished, they'd lived by the shore, in Cornwall, inside a ramshackle house on a promontory high above the sea, raising a herd of prizewinning cattle. Though no longer wealthy, they had hobnobbed with Diaghilev, Léger, and Picasso. Gertrude Stein and Peggy Guggenheim had vacationed in the summer cottages at their seaside farm. Ballet dancers in trailing, modernist dresses had quaffed champagne, collecting seashells. It was a pretty photograph, in an album, that she'd shown him.

At 11:00 A.M., Dan left the diner and drove home. The house looked wan at this hour of the day, deserted, without the usual colorful accoutrement of cars, bicycles, basketballs, baseball bats, croquette balls and mallets. Only one brown rabbit sat near the brush, ears back, on its haunches, as still as a wood carving. He stood in his driveway staring up at white and yellow structure, built of clapboards, with its high peaked roof and its turreted hexagonal attic. He turned down the path that led to Red Barn. It would be empty today; Nadia was at Town Hall. She had a weekday wedding to shoot.

For the past forty-eight hours, Dan had been struggling to develop a useful mathematical formula. He needed to crack a code. Across the field, on the first floor of Red Barn, he'd discovered a custom-built safe installed in the wall, behind the wainscoting.

So, This Is Art?

In Unit B, Christopher was touching the art supplies. The paints, pastels, and brushes were neatly arranged in plastic containers in the center of a long table in Meeting Room 11. Anyone in Unit B could use them. Unit B was populated by thin, polite men. The Unit B men had cheated on their income tax or conspired illegally to raise the price of stocks and bonds. Christopher had joined them because he'd officially become a model prisoner. At Nelson's recommendation, and with Brother Bill's letter of support, he'd been transferred to the minimum security facility.

Christopher was beside himself with excitement. He couldn't make up his mind—oils or acrylics? Paints or pencils? He didn't know how to choose. He sat close to the art supply containers and took a yellow pastel into his hand. He pressed its oily surface between his fingers. He put it back and took an orange pastel instead. It was impossible, after all this time, to begin. He put the orange pastel back in its container, closed the container, and opened a canister of clay. A full five-pound wedge of clay sat inside, untouched, just purchased, fresh. He pinched the virgin clay, then dug his fingers into it. The balls of his fingertips made circular craters in the soft gray substance. His throat closed. He swallowed again and again. Now he sensed it, like the smell of spring coming: He might actually have a fucking chance.

If Christopher was allowed to make art again, he might be able to leave Triton, one day, not long from now. But he could still blow it; nothing had been decided. He had to be prudent.

Christopher made a small clay figure, the size of his pinky, in the shape of a woman. He kept his little woman to himself, sheltering her in the boat of his cupped hand. He only looked at her for a moment and then he folded her in half, like a contortionist, grinding her feet into her face. He flattened her out with his hand and rolled her around and around on the tabletop. He made a ball of her. He changed the motion of his hand, forward and back instead of around and around. He turned her into a sausage, then a string bean. He kept rolling her out, thinner and thinner. He looped her into a coil, like a baby snake swallowing its tail.

"I see you found the clay," said Arnold Kroll, the art therapist, coming up from behind him.

Christopher was so startled, he jumped. He glanced over his shoulder, but Arnold wasn't even looking at him anymore. The idealistic young man's horn-rimmed glasses seemed to come from the Salvation Army supply room like everyone else's. Arnold was sitting in front of an easel, staring fixedly at the African violets on the worktable. His hand moved across his sketchpad while his eyes examined the petals and the leaves. Arnold had brought the luscious purple and white violets with him. They came from the Outside—not just from out in the prison yard, not even from the prison town of Triton, but from out in the real existing world (the world that was rumored to exist, half-forgotten) where Arnold walked around like a normal noncriminal person.

Every week, the men said, Arnold brought something different with him. One week he brought a violet snail shell from a beach in Maine, where his grandmother lived. The next week he brought a crow's feather that his wife had found on a hiking trail. He brought a paper bag full of ripening peaches; a single smoothly polished pebble; a piece of blue sea glass; the branch of a beech tree, broken in a rainstorm, with the bark peeling and the green leaves still attached. The objects were offerings to the men. They were reminders of life past the gates, where seasons changed, birds migrated from north to south, the sun rose and fell, the tide came in and out, the moon waxed and waned, and shit like that.

On the Inside, of course, where the fluorescent lights buzzed overhead, the men saw none of these earthly things.

"I found the clay," Christopher repeated, dumbstruck.

"I'd be glad to bring out the pottery wheel if you'd like me to," said Arnold. Unlike some of the other instructors in Unit B, Arnold seemed comfortable with the men at Triton. He just sat underneath the weak light bulb, nodding congenially at the white-collar criminals and the successfully reformed violent felons who wandered into Meeting Room 11. They were allowed to do that from three to five every Thursday afternoon.

"What is going on in here?" said Christopher's cellmate, Angel, flaring his nostrils as he waltzed in. "Lace-making? Macramé? Tupperware party?" Angel still spoke in the throaty, cocky, threatening tone that scared the hell out of everybody.

"Come on in, have a seat. This is art," said Arnold cordially. "Hello, by the way. I am Arnold. Call me Arnie, please. What's your name?"

The niceness of Arnold was emphatic enough to be disconcerting. "My name is Angel," he said. "But I never could live up to it."

"Pleased to meet you, Angel," said Arnold.

Angel said. "So, this is art? I have to go. I'm in the wrong room. I signed up for woodwork."

Nelson said Arnold had begun the Art Therapy Project for the men in Unit B. They'd been granted special privileges. They could complete a high school equivalency degree, become fluent in English as a Second Language or enroll in college-level courses. They could take crafts classes with a "therapeutic self-improvement component." There was "Woodworking for Anger Management," "Basket-weaving and Impulse Control," "Conflict Resolution in Photography," "Creative Writing and Compassion," and "The Emotional Vocabulary of Watercolors." But every Thursday at five minutes to five, Arnold began packing up the supplies. He took away the pastels and the paper, the oils and the clay.

Christopher took a pad of drawing paper and tucked it inside his jumpsuit, zipping the zipper up to his chin. That night, by the security light outside the small hole that was his window, he drew. He drew a nude figure, lying on its side. It would be impossible for anyone looking at that figure to tell what it was. Christopher had illustrated the death of a person. The dark, intense crosshatching that surrounded the body might easily be mistaken for artistic shading, but he'd meant it to be blood. Christopher had drawn the body bathing in pools of fluid—rendered in gray, innocuous in pencil—which had come out of its orifices. The wrongness of this pleased Christopher. It was always the wrongdoing that boosted his mood.

The image of his best friend's corpse, punctured and lifeless, gave him a peculiar feeling of satisfaction. It was the happy chaos of rule-breaking that he'd enjoyed as a young man illustrating underground comics. In reality, he wished no harm upon anyone. He didn't think he did, anyway. (Not really. Did he? He didn't know.) It was true that he'd sat in his cell more than once envisioning his best friend's torture during the long night, in sickening detail. This had been a mental exercise, allowing him to let off steam, to express his outrage. Now, thanks to Nelson, Arnold, and the Art Therapy Project, Christopher was doing new exercises. He was learning about empathy. He'd balked at first until he began to see its implications. He could get inside another person's skin and take a nice, long, liberated walk in someone else's shoes. Unrestricted, he could explore wherever he liked. He could get into Jenny, shedding himself.

Being in solitary confinement all those years, he knew, had steadily deformed him. He was pretty sure he hadn't been like that before. Some slippage had taken place, certain critical distinctions were no longer obvious to him. Things he'd never really wanted on the Outside, he'd wanted while he was living in Unit D. Even now that he was inside Unit B, living in relative comfort, he daydreamed that he felt the sensation of someone's racing, excited pulse under his hand. Was this a good fantasy? Or bad? Sometimes it was just the hot throbbing heartbeat of that lame pigeon he'd captured in the playground when he'd been eleven years old—on a dare he gave himself to terrorize his au pair, Beatrice. She'd shrieked as she ran around the sandbox after Christopher as he scampered away from her, jeering, clutching the pigeon firm in his grip, wickedly thrilled by its frantic pecking and its writhing. He'd had no interest in killing that bird. It was only a feint, a bit of posturing to disconcert Beatrice. But she'd believed him. On that day, Christopher had chosen sides.

"Assassin!" the rosy-cheeked Belgian babysitter had said, in her pretty accent, her face a cartoon of disgust. Christopher had felt electrified by her agitation. With a thrashing of feathers and a squawk, the pigeon had beat a retreat, scrambling under the shrubbery. What a commotion. Melodramatically enough, Beatrice had thrown herself down on her bare knees in the playground, calling to the bird, cooing in soft tender tones as if she were its parent. The pigeon, its orange eyes glowing faintly, had gone catatonic, spreading its scraggy gray feathers. Tucking its head to its breast, it seemed to sink into the dirt.

"She is dying," said Beatrice, turning to him. "How do you feel now?"

Whatever Christopher had said or done in response, he couldn't recall. Beatrice came unglued. Flushed, panting, she'd cupped her face in her hands and had opened her mouth. She'd looked like the figure in Munch's *Scream*, a painting that Christopher had seen in the fifth grade, on a guided tour of Norway.

Christopher must have laughed at Beatrice, or worse, because she pounced upon him in the playground, raised her hand and dealt him a mighty blow across the jaw. The strike was bracing.

"I'll have you fired for that, Beatrice," he'd told her. Later, he'd showed his mother the welt left by Beatrice's silver rings. Beatrice was gone by the end of the week. Many times since, he'd revisited the murderousness that had arisen between them—the charge of their opposition—and he'd parsed what he'd wanted to do after Beatrice smacked him. The incident had posed a riddle to him.

He'd even told the story of the pigeon to the men in Group. Nelson had said: "Everyone has these feelings." People imagined committing odious crimes a hundred times a day. Aggression was a natural instinct. To be allowed Outside again, Christopher needed only to refrain. Thinking it and doing it were two different things. No one went to jail for thinking a thought. Not even under the new legislation.

Christopher stretched out on his mattress, narrowing his eyes, letting his lids fall closed. His eyelashes formed a feathery curtain; amorphous shapes shimmied and flicked like a school of fish darting across his eyeballs. His sight blurred as he gazed up at the ceiling. He could see bodies and faces rushing across the concrete. If he pressed the heels of his hands against his eyelids, hard, dazzling neon lights flared up in kaleidoscopic pinwheels, fireworks of green and pink.

This was a prisoner's home entertainment system. Christopher's old girlfriends flitted across the screen of his solitary mind, dressed like showgirls in gaudy outfits. His former fiancée was the warm-up act, decked out in a bejeweled headdress and an eight-foot ostrich plume. Choreographed in formation, his chorus line of booty-calls danced around his one-time bride-to-be. G-strings sparkling between their legs and tassels shimmering from their nipples, they performed on the private stage of Christopher's imagination. The grand diva made her entrance, sashaying in in four-inch heels encrusted in silver glitter. Tonight was Jenny's night. Every night, in the end, belonged to her.

With the first light of daybreak, Christopher took Jenny's photo out from under his mattress. To be sure no one would steal it, he tucked it into his shoe every day, though it bothered him to think that he was stepping on her smile. It was the only way to keep her safe. It was this photo of Jenny which had saved him. Nelson had given him her picture two years ago, and her face had made a suggestion that inspired him. She'd told him to get out. By now, the photograph was creased. Even if her visage had remained undamaged, Christopher no longer could see it clearly. Like most of his fellow inmates, Christopher's vision had deteriorated.

The lighting at Triton was inadequate. He'd spent hours reading beneath the dull greenish glare of a fluorescent bulb. Prescription lenses weren't available to any of the men. Every couple of years, he was given an eye exam in the infirmary—by the alcoholic dentist, Marlowe. He was then allowed to choose a pair of eyeglasses from a bin. These glasses were discards, the lenses ground for someone else. They came to Triton from the Salvation Army, which collected them. Everyone despised these glasses. They were, the men felt, an insult. They actually made one's sight worse, allowing the left eye to focus while straining the right one. These eyeglasses were cast-offs that no one else wanted; the frames were ludicrously out of date. "I can't wear these," objected one inmate, a soft-spoken felon named Ryan. "They destroy my self-esteem." With that, Ryan had pitched his donated eyeglasses through the chicken wire that covered an open window in the mess hall.

"Now you won't see nothing," a failed bank robber named Sonny had said.

"At least I won't look like a retard," said Ryan. "I have my pride."

Christopher preferred to see what he could, but he agreed with Ryan. Anyone at Triton who wore eyeglasses looked like an imbecile. From the day Christopher had put on his first pair of prison spectacles, something had gone out of him. It restored him to close his eyes and greet Jenny in his imaginings. He saw her anew, in another light. He came to know her thoroughly and intimately—every subtle facial expression, hand gesture and mannerism. He spoke to Jenny each night before he went to sleep, talking now sweetly, now angrily. He held whispered, feverish conversations in which he played both parts, his and hers. Christopher poured out his fears to her, his grievances and desires, the things he couldn't tell other people. He conducted long, heated mental arguments with Jenny. He almost believed that she could hear him, wherever she lived now, and that it was her voice in the night, talking back to him.

After his transfer to Unit B, he'd been convinced that Jenny had tried to visit him. He'd felt her presence. The first day it happened, he'd been in Group while Ricky Mack had droned on about the beatings he'd gotten as a kid, a topic he dwelled on every Wednesday and Monday morning, at length, in the session room. The other men muttered and grunted in sympathy. They were all sipping at instant coffee, dispensed by an automated machine which poured a waxy brown substance into clear plastic cups small enough to contain a shot of Nyquil. An optimistic label next to the coffee spout said: *Café con Leche*. Christopher refused to drink the *Puke Con Crap*, as he called the coffee in Unit B. (Weirdly enough, the coffee over in supermax had been superior. Everything was more concentrated there—purer coffee, meaner guards, heightened security.) Christopher had lolled on a chair with his knees draped over the busted brown vinyl arm, chewing on a hangnail. Now and then, in response to Ricky Mack's litany of complaints, Christopher lifted up his hands and pantomimed a musician playing the violin.

"Your dad hit," he interjected at one point. "So that's your excuse." Ricky Mack had shot a man dead in a gas station during a botched robbery. He'd gotten away with two hundred dollars, giving himself up the next day. The sum of $200 as the price of the gas station attendant's life had nagged at him. More pertinently: His girlfriend had seen the bloodstains on his sweatshirt and had promptly alerted the cops, who'd launched a manhunt for him. He'd wandered around Detroit for thirteen hours, evicted from his life, until he'd finally walked up the steps of the nearest police station and surrendered.

Christopher wondered aloud whether adding a few zeroes to the end of those three figures, 200, would have justified the murder.

"Ricky has the floor right now, Christopher," said Jake Dole, a check-bouncer with a faint birthmark, the size of a fist, spread across the middle of his face like a new continent.

"Plenty of kids get hit," said Christopher, without looking at any of them. "And they don't shoot people. That's all I'm saying."

"He's invalidating my experience again," said Ricky Mack, affronted. He turned from one face to the next, incredulous. "Can you see? He did it again. He does it all the time. Christopher just invalidated me."

"Fuck you," said Christopher. He spat out his broken bit of thumbnail, which he'd bitten off, onto the floor.

"How are you feeling right now, Christopher?" said Nelson. "What's going on with you?"

"I'm feeling like I'd like to get the fucking fuck away from you," said Christopher. He nursed an urge to tell them his tragedies, but he resisted it. He didn't believe in any of this soul-searching, this cause-and-effect twaddle, digging around for reasons, for people to blame for one's mistakes. Instead of suffering in tandem with the other Group members, as Nelson had insisted they do, Christopher stretched out in his chair, lying back as if he were in bed and, obstinately, began to indulge in his secret store of sadistic fantasies.

Nodding thoughtfully from time to time to show he was paying attention to the men's elegies, Christopher stared out at the prison grounds. His view was obstructed by thick wire mesh; it was embedded inside the double-paned, soot-streaked window. A car had pulled up to the parking lot and had begun circling. Fast as a jack-in-the-box, a lady popped out of the front seat.

Christopher's breath caught. Had he dreamed her up? He'd imagined her so vividly, wanting to see her, and now, maybe, here came

Jenny. He had to prevent anyone else in Group from taking notice. He kept himself still, lounging in his armchair, furtively watching the woman in the parking lot. She had raised her head to stare at the brick towers. She gazed up at the penitentiary windows, or so it seemed. She appeared to Christopher in a glimmering orb of twilight.

Looking at the visitor through his crap eyeglasses, Christopher could just make out the form of a woman in a straw hat and a shapeless dress. His surroundings had the soft focus and muted hues of watercolors. A halo of blonde hair framed a clouded face. It could be Jenny, or it could just be a lost suburban housewife. Within minutes, she had driven off, and her rumbling engine was only a sigh, an undertone. But the sight of this woman had filled his head with commotion. Wanting to fly to her, it was all he could do to stop himself from hurling his body through the window.

"I have something to say," Christopher announced to the room. After that day, he threw himself headlong into Group.

PART TWO:

Jenny and Christopher

Standing in Good Shoes

Christopher had only to reach out and untie Jenny's long scarf, pull it from her neck like a boa constrictor that travels slowly over and down, across her shoulders and along her side. She'd stared at his mouth, as if entranced, while he undid her buttons, one by one, starting from the Peter Pan collar at her throat, to the one above her breasts, downwards, seven white buttons that began at her neck and ended at her navel. With neither of them speaking, her response had been to clasp his extended hand, following him down the hallway of that grand apartment with it black and white tiles. Off she went with Christopher up the stairs, tugging at his belt loops, her arms circling his hips, without conversation. She'd followed him through the carpeted hall into the clean, tidy bedroom he'd grown up in.

In memory, Christopher saw himself as handsome, as young, as an art student, dressed in the low-slung pajamas that fell off him at the pull of a drawstring. His expression, he imagined, had been intent but impersonal. A growth of beard darkened his sunken cheeks. He kept his eyes open in bed, while Jenny closed hers against him. She had turned her head to one side, even as he got into her, as if she were shutting him out, leaving him behind. As he rolled off her, he made a grab for Jenny's purse. Like a misbehaving boy, he dumped its contents onto the bed where Jenny lay naked, her big breasts partly hidden by her flabby arm. She rested on one elbow, her double-chin propped up by her plump hand, like a nude odalisque by Rubens. She looked on while Christopher, without asking permission, sorted through her personal effects. He had met her, briefly, just twice. He had known her, all told, for less than an hour. Looking through her handbag was a demonstration of ownership.

"Let's see what we have here," Christopher had said, poking at her things. He pulled a crumpled heap of bills out from her bag.

"Seven dollars," he said, catching her eye. "Is that all you have on you?"

"Don't tell me *you* need money," Jenny said, her tone sharp.

"I'm on a fixed income, you might say," said Christopher.

"Great. Lucky me," said Jenny. "I fuck the senator's son on Fifth Avenue and he asks me for financial aid."

"Very fixed income, that is," said Christopher, liking her, the way she snarled, the way she didn't kiss up to him. Self-possessed for a girl of fifteen, she was as combative as an equal. "I depend on the upper class for handouts," he said.

"You *are* the upper class, stupid," Jenny explained.

"Not exactly. They've got me on an allowance. It's not as easy as it looks, Jenny."

"What isn't?" She examined her toenails. "You don't have any nail polish around here, do you?"

Christopher searched through the drawers beside his bed, found a bottle of nail polish that his fiancée kept there together with her tampons and a spare diaphragm, and began to open it. He had twisted off the plastic cap, had taken the little doll-sized brush out, and had wiped it free of excess nail polish. In a gentlemanly mood, he had taken Jenny's ankle in his hand, prepared to paint her toenails for her.

She kicked him.

"Ouch. What was that?" said Christopher.

"What are you doing?"

"Painting your toenails. So you can show off your toes in the sandals you stole."

"First of all, I never stole sandals," said Jenny.

"No? What are those in your bag?"

"Those happen to belong to me," said Jenny. "Your mother has no idea how many pairs of shoes she has and I am simply recycling something that isn't being used."

"I wasn't going to tell on you," he said. "Relax. I rip my parents off all the time. I take cash, silver, jewelry. You prefer shoes, whatever. To each his own." He once again began to try to apply some nail polish to her pinky toenail.

"That color is low class," said Jenny, pulling her foot away.

"Like you know."

"You don't need money to have taste," she said.

"My fi..." He began, and stopped.

"Your fee?" said Jenny, skeptically. "This just gets better and better. You're a gigolo. You're charging me?"

He had been on the brink of telling her that his fiancée had left the nail polish there, and that she was from an aristocratic European family. She had perfect pitch when it came to classy nail polish. His fiancée was a doyenne of fashion. She had designed their wedding clothes, selected a remote beach resort in Morocco for their honeymoon, hired a graphic artist to print their wedding invitations, and chosen the monogrammed silverware for their wedding registry. He decided against it. "I'm charging you," he said, playfully, applying the polish to his own toenails instead. "I told you, I'm dead broke thanks to the Antichrist and his concubine, otherwise known as the Senator and Mrs. Benedict, my parents."

"Fantastic," said Jenny. "You're knocking on the wrong door." She began lighting a rather expensive hand-rolled cigarette of Christopher's—Thai stick laced with opium—which she had found on the dresser. She coughed a little as she inhaled. "You're Manhattan royalty, for fuck's sake," she said after a while. "If you need money, don't look at *me.* I'm the last person on earth who could help."

"I'm living in genteel poverty," Christopher said, removing the joint from her hand.

"I don't even think that such a thing exists. That's a load of shit. You want to see the other side of the tracks, you ought to come over to my place."

He smiled. He was intrigued by the disparity between them. Small tokens would go a long way with Jenny, he thought. If she wanted a necklace, he could simply walk into his mother's bedroom, open the top drawer of her dresser, take out one of the four lacquered, multitiered jewelry boxes, and present her with one. Compared to a tropical parrot or a python, a girl like Jenny would be an easy, low-maintenance pet.

"This your mom?" he'd said, finding a photograph in her wallet and removing it for study.

Jenny had made a grab for the photo. "Give that back."

He took a long drag from the joint, then stamped it out carefully in a china saucer that he was using as an ashtray. His eyes alighted on hers. "Let me guess," he said, craftily. "Your father's not around. You were an illegitimate child, born out of wedlock like half the Second Chance girls. Generational delinquency. The culture of poverty. You don't even know who your father is. Am I right? Do you?"

"Fuck you. You're detestable," she said and began to gather up her clothes.

"The truth hurts, I guess," said Christopher, smiling to himself. He placed the remainder of the joint inside his leather portfolio, saving it for later.

Jenny, obviously offended by what he'd said, reached for her bag. A cache of cosmetics fell out on to the floor—lip gloss and mascara, blush and eyeliner. Christopher, pretending to ignore her impending departure, opened a lipstick and applied some to his lips, checking in the mirror to study the effect.

"Give me that," she said, and snatched it away from him.

"Oh, calm down. I'm on your side," he said, handing her her lipstick. "Why don't you wear any of this? Is there some kind of rule they have against painted ladies? Did they make you give up makeup and start dressing like a prim little spinster nun over at the Second Chance Society?"

Jenny shrugged. He watched her appraising him, deciding whether to befriend him or turn against him. Her emotionalism excited him.

"My counselor at Second Chance encourages us to look natural," she said. "No heavy makeup. We're not supposed to invite. You know."

"No, what?"

"Male attention," she said, collecting her stash of makeup and tucking it back into her bag. "It distracts us from our studies. We all. We all fucked up," she stammered. "The girls at the Society were fast. And we. And I." She didn't continue her confession. He'd already discussed her early teenage pregnancy with her the first time they'd met, a week earlier.

"You were a teenage whore?" Christopher offered, helpfully.

Her expression darkened.

"I mean that in the nicest possible way, Jenny," he assured her. "Not an insult. A compliment." He'd had a thing for the Second Chance Society girls, ever since he'd first found out about them. Bad girls. Loose girls who, by the age of fourteen, had already racked up a prison record, lost a friend in crossfire, or given birth to a child. They were shining examples of deviance. Christopher admired them on principle.

"Jenny the Whore," he said, in a singsong voice. "X-rated Jenny."

Her face changed, and he read it, first surprise and, there, the sting, he'd struck a nerve. Without saying another word, she'd begun to get dressed, her gestures fast, limbs slicing through the air, no longer relaxed and languid. Even a proud girl could be played. Even a cocky girl had strings to pull on, to make her jump and jerk.

"I was just kidding around," he'd told her, touching her wrist.

Jenny whirled around, shaking her finger at him. "You listen to me, you little fuck. I'm warning you not to disrespect me. Never underestimate me," she said. "Do you hear? If you don't treat me right, I swear to God, you'll live to regret it."

Her eyes had glowed and sparkled in a way that he'd liked. He liked her fuming, this plump small girl, full of pride, as hungry and hostile as a stray dog.

"You're cute when you're angry," he said.

Arms Around a Memory

Like everything else that's bad for you, it had been sublime in the beginning.

Alone in the hexagonal room, looking through the blue and yellow stained glass window, Nadia tore open Christopher's first letter. As she read, she began turning him over like one of the twenty globes, the turn-of-the-century paperweights she collected and arranged on the two shelves above her desk. She turned him and turned him, looking at Christopher from every angle. She interrogated and cross-examined. And she admitted, if only to herself, her capacity to experience an ecstatic abandon. She had felt it only with Christopher and no one else, before or since.

He had goaded her on to new dangers and misbehaviors. Christopher had no fear of death. When she'd been with him, she'd absorbed his barbarism and, with it, a certain innocence. It had something in common with the rambunctious bliss of her sons, that weekend on the beach in Montauk, when they'd each broken free of her hands and had run along the shore, kicking in another child's sand castle, stomping on it gleefully while the kid had shrieked, happy until Nadia had caught up with them and informed them they were being punished for it, that they wouldn't be allowed on the boardwalk or in the bumper cars, that she wouldn't buy them any cotton candy.

She could remember the surprise in their eyes as they tried to sort out why it was wrong to destroy.

With Christopher, she'd discovered the childlike delight of wrecking things.

One afternoon, at Christopher's warehouse, he and Jenny began making calls to the phone booth on the corner of President Street and Bond, to see if any passersby would pick up the phone. They could hear the ringing phone from where they sat on the window ledge. It rang forever, or so it seemed, incessant, like an alarm, roiling. Even though they were the ones making the call, the sound jangled her nerves, an unheeded plea for help. With no one around, ringing insistently on a desolate street, that phone seemed to announce some encroaching disaster.

Jenny had said to Christopher: "Forget it."

But Christopher had persisted, letting it bleat. When a patrol car drove by, Jenny tried to hang up the receiver, wary in the presence of police. But Christopher held firmly to the phone. A cop got out of the front seat, walked to the phone booth, and answered it.

Jenny pressed her ear against Christopher's head. He turned the receiver so they could both listen.

"What's happening?" the cop said in a casual, almost flirtatious, tone that Jenny did not associate with the New York City police.

Jenny listened, horrified, while Christopher, imitating the other man's conversational manner, said, "Hey there, this is Christopher. Who am I talking to?" He sat up straight, on the windowsill, one leg crossed over the other. His comportment was as assured and graceful as a dancer's. He didn't look in Jenny's direction, so he couldn't see her desperate gesticulations. She wanted him to hang up.

"Hey, I've got a fifteen-year-old girl here without any clothes on. If you look up at the window of the third floor, the second building across the street—the one with trees on the roof garden—you'll see her standing here."

Christopher reached out to Jenny and grabbed at the obi of the silk kimono, until he'd pulled the wide strip of patterned material off and the folds of the kimono fell open. He stroked her shoulder blade as he pulled the fabric, ever so gently, peeling her outer covering away until the husk of the kimono slithered off her skin, landing at her feet. Jenny, being Jenny, hadn't stopped him. Breathing fast, she'd stood by the window as Christopher said, waiting for the one thing, the only thing, she cared about. To see what happened next.

Officer Moore looked up at Jenny in the window.

Disjointed scenes filled her head. She saw herself at the police station, in custody, in trouble. She saw herself in a courtroom, talking to a gray-haired lawyer in a suit and tie. She saw Christopher stepping into the patrol car and waving to her as the car took him away. They had broken some laws together and she had no sense at all of who was innocent, who guilty.

Christopher gave Jenny an encouraging push, caressing her hips, lightly smacking her ass. She stepped closer to the window to display herself naked to two uniformed police. Three stories below, the street was empty. Dozens of overstuffed black garbage bags gleamed beneath the streetlamp.

I am crazy, Jenny thought. I'm losing it. It wasn't the worst thing she'd ever done, or the hardest, but it may have been a close runner-up for stupidest. She hadn't known, yet, that the police were fallible, human. She hadn't known about the porous mesh that is the law. For the first few seconds, she felt suspense. Maybe Christopher, right then, would be hauled off and placed under arrest. Swiftly, though, the shock of her nudity began to be absorbed by the ravaged streets of an outer-borough industrial zone, where old brick buildings are acquainted with sheltering illegal activities. The factory across the street had no windows. As far as Jenny could tell, it conducted no legitimate business and had no employees, no inhabitants.

To see if she could get away with it—that was half the fun of tearing her clothes off. Stripping off her clothes, pulling up her dress. These were routine activities for Jenny.

Police, however—that was a first. She'd never flashed her breasts at cops.

"Nice, isn't she?" Christopher had said into the phone.

"Would you like to come over and hang out with us?" Christopher said, and again the feeling came to her stomach, a pleasant sizzle, a vibrating anticipation, of a good or bad thing, which one didn't matter. "Come see her up close," urged Christopher.

By this time, he called himself her boyfriend.

With a smirk, Christopher hung up the telephone. "Officer Moore and his partner are coming over," he told her.

"What? Are you deranged? When?" said Jenny.

Christopher gazed serenely down at the patrol car. "It'll take them a minute or two," he said, amiably.

Jenny began running around the bedroom, frantically cleaning up, gathering discarded lingerie, socks, drug paraphernalia—the plastic sandwich baggies filled with dope; the crinkled scraps of tinfoil; the glass pipe stained black; the red, orange, pink, and blue pills of various sizes and shapes, scattered over the tabletop by the handful, like so many jelly beans; a tiny transparent envelope with a last pinch of brown powder stuck at the bottom, like grains of dirty sand.

"Let's not let them in," Jenny said as she threw their belongings into the closet. "Christopher, it isn't funny."

"Who said it was?" Christopher raised an eyebrow.

"I mean it. Just don't answer the door. My aunt could lose custody, don't you understand? They could take me and put me in a foster home. This is my life we're talking about here, asshole." Jenny's mother had gone traveling with a new boyfriend, leaving Jenny and her aunt in the East Harlem apartment.

"Such drama. No one's taking you away," said Christopher, in the way he had. Whatever ailed her, Christopher, the indestructible, was immune.

"Please don't open the fucking door," Jenny said. "This is non-negotiable."

"No one's negotiating. I invited them and they're coming over," Christopher said, in a voice that brooked no argument.

"They can't open anything inside a closet or cupboard without a warrant," Jenny said and she knew, when she heard these words, that she'd already given in.

"What are you talking about, woman? This is a social call. I don't open the cabinets when I'm invited into someone's apartment, as a guest, for caviar and cocktails. Do you? Let's give these boys some credit. They're not heathens." Christopher gave her his profile, as if posing, staring out the window.

Jenny threw another handful of things inside a drawer and slammed it shut. Out of breath, she spun around the room, looking out for anything else that might be illegal or embarrassing. A pink rubber sex toy, gathering dust, peeked out from under the bed. Jenny pounced on it and threw it in the drawer.

"God!" she said. "You've gone over the edge! Why are you doing this to me? You're demented!"

"Relax already, sweetheart," Christopher said.

"Oh my God, oh shit, oh my God," Jenny said, crooning the words softly to herself in a chant, opening and closing the cabinets, stashing pornographic photographs and illegal substances, condoms and satin negligees and thong bikinis, body oil, kinky accoutrements, leopard-print panties, underground comic books and anything else incriminating. "You're kidding me, right?" she said, going to the window. "It was a joke? This is you, being an asshole? The cops aren't coming, are they?" But the patrol car had parked, and the two young policemen, their hair shorn down to the scalp in military-style crew-cuts, dressed in blue uniforms, were loafing around on the sidewalk, stretching their legs. They began sauntering towards Christopher's front door, in slow motion, dream police from Jenny's nightmares.

"Aren't they cute?" said Christopher, drawling.

Jenny let out a shriek.

"Don't do that, please," Christopher instructed. "Quit worrying about it. If you aren't into it, be boring. Who cares? I'll handle it." He handed her a quart of gin.

She accepted the bottle, drank from it and, retrieving the silk robe, she ran into the bathroom, half-undressed, the folds of the Japanese kimono streaming behind her like the train of a gown. She locked herself in and proceeded to gulp down the gin as if it were no stronger than ginger ale. Through the door, she heard voices, small talk, footsteps walking into the kitchen. The sound of their chitchat was soon drowned out by music. Christopher had turned on the stereo. A rhythmic electronic pulse rose and fell as Debbie Harry began to wail and burble in her clear high soprano, her delivery indifferent, the embodiment of blasé chic.

> once had a love and it was a blast/soon found out
> had a heart of glass/seemed like the real thing and it was divine

Jenny retied the obi around her waist and waited, channeling Debbie Harry's aloof cool, for what felt like an eternity. At some point, curious and impatient, she unlatched the small metal hook that locked the bathroom door. She opened the door a mere crack, no more than a quarter of an inch, just wide enough to see Christopher on the floor before Officer Moore, whose unbelted trousers had been pushed down along his hairy thighs. The other cop was standing with his back to Jenny, holding a pair of handcuffs and a nightstick. Whether to smile at this or to frown, to be impressed or distressed, Jenny couldn't tell. Christopher, as usual, had cracked open the city like a piñata to get the goodies inside. Nothing functioned there in that factory on the Gowanas Canal quite as it was supposed to. Cops took prank phone calls from strangers and delivered themselves to the door like pizza boys, like call girls. Christopher's city was diabolical and boundless, peopled by characters like him. Whatever he did, wherever he went, he found new converts. Aktionism was his religion of sensation.

Jenny shifted her weight. Now she could see Officer Moore's jaw and, as she moved back, his neck and shoulder came into view. When he turned, she saw a bright crimson slash: an armband. She moved away from it, repulsed, before even seeing what it was, before her brain had translated. He no longer wore a police cap. What he had on his head was similar, but instead of the plain shiny black bill, his new cap had an eagle and a swastika on it. Jenny shut the door with a click and sat down, heavily, on the rim of the bathtub. She didn't know where this Nazi shit had come from. She wanted to believe, but didn't believe, that New York City cops were in the habit of carrying Third Reich memorabilia around with them. She couldn't accept that it had anything to do with Christopher, he of the pink satin smoking jacket, he of the anarchist revolution, he of that insouciant cult of the senses.

Jenny climbed inside the bathtub and pulled the shower curtain closed. She laid back, her vertebrae pressing against the flat hard porcelain. She clasped her hands behind her head to form a cushion and stared up at the ceiling lamp, its white glare softened by a red paper Chinese lantern, four gold tassels swaying beneath it, trembling, each attached to a pale green bead. Now she was trying not to listen for sounds coming from the bedroom, but she caught herself straining to hear. With the bottle propped between her knees, she covered her ears with her hands. Even so, she imagined too much, sensed too much, attuned to fugitive noises that ran beneath the music, low and faint, like someone sighing. Blondie's voice dominated.

"Once had a love, and it was divine, soon turned out, to be a waste of time," came the words in their inimical, offhand, nasal whine.

Blondie was trying to tell her something.

Jenny lay down on her back and stared up at Christopher's skylight. It was shaped in a circle, and the design he'd painted around its edges made it look as if he owned a piece of sky. It was the middle of July, and the window was full of blue sky with one streaky white cloud stretched thin over it, like a phantom hand whose bony white fingers reached ahead towards something Jenny couldn't see.

When she opened her eyes again, the factory was quiet and the sky was the color of ink. Jenny had drifted off to sleep.

"It's safe to come out now, you chicken," Christopher called as a sliver of moon slid out from behind a darker cloak of cloud.

"Bluck-buck! Bluck buck-buck!" Christopher was imitating chickens clucking. He rattled the doorknob. "Any chickens in there?" he said.

Jenny climbed out of the tub and unlocked the bathroom door. There stood Christopher in jeans, sneakers, and T-shirt, his long straight hair combed neatly as a schoolgirl's. He was shrugging on his black leather trench coat, ready to go out to dinner at the local Chinese restaurant, as they often did, as if nothing unusual had happened. With a bemused, cynical expression on his face, he said, "I'm sorry you didn't meet the officers, Jenny. What nice police!"

Call Me Any, Anytime

"Careful. Jeremy! What did I tell you?" Nadia said.

Reaching for the telephone, which had begun to ring, Jeremy tilted his chair backwards. Suddenly, he lost his balance, tipping sharply towards the floor. Nadia rushed at him, grabbing the wooden ladder-back slats and holding the chair steady.

"What's the matter with you?" she snapped. "Honestly, Jeremy, you're regressing," Nadia muttered. "This is the sort of thing you did when you were a toddler." She pictured what could have happened—the back of her son's skull colliding with the terra-cotta tiles that extended in an arc around the fireplace. The horrid thwack of bone on stone. This was the one thing she hated about being a mother: premonitions of her children, mauled, injured, getting into accidents. She retained the memories of frightening dashes to the emergency room, holding a bloodstained child in a bundle, the gash on the forehead, the tooth knocked out in a playground collision, the helpless shouts of "Stop right now!" as Jeremy outran her while she rescued his younger brother from a hornet's nest, just in time to see her older boy throwing himself, like a little Hollywood stuntman, recklessly, headfirst, down the slide. A sprawl across a black rubber playground mat, a howl and a wail, a nosebleed, a fear of concussion, fear of brain damage, fear of blindness. Motherhood was harrowing.

Nadia's nerves were frayed. A year had passed since her ill-starred visit to the penitentiary, but Christopher's letters had kept arriving. He cajoled and flirted, he threatened and flattered. The last letter was the shortest and most devastating of all. It warned her of his release.

Baby doll,

I want to see you. Look for me, Outside, before the fall.

Whether this news was true or false, Nadia expected him to call—or even to show up uninvited—at any moment. She could no longer be certain that Dylan had kept her alias and address safely out of Christopher's hands. Dylan's hero worship of Christopher had dissipated over time; the attachment between the two men had once been ferocious. Dylan still visited Christopher twice a year, promising Nadia that he'd never mention her whereabouts. She knew Dylan was sending the letters to her at Christopher's insistence. She'd asked him again and again to stop. Even now, Christopher held Dylan in his thrall.

During the near mishap with Jeremy and the tilted chair, the phone had stopped ringing.

"We missed the call," said Jeremy, mournfully. He had a rubbery face, always mugging and hamming it up, full of exaggerated expression. He'd righted himself just in time, grabbing at the table and scattering hundreds of dollars on the floor. It was dark outside. Nadia and her sons were alone in the house, on a Thursday night, playing Monopoly.

"It was probably Dad," said Will. "He'll call back."

"What if it wasn't?" said Jeremy, who tended to dramatize minor events. "What if it was a crucial call for me?"

"How crucial could it be?" asked Will. He had an open book

propped up on the table before him. Will had earphones on. He held his cell phone in his hands as his fingers moved across the keypad while he typed, read, played Monopoly, and listened to his band. Nadia had given up her naïve parental attempt to get her kids to do one thing at a time. They were incapable of this. They were fast-thinking twenty-first-century children who burned through electricity as quickly as they hemorrhaged cash, watching television and downloading and uploading songs, short videos, and photographs into their hand-held gizmos, their state-of-the-art computers. Music came through the two new speakers that the kids had set up on either side of the fireplace, but the den, sparsely furnished, felt empty. Nadia loved the emptiness, and it was why she gravitated towards this funny, ugly little room. It had an echo that reverberated when anybody spoke; wind whistled through the loose old windowpanes. The den was built crookedly, haphazard and off-kilter; none of the walls met the ceiling at right angles. Blondie's ball rolled swiftly along the sloped wooden floorboards, rolling, rolling of its own accord, through the den, over the carpet, and out the door into the dining room, like a toy possessed by a demon, making the dog wag her tail rapturously and bark in surprise each time. Outside, lamps lit the front and back porches, throwing circles of light on the meadow that stretched all the way down to the shore. On either side of the house were woods. Straight ahead was a field planted with wild grasses and, past that, the dark, fast waters of the river. Though the house felt secure, Nadia could imagine what it might have been like to be a settler hundreds of years ago, gathered around a fire in the enormity of the wilderness. A wolf bayed, or a dog. It was a quiet night, with rain pattering on the roof. Sitting by an open window, Nadia jumped when a twig broke in a thicket of trees. She detected other, fainter noises outside among the leaves. The back of her neck began to prickle. She sensed someone standing in the copse, hidden by the trees, but when she stared out the window, no one could be seen.

The phone rang a second time. Will didn't notice; he had his headset on. Nadia and Jeremy stared at the phone without touching it.

"Should I get it?" Jeremy asked, and Nadia had the strange feeling that she had no secrets from her oldest son, that there were things he knew.

Jeremy reached for the phone. And once again, he let his chair careen backwards, attempting to balance on the two back legs.

"What is wrong with you!" barked Nadia, who had repeatedly told him not to do this.

"Nothing," said Jeremy, blinking at her. He caught himself, preventing the fall, the fracture, the stitches. He picked up the telephone receiver with his adolescent male hand, larger, thicker and more pawlike than the child's hand he'd always had. It was slightly disconcerting to watch her children growing. She felt proud of herself, as if she'd sprinkled magic dust over him. But Jeremy's enlargement, his maturation, also worried her. His big adult hand seemed to warn her, in sign language: Good-bye mom, I'm moving out, very soon, I'm leaving.

"Halloo," Jeremy said into the telephone receiver, "Tobacco Shop. We've got Sir Walter Raleigh in a can."

"Give that to me," Nadia said, exasperated, and stretched her arm across the Monopoly board, knocking over Will's piece. The horseback rider crashed onto Park Place.

Jeremy didn't give Nadia the receiver, but kept talking in this new, sardonic, teenage tone. It had crept into his innocent childish voice only recently. "Nope, sorry, you're out of luck," he said. "Miss Jenny Underground?" He made a face. "Um, no. No. You've got the wrong number." He frowned. A giggle escaped him. His face turned red. "Woah, no, no," he said and slammed down the telephone.

Nadia held a stack of phony, bright orange cash in her right hand, but her muscles had gone weak, she had no grip. Mute, she continued to listen to the telephone conversation, replaying Jeremy's response over, slowly, in her mind. Somewhere near the house, an owl hooted, its guttural call soft and eerie. Dry leaves rustled by the back stairs, and Nadia thought she heard the faintest knocking.

"Jeremy," Nadia said, "what are you doing?"

Will, who'd been paying only intermittent attention to the game, was reading *Captain Pettypence and the Dark Island of Toots* for the thirtieth time. He'd never read any other novel, as far as Nadia knew, but he read and re-read the *Captain Pettypence* books, rapt each time, shaking his head with appreciation, murmuring "awesome," to himself every few minutes, as if these books contained Confucian wisdom. Now he lowered his paperback to gaze steadily, for an interminable minute, at Nadia and Jeremy. Will had a round, wholesome face, peach-brown from racing noisily up and down the river on water skis for hours, abetted by the neighbor's speedboat and the two Hanover girls on water scooters. He smirked at Nadia. Will smirked at Nadia almost continually, about eighty percent of the time she spent with him. When Will wasn't smirking at her, he was lifting his eyebrows in mild surprise. Sometimes he laughed, giddily, showing large, even, healthy white teeth covered by the silvery barbs of his braces. Aside from these basic expressions of feeling, Will had a poker face. Taking after Dan, he was a smart, confident, self-possessed child who did well in school and who listened to his parents. Will kept his thoughts to himself. His inner life was inaccessible to Nadia.

"Problem?" Will said, his eyes gleaming with the special glint that meant: My older brother is in trouble.

"Jeremy, since when do you just hang up on people?" Nadia said, aware of a heightened tension in her voice. She felt a whirring inside her, an electric current in the back of her knees.

Appearing not to have heard her, Jeremy was enraptured by his impending real estate deal. "Don't look now," he said, waving the card he'd just picked from the Community Chest pile, "But I've just received an interesting offer."

Nadia spun around to look behind her, convinced for a fraction of an instant that a moving shadow had scurried across the room. There was nothing. "What offer?" she heard herself say to Jeremy, her voice tinny and brittle.

"Emperor of the rails, ladies and gentlemen," said Jeremy. "I'm afraid to inform you that I'm now poised to acquire all four railroad companies. Hmm. Maybe I'll build, too, on my other monopolies." He wielded his cards. "Marvin Gardens would look way better with some little plastic green houses covering the open land, don't you think?" he said, pretending to twist the ends of an invisible mustache, like a dastardly villain on a television cartoon they'd watched together when the kids were in elementary school. "Or even a big red plastic hotel or two." He thumbed through his stack of property deeds and made his purchases. He plucked out the four white cards printed with the logo of the black locomotive, laying each of them out on the table, one after the other.

"Jeremy, you didn't answer me," said Nadia. "What were you talking about just now, on the phone?"

"It was just some townie, Mom," said Jeremy. "A drunk, I think, making a prank phone call."

"You *think*," said Nadia, frostily. "You think?" She was deeply angry with him. "Was it a man or a woman on the phone?"

"A guy." Jeremy had picked up the pamphlet from inside the game's box-top, as if he'd found a need, just then, to consult the Monopoly rulebook.

"What did he say to you?" Nadia said.

"Nothing, Mom," said Jeremy, the tops of his ears reddening. "Forget it. He was speaking gibberish. Not making sense."

"Who called just now?" she demanded, and she felt herself sliding, by the second, into a tar pit.

"He didn't give a name," said Jeremy. "Have you seen the Jenny Underground, he said. Or something like that."

She allowed herself to inhale. "Are you sure that's what he said?"

"Yeah, Mom. I forget. What's your problem already, Mom? What's the difference?"

"Has that happened before? That caller?"

He didn't respond directly. "No one like that's living here. And that's what I told him." Jeremy, who had been closely examining first the rules, then the stack of cards, and now his Monopoly money, looked at Nadia out of the corner of his eye. Her son's glance was unnerving. Again, she had the nagging sense that he was on to her, that he knew more about her situation than he'd reveal.

"Did he call here before?" said Nadia, aware that she was acting strangely.

"Maybe," Jeremy admitted.

"Tell me what he said the last time," said Nadia, her breathing seizing up.

"Some crazy shit. Look, let's just forget about it. I'm trying to win here, Mom. Get out of my way. We have a *game* to *play*." Now he faced her with large, puzzled, pleading eyes. It had often happened that Jeremy overreacted. He'd always been a sensitive and insecure boy, with a tendency towards hypochondria, thrown by the slightest ailment, regarding every minor cut or bruise as a sign of gangrene and contagion. More than once, he'd come to Nadia with a scrape that he claimed "wouldn't heal," and had begged to be tested for leukemia. When he contracted athlete's foot from the locker room at his school, he'd been convinced for days that it was leprosy.

"Tell me exactly what the caller said to you," Nadia insisted. "Let me decide whether or not it was nonsense, or an urgent matter."

Will's heavy brown eyebrows, indistinguishable from his brother's, appeared from over the top of his paperback book, like two furry caterpillars nosing each other. Gazing into his brother's eyes, he and Jeremy conferred. They silently asked one another: What's up with our mother?

"Urgent, like what?" said Jeremy, making a face that managed to suggest Nadia was a little off.

"Like a magazine assignment," said Nadia, though she'd dropped out of the competition for *National Geographic* gigs years ago. The hustle of it, the jockeying for position, the office politics—these had been enervating. "It might have been a commercial photography job for me, or an ad campaign," she said, pretending that was what mattered here. She'd done an advertising shoot only once, in the past year, for liquid soap: two days shooting six small droplets of dew, made out of rubber cement, glued onto a handful of wild strawberries. What this had to do with liquid soap, she didn't ask. Not very ennobling, though it had paid so well that she'd bought Simone a carpet, stove, and refrigerator for her new apartment.

"It wasn't," Jeremy said with a shrug. Something in his body language conveyed that he thought little of Nadia, her questions, her career. In his view, she needn't work for magazines or advertising agencies. She needn't participate in gallery exhibitions or win photography awards. Nadia's primary purposes on earth were: cook Jeremy dinner; provide copious snacks; purchase sneakers and computer games.

"Maybe it wasn't just Jenny Underground he asked for," Jeremy said, moving his piece—the miniature car—in an orbit, slowly, slowly, over the Monopoly board. The four wheels of the tiny metal car scraped against the cardboard.

Nadia said nothing. Under the table, she grabbed at the thick outer seams of her jeans and pinched, hard. She held on to this rind of denim as if afraid, suddenly, that her pants would fly off, taking the lower half of her body with them.

Swoosh, swoosh, came the noise of his miniature automobile sledding across the Monopoly board—warm, warmer, hot, hotter—closer and closer to Nadia.

Nadia watched breathlessly as the car moved uncannily towards the deadly corner. The haggard face behind bars, hands gripping, eyes imploring. Go to Jail.

"He might have said something weird to me," said Jeremy.

"Oh?" Nadia said, in retreat, ready to drop the subject. Further discussion would be impossible.

"He might have asked me if I'd seen any gold-digging bitches."

"A gold…" said Nadia.

"Yeah. Nuts, right? So I just hung up on him. Just a wrong number. Right Mom? Right?"

"Right," she said, exhaling, wordlessly freaking out.

No one moved. The apparition had floated through the window and hovered between her and her children there in the room. Nadia looked from one son to the other. A creeping hysteria seized hold of her. "Do you have something else to say to me, Jeremy?" she said, hazardously.

"Nooo," Jeremy said, with an unsettling inflection, extending his lips like a chimpanzee.

Rage took hold of Nadia. The boy sitting beside her seemed like a rude lout, unrelated to her. She lunged at Jeremy's collection of deeds and grabbed the pile away from him. "That's it," she said, slapping them against the table.

Neither of them looked at her.

Will took his earphones off, his eyes widening. He stared at the Monopoly board.

"How dare you disrespect me," said Nadia.

From either end of the dining room table, Will and Jeremy were locking eyes. Will continued to hold his cell phone in front of him, manipulating it, tapping at the keys, his fingers moving almost stealthily, nervously.

Beep, Nadia heard. One brief note. It meant, she knew, that Jeremy had received a text message on his cell phone.

Jeremy looked over at Nadia, for just an instant. But it was too late. She knew what they were doing.

"Give that to me," she said in the cold voice of a secret agent, someone inside her that she didn't recognize.

"What?" said Jeremy, too quickly, too innocently, raising his eyebrows high on his forehead.

"Your cell phone."

He patted his front pockets. "I don't know where it is," he said. "I must have left it upstairs."

"Now," said Nadia.

He laughed. "Come on, Mom."

She slammed the table with her fist. The dice jumped.

Jeremy reached into the side pocket on his cargo pants, pulled the Velcro tab open with a faint but distinct screech, the sound of synthetic fiber teeth being torn apart. He handed her a sleek black cell phone that she hadn't bought for him.

"Where did you get this?" she asked.

"I bought it," said Jeremy. "It's the one I wanted and you said it cost too much money, that there was no reason to replace my old one."

"How did you pay for it?"

"I had a job, you know." He spoke with the arrogance of someone much older than he was. During the school year, he'd bagged groceries at the supermarket for three hours on Saturdays. She wanted to ask him how the pocket money from that minimum wage job could possibly cover the cost of a high-tech phone like the one in her hand. Appalling possibilities came to mind. Instead of questioning him, she opened the flip-top and stared at the tiny blue electronic screen. The symbol of an unopened envelope appeared at the top, the light beside it blinking. "You have one message," the words said, in their anonymous digital lettering.

The message was a "repeat," which meant the same sentences had been sent and received more than once. There was no mistaking what it said; there were no abbreviations to obfuscate it.

THE 'HO IS ON THE RAG.

For one terrible moment, Nadia thought Christopher had sent this. When Nadia glared at Will, he hid his face behind *Captain Pettypence*. A boy, wearing a mask and cape, flew across the cover.

"You will not," said Nadia, "refer to your mother, or any other female, ever, as a 'ho. If you do this again, I will ask you to leave this house. I mean: Leave. Permanently. Don't push it. You will not be a part of this household." She'd actually told her own dear sons that she'd cast them out onto the streets. Like a cruel stepmother from a folktale, banishing the children into the woods, she might have meant it.

"You'd be asked to move your things into the guest house," Nadia said more gently, shaken by her own words.

"You don't want to do that, Mom," said Jeremy. He was a smooth little operator, she saw. A natural-born politician. A fast-talking manipulator of females.

"You watch me," she said, her anger rising again.

"What I mean is that wouldn't *work* as a punishment, Mom," said Jeremy. "You know? Moving out into the guest house? It would be pretty cool."

Will tittered.

"This isn't funny, William," said Nadia. "And I'm not sure that the guest house would be so 'cool' without any computer games, without any television, without any music or telephone calls. Or electricity. Or heat. Or running water. But maybe I'm wrong." Never before had she said such things to her children. But in her mind, tonight, they'd aligned themselves with something bestial.

"We're sorry, Mom," Jeremy said, hastily, as his eyebrows knit themselves together. "We're really, really sorry." His voice was insincere. It was a showy display of repentance.

"You're not sorry," she said, her voice hard. "You two don't know what the word means. You've never been sorry and you never will be sorry in your lives."

With some small satisfaction she watched their expressions change, the dawn of understanding. Yes, she thought, there is a part of me that looks down on you. Yes, she thought, I could almost do it: I could almost desert you. You're not like me. You have no weaknesses. You come from the land of the lucky ones.

"We're really sorry," said Jeremy, breathlessly.

"Really, really so super totally sorry, Mom," Will chimed in.

She'd frightened them, finally.

"Now you're sorry," said Nadia. "Now!" How had she raised such pigs? Her thoughtful, well-mannered boy was apologizing belatedly, desultorily, and only after she'd threatened to take his precious computer games away from him.

Her children had called her "ho."

"We'll discuss this another time," she said, turning away.

After she'd sequestered the boys in their rooms to complete their homework, Nadia stood in the kitchen, staring out the window. Rain pummeled the magnolias. A wind stirred the branches. The sun was setting out on the river, a glowing orange fireball swallowed by moving water. In the kitchen, she let it go. She let the dream have its say. Nadia's dream: She would climb into her jeep, alone. She would bring only a single suitcase, taking nothing but what she'd started out with—the denim dress, the leather coat that didn't belong to her, and a pair of motorcycle boots, two sizes too large, which she had borrowed from Christopher. These had been the spoils of her private war. She'd leave behind all her earthly possessions, her pile of jewelry, her shoes, the clothes, the mountains of coffee-table art books, her cashmere, her silk, her crap, her makeup, her nail polish, her skin creams in their jars, her imported French perfumes, her scented milled soaps. She'd leave behind her children and husband. She'd drive to Triton, park the jeep on a quiet road and wait for an appointed time—two o'clock in the morning. Christopher would be released. He'd rise up from a bench at the bus stop and approach Nadia, leaning to push the hair out of her face. His hand would be warm on her cheek. As if no time had passed, he'd say, "How you been, babe?" They'd use fake drivers' licenses with false names so no one could ever find them. They'd sleep in motel rooms in Phoenix and Santa Fe. They'd drive out West, crossing the border into Mexico to live in Baja, where ex-cons can intermingle with vacationers, where runaways pair up with unfaithful wives, accepted and unnoticed.

The phone rang, startling her. She picked up the extension in the kitchen. "Hello?" she said.

No one was on the line, no one answered. But she heard no dial tone.

"Who is this?" she said into the phone. "Hello, hello?"

A soft breath, in and out.

"Christopher, is that you?" she said.

Far away, in a strangled whisper, someone said "Jenny?" She heard a thud and a bang. The phone went dead.

If We Ever Get Out of Here

Christopher was carrying a length of fishing line inside the waistband of his shorts. He'd bought the fishing line at a sports equipment shop in Triton, early in the morning, on the day they'd let him out. Now here he was, a fortnight later, lolling in the warm waters of a heated swimming pool. The pool belonged to Dylan.

This was the same Dylan who'd screamed for mercy in Christopher's gory, vengeful daydreams.

It was the same Dylan whose imaginary face had turned purple and whose eyes had rolled back to show the whites.

He suspected Dylan had been the one to turn him in to the cops twenty-three years ago. Even as Christopher swam around here, paddling back and forth and up and down in Dylan's pool, ate Dylan's food, and stayed as a guest in Dylan's house, Christopher kept the coiled thread of fishing line tucked inside the elastic waistband of his swimming trunks. It was reassuring, even thrilling, for Christopher to think: Whenever I want to, I can strangle him: my ultimate Aktion. Just a daydream.

A lot of killings were accidents, Nelson had said. Murderers made mistakes and had the guilt, the regret.

"Do you ever hear from any of our old friends?" Christopher asked, spreading his arms out on the tiled rim of the pool. The wind made him shiver. The night air smelled of chlorine, charcoal from a barbecue, and freshly cut grass. He let his hands fall back into the water, plopping like tossed stones as they broke the surface.

In the moonlight, beneath the stars, Dylan took a sip of white wine from a slender glass. "Our little group disbanded," he said. "You know that." He was heavyset, with jowls and squinty eyes. He had a pleasantly handsome, sunburned face.

"How is Jenny?" said Christopher, after a moment. It was more difficult to say her name aloud than he'd expected. A subtle quaver reverberated in his belly. It started in his groin and radiated outwards, as if he'd swallowed a tiny extraterrestrial who would burst, momentarily, out of his chest.

"Jenny who?" said Dylan, his voice nasal.

"Jeez. Give me a break," said Christopher.

"Oh, Jenny, what's-her-name, you mean? That Jenny?" The reedy voice went up, piping.

"Yes, Dylan. My muse. The little hellcat who dined on my heart. Jenny. My old girlfriend."

"I wouldn't know how she is," said Dylan.

He was lying. Christopher could tell. "I thought you were friendly at one point," Christopher said, sounding unconcerned.

"Yeah? I guess. Long time ago."

"I find myself," said Christopher, "thinking about her." He cupped his hands and let the water fill them. He splashed his face. "Do you, ever?"

"No, I don't," said Dylan. "If I looked back, I'd start to think about what went down at Lucidora. Dude, let me explain something to you. I run a business that nets 73 million bucks a year. I have ten high-end spas, bring in 7.5 million each week. I manage 429 employees. I've got two kids in private colleges, a vineyard on Long Island that's trying to turn a profit. Still in the red there. I've got a sailboat at my marina, a second home in Colorado, a vacant condo in Manhattan that's been broken into by my marauding teenage offspring every other weekend. And an obligation to pay sixty percent. Yes, you heard correctly, my friend. Six oh. Almost two thirds of what I earn every month goes to my ex-wife. The Red She-Devil."

"But we were talking," said Christopher, "about Jenny. Don't you remember her?"

"Look, I have better things to do than hang around and reminisce."

"Of course you do," said Christopher. He took a breath. Dylan's smugness was unpleasant. That smugness could be eradicated, quite easily. Christopher had only to come up behind Dylan with his fishing line; the length of thread would be virtually transparent, invisible after nightfall. Dylan would hardly have time to comprehend what had happened—that Christopher had turned against him—before Christopher garroted him. The possibility of taking this action, however far-fetched and unlikely it was that he'd go through with it, gave him a sense of dignity. Since his release, it was dignity he lacked.

"So then, I'm figuring you don't know what became of Jenny," said Christopher.

"I have no idea."

"I take it you didn't forward any of the letters I wrote to her."

Dylan did a good impression of being a disinterested party. "Me? I told you I couldn't help you out on that one."

"How long, exactly, has it been since you had her address?"

"It's been, oh. Many years," said Dylan. "She cut out, you know. Jenny overreacted to the news of your arrest."

"Ah. Jenny was upset?" asked Christopher. Jenny-Jenny-Jenny. It was getting easier to say her name. Every time he heard it, Christopher felt an opening.

"We were both pretty freaked, to put it mildly," said Dylan. "After what went wrong in Lucidora, Jenny was devastated. She thought she was next."

"Yeah, I remember you'd mentioned something like that."

"She got me to help her," said Dylan, examining the bottle of wine, holding it up, shining a thin ray of light onto it. He had a fancy gold pen with a flashlight, a stopwatch, and even some sort of camera inside of it. Why? He kept this slick, showoffy gadget close at hand, lying on the tiles that ringed the swimming pool. Beside the pen-watch-camera, Dylan had a collection of toys for the nouveau riche. Recording devices, computers, who knew what. The technology left Christopher bewildered. Now Dylan continued to shine the beam on the label, as if checking the vintage. It was a crappy Merlot from Dylan's own vineyard but just then it tasted ambrosial. Still, the Merlot's poor quality was apparent even to Christopher, who'd learned about wine through a process of osmosis, picking it up as a kid from members of the Parallel Club on Fifth Avenue and the other Republican-Democrat-Republicrat turncoat chameleons who had toadied up to his Dad. Just a bunch of winos in tuxedos, winos with portfolios. Not that he was interested.

"So, you *helped* Jenny," said Christopher, caressing the word ever so lightly. "Good for you, Dylan. What exactly did you *help* Jenny do?"

"To get away. Start over. You know this. We've talked about it."

"Jenny Underground," said Christopher. "That's what I started calling her."

No one said anything.

"You signed our Jenny up for her own do-it-yourself witness protection program, I gather, Dylan," said Christopher. "That it?"

"I'm not going to talk about her."

"Ah," said Christopher. He could reel him in now by ignoring the rising friction between them, playing it relaxed and casual.

"Hey pal," said Christopher, "you're hogging the wine there. Pass me that."

Dylan, who had grown large and soft as a walrus since the days of their close friendship, stayed in his corner of the pool. He reinserted the cork and placed the wine bottle inside an inflated rubber wine-cooler—a raft, filled with ice. It had been specially designed for this purpose. The raft had four circular holes in it, drink holders, and an inflatable ice bucket. Cute shit for men like Dylan, who spent their leisure time drinking wine in swimming pools. Dylan gave it a push and the floating wine cooler bobbed over to Christopher's side.

Christopher retrieved the raft and pulled out the chilled wine bottle. "This is cold and the water's hot," he said. "One is expanding from the heat, the other contracting from the frozen ice. The glass bottle might crack."

"Well, Christopher, deepest thanks for the physics lesson. To prevent the glass from cracking, I suggest you keep my fine bottle of wine out of my eighty-three-degree pool," said Dylan. He spoke angrily.

"Sure thing. Just curious, though, what did you do for our lovely Jenny? That's all I'm asking you. Easy question."

"Why do you keep calling her ours?" asked Dylan.

Sniff sniff.

Nibble nibble.

He was coming forward, like a mouse, nearing the cheese, taking Christopher's bait.

"She told me once how she felt about you," Christopher lied.

Dylan must have sensed a trap. Pretending not to hear him, he whisked away, began swimming laps, and the moment to get to Jenny passed.

Christopher slapped his hands against his upper arms, rubbing his skin. The chilly air had given him goose bumps.

"Hey. You feel like watching a movie or listening to some music or something?" Dylan rested against the rim at the deep end. "I got a cool new projector hooked up out here. Wait'll ya see it. I gotta show this to you."

"I'd rather continue our discussion."

"I can't believe this," said Dylan. "Do you comprehend how much time has passed, here? You're not still stuck on her after all these years, are you? I mean, get real. Until you blew the operation at Lucidora, Jenny meant very little to you. You never even liked her. Admit it. Did you?"

"Shut up or I'll kill you." The words escaped. His fingers slipped inside the waistband of his swimming trunks and grasped the fishing line, rolled into a loop.

"Listen, Christopher, I've got a tip for you," said Dylan. "Out here in the countryside, in this quaint old rural town, we have certain customs. You might like to know about them. Folks here don't go around casually threatening their dearest fucking friends."

"It's just a manner of speech," said Christopher. "Bad habit I picked up."

One useful lesson Christopher had learned in prison: Upon re-entry into society, it's best not to mention one's hankering for revenge. Christopher had daydreamed about repeatedly plunging a carving knife into the abdomen of the person who'd betrayed him. He'd pictured choking the traitor. He wasn't certain, however, who that person was.

The question had come to obsess him.

"Thou shalt not kill," said Brother Bill, the prison chaplain.

"Says who?" Christopher had replied. An argument was going on in the back of his head now, all the time. Since boyhood, Christopher had despised being told what not to do. From the safety of his prison cell, murder had taken on the delectable flavor of forbidden fruit. It had beckoned to him the way mayhem always had. Taking a life had a provocative allure, like sleeping with his mother's bridge partner, Mrs. Florence Atkinson, or exposing himself to passersby on Fifth Avenue through the window of a limousine.

He rejoiced in the memory of his petty crimes and misdemeanors—skateboarding indoors, on the sly, up and down the hallway inside the duplex he'd grown up in. That had been a fine childhood transgression. He'd graduated from that infraction and he'd climbed the ranks, up and up, from "bad boy" to "black sheep." Now he was on the Outside. He could, if he chose, rise to "great criminal" by choking the life out of whoever had double-crossed him. It would be a revenge killing.

In the upside-down world of Triton, murderers had been accorded an extra measure of respect. Now, two weeks after Christopher's release, the fantasy of retribution held him in its grip. The mirror told him he looked old, pliant, and docile. Christopher wasn't sure he wanted to be good.

Dylan heaved himself up out of the pool like an orca, made a grab for something and waved it in the air at Christopher. "How about we watch *L'Avventura?*" said Dylan, cheerily. "Check it out. At the push of a button…"

From inside Dylan's house came a strange noise. It was the whirring of gears grinding. A movie screen began to rise. Large, square, flat, and white, it came up from the ground-floor window that faced out onto the lawn.

"I have weekly film screenings out here in the garden on Sunday nights in the summer," Dylan said. "Cool, no?"

"Cool, sure. Very," said Christopher.

"I have the entire Odyssey film collection—fully restored originals—on DVD," Dylan boasted, obviously pleased with himself and his acquisitions. "The 230 top classic films, the 78 best foreign films and 113 MGM musicals in black-and-white. I've got all of Kubrick, Lang, Hitchcock, Buñuel, Godard, Cassavetes, and Renoir. Are you still a film buff, Christopher? Pick whichever director rocks you. We can sit back and relax here, bro. It's your choice. We'll watch whichever one you like."

"You don't generally get a lot of opportunities to go to the movies at the federal penitentiary," said Christopher, dryly. "Best they did for us guys, Inside? A couple broken DVDs. Those directors you mentioned, I can't remember half of them."

"That's what I figured," said Dylan, glossing over the nasty edge in Christopher's tone. "You've been deprived of a proper cinematic experience. You must be missing it."

"You can say that again," said Christopher, grimly.

"Get ready, get set. And. Here. We. Go," said Dylan. He pushed a button on his electronic toy. Gray shapes appeared on the movie screen. Random film clips: a narrow window; a ship docked in a harbor; a girl at the edge of the frame, windblown, young, alone.

"What I'm missing most of all. What I'm missing is the answer," said Christopher.

"Mmm," said Dylan, opening a pack of cigarettes. "I gave up smoking on doctor's orders," he said. "But I'm lighting up in your honor. To celebrate your release. It's a special occasion. Want one?"

"Not for me. I don't need to make the tobacco industry any richer than it is already. Dylan, don't let me get this idea into my head, here."

"What idea?" Dylan lit his cigarette with the lighter he liked to flash. It was made of white gold.

"If you don't want to arouse my suspicions, you should answer my question. About Jenny."

"What?" asked Dylan. "I helped Jenny get a passport off the black market. That guy we knew stole them, altered them, and resold them. What's-his-name, the forger. His nickname was the Badger."

"I remember the guy."

"Jenny started her life over again. So? It wasn't only Jenny that had to scratch out her whole persona and trade it in for a new one."

"Got it," said Christopher.

"Do you? I hope so. Can't we watch the movie here? I'll make some popcorn, Christopher. Are you listening? Because I'll put the veggie burgers on the grill is what I'm saying. Just like in the old days. We used to love Antonioni, me and you. We're going to watch an Antonioni film. Okay? Remember?"

"Sure I do," said Christopher, but he could only remember seeing one movie with Dylan, and it wasn't this one.

They watched the opening credits roll, white letters on a black background.

"Wait until you see the razor sharp image I get with my equipment in this restored DVD of *L'Avventura*," Dylan boasted. "This is Michelangelo's masterpiece. The subtle gradations of light and shadow are a revelation."

"Didn't Jenny tell you who she is nowadays?" asked Christopher. "She must be living under an assumed name."

"*No*, already," said Dylan. "No, no, no. If you ask me that question again, you're going to have to hit the road. You can sleep at the homeless shelter. The topic of Jenny is over."

Christopher's hands swam aimlessly around his body. They landed on his hamstrings, taut and muscular from the rigorous daily regime of prison exercise in Unit B, one hour in the morning, one hour before lunch, one hour before dinner at five, and again at nine at night—running on the track in the yard. Around and around they ran, in the gymnasium on rainy days, until they wheezed and collapsed on the mats, to prepare them for their reentry into society, to give them the musculature of racehorses and the blank complacent minds of lambs.

"I don't believe a single word you're saying, Dylan," said Christopher. He gave his own thigh a friendly squeeze. It had been too long since anybody besides himself had touched his leg that way. He imagined it was Jenny doing the touching and patting, soft, sweet, a nebulous Jenny whose age and body underwent a continual metamorphosis, back and forth, older and younger, larger and smaller, a girl's hand on him, and then a woman's, a child's hand, a grandmother's. Good touch and bad touch, they carped on that. What a stinking dump of crap. All touch was heaven, all touch was God, he'd take a geriatric geezer, man. He'd take a 102-year-old pinching his fucking cheek and cooing at him, chucking him under the chin. He'd been denied it, barred from the kingdom of physical contact.

"What reason do I have to lie to you?" said Dylan, punching buttons on his fancy gadget. It was a remote control device, no larger than a deck of cards. It allowed Dylan to turn things on. "Popcorn's cooking," Dylan said. He could toast a bagel or warm a vegetarian burrito without even leaving his heated swimming pool. Dylan could make himself a decaffeinated cappuccino with steamed milk and cinnamon. He could watch movies on this blank white screen that popped up, at the flick of a switch, from beneath his living room's picture window. He could listen to Brahms or Blondie. He lifted the device now and here came hundreds of flickering glow worms: dozens of twinkling white lights, threaded on wires through the branches of the oak trees. The patio lamps around the pool switched off.

Fairy lights under the dark open sheltering sky. Looking at them, Christopher almost began to cry, snuffling in the night. For his old friend, Dylan, the lights, the lawn, the pool, the movie screen, the popcorn, the cappuccino—all of it was taken for granted, simply a regular part of life.

"You're protecting Jenny," said Christopher, his voice unsteady now because he was feeling his fucking feelings again. It was getting to be a habit with him. Darkness had settled over the backyard, cocooning him. Only the fairy lights twinkled. "That's what I think. But you never were very good at that. Protecting Jenny. Were you, Dylan? You watched from the sidelines. You weren't what I'd call a hero."

"Don't blame me for your mistakes, you prick," said Dylan, quietly.

Inside the house—an immaculate ten-bedroom mansion whose only flaw was that it was identical to every other mansion on the lake—a ceiling fan had begun to spin. Dylan was playing with the remote, raising and lowering the volume, turning his grown-up toys on and off, off and on.

"You really sucked at saving her from... how shall I put this?" said Christopher. "Her lowest impulses."

"May I remind you, Christopher, that you're the ex-offender, here, not me? I've opened up my home to you. Now I've offered you a goddamned job. I did that willingly, but don't push me any further. Don't yank my chain. Do you read me?"

"I'm not sure that's going to work," Christopher said. "As much as I appreciate your offer. Designing tattoos for suburban professionals at a private health club..." Treading water, he kicked his legs in the pool, in and out, in and out, staying in place, flexing his thigh and calf muscles like a frog. "It's not for me," he said. "I have no plans to surrender."

"Surrender to what, Christopher?"

"To the golf-playing, club-joining, networking, Rolex-wearing nation of shit-shovellers, pal. Call them what you like. Since I've been gone, Dylan. They have bought you out."

"You need a job."

"Not with you. Doing what *you* do. I'd rather go live at the homeless shelter than lower myself. It's against my ideals."

"You have no ideals left. Look, can we please shut up now? Here she is, Vitti." On the movie screen, the composed blonde actress waited on a cobblestone street. She was not as Christopher had remembered her. She'd been the most resplendent star in the sky, and now she was different. He watched her celluloid face for a few moments, trying to understand what had happened.

"My God. She's an ice queen," said Christopher.

"You don't love her anymore?" Dylan asked.

"No I don't. No, warmth. Vitti is all gold and frost."

"She's a fucken goddess," said Dylan. "Shoot that bottle back to me over here, would you?"

In this exchange of opinion over beauty and desirability, the unpleasant thing between Christopher and his old friend grew wider.

He felt the rift. "No can do, babe," said Christopher. He held the bottle upside down and shook it. "Looks like we're through."

"When I was down in my wine cellar, I should have brought up a few," said Dylan.

Christopher mewed in a high, nasty voice: "When I was down in my *wine cellar.*"

Dylan acted like he hadn't heard him. His hand caught the light as he gestured towards the movie screen. Handsome and placid in his white shirt, black tie, and black suit, the Italian actor Gabriele Ferzetti debarked from a yacht, strolling down the plank to a harbor outside of Rome. Ferzetti greeted Lea Massari, his on-screen lover, with a nod.

"Here comes the soulless seducer," Dylan said. "Cad. No wonder his girl walks out on him. I don't blame her a bit. What a bloodless, heartless, reptilian little prick."

"You're wrong about me," said Christopher. "I do have an ideal or two, unlike you. You're just a businessman now, Dylan, a number-cruncher. Myself? I continue to resist. And, honey, I refuse to tattoo."

"That *means* something? Not to *tattoo*?"

Christopher cleared his throat. "Tattooing is just one banal example, the tip of the iceberg, of what it is about America these days that I despise. For me to start earning a living as a tattoo artist would be to buy into Their mechanism. It would be an admission of failure. Transgression gets cleaned up and commodified."

"You *are* a failure," said Dylan. "Last time I checked." Waving the subject away, he pointed to the movie screen. "What I love here, in this scene, is the terrible sex. This is the worst sex ever filmed! Disconnected. She's not even paying attention to Gabriele Ferzetti! She feels nothing. Nothing for him. See? Look, there. Her face, impassive. Her body, languid. Her thoughts are wandering. She definitely doesn't love him. Why should she? He's a shit."

Up on the screen, the brunette, Lea Massari, was half-dressed in a bra and lacey slip, supine on an unmade bed. Nothing moved but her eyes. They were searching the room, fleeing to the wallpaper, inspecting the closed door, gazing longingly at the open window.

He knew the feeling. The scene triggered an excruciating thought, for Christopher, not just the memory of Unit D, the Hole, in solitary, but a hurtful memory of Jenny.

"I see," said Christopher, softly.

"Let's speak plainly," said Dylan. "A failure is what you are. People who've been in jail for more than twenty years are, by definition, unsuccessful. Don't get me wrong, Christopher. I love you, man. It's not an insult."

"On the contrary, I take it as a commendation," said Christopher. "To be a failure was what I always wanted."

"Christopher Benedict is a failure. It's a simple statement of fact," said Dylan. "The beautiful part of America is: You can change that. Fitzgerald was wrong. Join my corporation. There is a second act."

In the kitchen, a bell rang out, high and loud.

"Popcorn's ready," said Dylan. "Now which of us two lazy fuckers is going to get out of the pool and go get it?"

"I will," said Christopher. "I have to piss. And I won't urinate in your pool. See what I mean? I have my ideals intact. I'm a person of moral integrity, just like my pop, Senator Benedict. I am a man of virtue."

"I never can tell when you're joking," Dylan called after him.

Christopher, skin damp, hair wet, chilly in the backyard, charged out of the heated pool and ran across the soft thick grass, which emitted the most delicious odor, a smell he hadn't smelled before, ever, though he'd run over grass as a kid, and he'd been the unit's gardener, overseeing the planting and the fertilizer, tending the prison grounds, for three consecutive years at Triton. The air was fresher here, and the island of affluence that Dylan had built for himself was full of tender blossoms. Ornamental pear trees were planted beside the pool and, beside them, cherry trees grew in rows. Tears ran down Christopher's cheeks, mixing in with the pool water.

The Outside was talking to him.

Christopher Benedict, you don't belong here, the glass sliding doors told him, hissing, as he opened them.

This isn't yours, the downy terrycloth robe said as he picked it up from the chair where Dylan had left it.

You're a relic from another era. You're a pterodactyl, prehistoric, jailbird, dinosaur, get lost, said the shiny appliances that lined the kitchen counter like an arsenal.

Christopher grabbed the popcorn. Hot from the microwave, it scalded his fingertips. He poured the fluffy little white corn kernels into a lavender glass bowl, the color of irises. Jenny had loved irises. She'd brought him some that day. The day he'd blown it between them.

Jenny was everywhere and nowhere. When he was on the Inside in his cell, he hadn't understood how much stronger Jenny's pull would be when he got out. Jenny on the Outside, wherever she was, was calling to him. The thought of her was driving him out of his mind.

He ate a handful of popcorn while his drenched bathing trunks dripped chlorinated water on the kitchen's marble floor. *Marble* tiles on the floor, even. Fucken Dylan. His ostentatious arriviste house was tricked out like a dead dictator's mausoleum. When Christopher had first met him, Dylan had been trailer trash. And now here he was, rattling around in this immense castle. Steam rose up off of Dylan's back, out in the pool, as Christopher stood watching by the window. Dylan appeared to be mesmerized by the Antonioni movie up on the screen. He wasn't looking at Christopher.

Turning, Christopher walked quickly down the hall. A row of doors lined the corridor, each of them shut. When he'd tried opening them that Saturday, while Dylan was out grocery shopping, two of these five doors had been locked. He tried again now. No luck.

Christopher slipped inside the room that Dylan had grandly called "the library." While he chewed on his popcorn, he flipped through the cards inside Dylan's Rolodex. He was searching for Jenny. Christopher had been looking for Jenny's address and phone number since Saturday. He was up to the H's and G's. She'd have a new name, now. But Christopher was certain that, when he saw her new name, he'd recognize it. She would have picked a name that contained a clue. It would be a name that referred to someone or something he and she had held in common. It might be the name of a film director or a rock band. It might be an artist whose work they'd both liked, or a character from one of Christopher's favorite novels. Jenny would have left a trail of crumbs for Christopher to follow.

If he had said "yes" to Jenny that summer afternoon, the catastrophe of Lucidora would never have happened. That girl, restored. The present moment, remolded.

The mansion would not belong to Dylan. It would be Christopher's. Jenny, in her bikini, would be out there waiting for Christopher in that heated swimming pool, with the wisps of steam trailing from her bare skin. Jenny—older, altered, but still in love with him. What she'd wanted had once frightened him. Things had changed since then. Being alone, abandoned by all—this was the one great human horror. He was Outside, but it did him no good. It was all too likely that Christopher—the ex-offender, the leech—would live out his life here in this sleepy town, dependent on handouts from Dylan. He would be a charity case. He'd be out here in the stupid world, for a few more years or a few more decades, until he died, without once getting laid.

Christopher's fingers, slightly damp, thumbed through the names and addresses, pausing to look more closely at one or two of them. Paula Goldwin, Diane Gould, Helena Gutner. Back in art school, Dylan had seldom had a girlfriend, but he sure knew a lot of women these days. Maybe the wine cellar and the gadgetry actually attracted them. But Paulas and Dianes were too humdrum for Jenny. She'd have given herself a cooler alias.

"So. Christopher," said Dylan, as Christopher waded back into the shallow end of the pool. "I invite you to reconsider that job offer I made you. I hate to break it to you, but you're not seen as someone who's set to orchestrate a meteoric rise." Dylan, on the steps of the pool, was stuffing popcorn into his mouth, dribbling some into the chlorinated chemical water. "You don't," he said, between mouthfuls, "Have unlimited options." The music to *L'Avventura* swelled as the film flickered, silver and white, on the screen across the lawn.

"Beggars can't be choosers," said Christopher. "Is that it?"

"You said it. Shhh, this is the best shot in the flick. There goes the boat, and she's on it. I love it."

They watched the actors climb the craggy rocks off the coast of Sicily. "This was where you hid out for a while, wasn't it?" asked Dylan.

"Yeah. Near there. The Aolian Islands."

"Desolate, harsh, beautiful," said Dylan. Together, the two of them had been art students. Dylan, penniless, had received a scholarship to cover tuition. Now he was a fucking mini-mogul. Christopher, meanwhile, well, he was a fuck-up, but at least he had stuck to his guns, his youthful vision. His actions, right or wrong, had been deliberate.

"You used to look up to me," said Christopher. "Now you think I'm a loser."

Up on the screen, Monica Vitti stood on the shore, barefoot, in her thin short dress, as the turbulent surf churned around her, lapping at the rocks, splashing on her legs. The wind ran through her full blonde hair. She let her head dangle on her neck, weakly. She was being blown about. She had no will. And yet she'd had more heart than the rest of them. She was the only one with a conscience.

"I don't think of you as anything," said Dylan. "You're just

Christopher, an old friend to me. But I gotta say, designing tattoos was good enough for *me*. It's how I earned a living for a lot of years. And I made a killing doing it. Now I hire guys to do the tattooing for me. You have this whole superiority complex lately. What's so special about *you*? It's not a little thing I'm offering. There are plenty of people who'd die to be an apprentice at my spa. I'd train you."

"What a sad piece of crap you've become. You're pricking investment bankers' bottoms. A tattoo is a consumer good, thanks to you. It's not subversive."

"Why do I get the feeling here that you're wasted?" Dylan asked.

In fact, Christopher had raided Dylan's medicine cabinet twenty minutes earlier. He'd found a few interesting psychotropics in there, and had helped himself to them with abandon, popping them in his mouth as if they were breath mints. He was feeling real well just about now, actually.

"If you'd ever had to work for a living, you'd understand," said Dylan.

"It has nothing to do with that." Christopher reached for his fishing line.

"It has everything to do with that. From where you sat—in that throne of yours on Fifth Avenue in uptown Manhattan—you'd say that earning a living means nothing. You can say investment bankers and attorneys are uncool. Well, let me tell you something, buddy. Investment bankers are my customers, and I like them. They have money to spend and that matters to me. Jenny grew up on food stamps. She stole canned food from the supermarket, hidden in the lining of her coat. And I grew up eating squirrel in a trailer park in West Virginia. Squirrel, man. You don't know what it's like to be that poor. You just wafted around in your privileged world."

"Relax, I'm not attacking you."

"First of all, yes you are. And second of all, you don't even know what's happening. The world you left, the day you went into your cell in Triton? Dylan, it's gone. It doesn't exist. You know nothing. If a guy like *me* offers you a job, Christopher, you ought to say thank you very much. And you ought to accept it. You take it from me. And you take it politely, and you take it gratefully and you do everything I say you should, and you do it responsibly and carefully."

"Oh, fuck," said Christopher under his breath.

"You have nothing at all now, Christopher, and no one to help you. You don't turn a job *down*. You're an ex-convict. 'I'm grateful to you for giving me a second chance.' You try saying that to me now."

"Why, Dylan, thank you very much," said Christopher. "And you can stuff it up your rectum. I'd rather mop floors for a living than kiss the Man's ass."

"But there is no 'the Man!'" Dylan sputtered. "There's a boss. Your boss who gives you weekly paychecks! And that boss could be me. See? Hey, if you'd rather be a cleaning man, no problem. Be my guest. Just go try it. *Try* finding an office building that'll hire *you* to push a broom around, sweep floors, empty trash baskets, wash toilets. But yeah, that's a solid plan, Christopher. You'd make an excellent janitor."

"I didn't mean to start a fight with you," said Christopher after a while.

"I didn't mean to either."

"We both know what's eating away at us inside, old pal."

"Nothing's eating me," Dylan said. "I'm fine. You're the one with the problem."

On the screen, the film had come to an unexpected stop. The image of Monica Vitti standing in the window, looking down at the villa lined with palm trees, had frozen.

"My housekeeper dropped this disc the other day," said Dylan. "She's a fucking disc-dropper. She scratched it up. Shit. This is the best sequence!"

"I never did know how to act," Christopher remarked, to no one in particular.

The movie changed color, the grays and blacks bleeding into tobacco-stained shades of brown, blue, and red. The picture was breaking up, the lines turning into a shimmering mirage of tiny multicolored cubes, pixels fragmented like the scattered pieces of a jigsaw puzzle.

"Bitch scratched the disc," said Dylan, clapping his hand to his forehead, in evident distress. "My brand new *L'Avventura*, with unseen footage from the scene Antonioni never used."

"I never learned how to behave myself in polite company," said Christopher, mostly to himself. "What I am is a pariah."

"This isn't polite company, man," Dylan said. "This is just me and you. So, let's forgive and forget. Can we do that?"

"Maybe," said Christopher.

"Maybe is for pussies. Give me a yes or a no. One of us is going to have to get the fuck up out of the pool, get off his ass and fix this."

"No, man, I don't think we can," said Christopher.

"And you, as a criminal offender, are the moral arbiter here?" said Dylan, his voice flat. "You've never even used a DVD player, obviously, so I'll have to play repairman."

"I'm not the moral anything," said Christopher. "I'm just not sure that sticking tattoo needles in the fatty dimples on chicks' asses is going to allow me to, shall we say, repay the debt I owe society. Supposedly."

"It's easy to criticize," said Dylan, while the image on the screen trembled to life, began to move, and got stuck again. "I pay my taxes. I made a contribution, and so can you. Shit. Brilliant. Look what I did."

A faint gurgling sound from Dylan's side of the pool, a kerplunk, suggested that he'd dropped the remote into the water.

"How much you charge those pampered fucks at your gym?" said Christopher.

"Damn, damn, damn," sighed Dylan, while the movie screen

went blank. "The casing is supposed to be waterproof. But is it working? No. How much I charge depends which spa package they choose, Christopher."

He actually took his idiotic health spa seriously? "*Depends on the spa package they choose*," Christopher repeated in a mocking falsetto.

Behind them, a loon sent out a high fluting call while Dylan shook the remote, blotting it dry with a beach towel. Christopher turned away to face the lake. At this hour, it was a negative, just the suggestion of a lake, invisible, a long black oval. The houses were set far back from the shore, offering fleeting glimpses of their lit windows through the pines. Only the lights from the docks, reflected in dancing lines on the rippled surface, told him the lake was real, that and the smell of algae and the sound of the posts groaning as the currents shifted in the dark.

"See, the spa package is the central concept," Dylan said, hoisting himself up on the ladder of the swimming pool and pointing the remote at his entertainment center. "Don't you make fun of the package, man."

"Wouldn't dream of it," said Christopher. The sequences were going by too fast for him to keep track. He saw a scrap of *Jules and Jim*, a hint of *Breathless*. How could a guy like Dylan be into *this*, when before he'd been so deeply into *that*? Spa package, blech. This was an America of "spa packages," a scene that Christopher detested on principle, and in this place of plastic packages, phony yoga mats and hard-bodied girls chained to gymnastic machinery, Christopher suspected there was no room for the likes of him. He was a former dreamer, former sex fiend, former offender, current nobody.

"Yes, indeed, it all depends on the spa package," said Dylan. "We have an array of options, Christopher. A range."

"An array, a range," said Christopher, in a tone of derision. These words people were using now, advertising lingo, bullshit terms, seeping into the language, where did they come from?

"I got all kinds of good shit for 'em to choose from," said Dylan. "Look, I've raised tattooing to a high level, Christopher. It's an art form and I excel at it."

"Ah, exclusive tattoos at the highest artistic level," said Christopher, softly. He had balanced himself precariously on a beach ball, swaying from side to side, unsteady, as it bobbed under him.

"You're not in any position to be such a snob," said Dylan. "You ought to take a closer look. My tattoos are extraordinary works of body art. They mean a great deal to my clients. They each have symbolic, personal significance. Look down your nose if you want. The fact is, you know I'm the better artist. You've always been competitive with me. You're jealous."

"That's right," said Christopher, tipping over. "Fuck." The beach ball shot out from under him. He hit the water's surface with a plash. "You win. Dylan, I agree."

"You're going to have to change your attitude," said Dylan.

"Guy goes to prison for a while," said Christopher as the movie screen came back to life and glowed an ethereal Martian red. "The guy comes out. Lo and behold. Everyone in America has started talking like Mrs. Benedict, my mother. Conservative socially, yet liberal on economics. Socially progressive, yet economically conservative. A bunch of bourgeois bohemians. Bo-bo, go-go, free market capitalists. Don't you see you've mushed it all up into the same gray prison stew? No one can tell the difference anymore between any of you."

"I'm trying to help you," said Dylan.

"No, no, man," said Christopher. "I'm trying to help *you*." He reached over the side of the pool and dragged a plastic float over the tiles, pulling it down into the water beside him.

"If you have a problem with me? Just come out and say so," said Dylan.

The sound of breaking glass, far away, disrupted the quiet night. Christopher took a breath.

"I do have a problem," said Christopher. "You know what it is. You know that I do." His fingers touched the fishing line, a lethal weapon tucked out of sight. He ran the ball of his thumb over the coil. He could maneuver the length of cord behind him, surreptitiously, and unwind it. Stretch the fishing line taut, one end in each hand. It took four and a half minutes to crush the windpipe and deprive the victim of his oxygen. Convicts had taught Christopher how to garrote a man.

"You were behind it, Dylan," said Christopher, quietly, boarding the float and lying on his back, face up. The rubber pillow felt firm and solid beneath his head. He was buoyed in the water, rocking comfortably. The motion lulled him. "Like the movie we saw, French film noir, the one by Jean-Pierre Melville," he said, his voice low, rhythmic, and hypnotic. "*The Red Circle*, it was called. *Le Cercle Rouge*. Staring the ultra-sexy Alain Delon. Remember? You watched that, in the theater, sharing a rum and Coke with me, sitting on the seat right beside me. And sitting on the other side of me in that theater was Jenny."

"Drop it now," said Dylan.

"Here's the plot, babe. I will review the plot of *The Red Circle* for you. A best friend takes a guy's money and steals his girl. The handsome guy goes to jail, and the girl and the friend run off together. With my goddamned motherfucking cash. You took her away from me. Dylan. Didn't you?"

"You're out of your skull," said Dylan. "You're one paranoid conglomeration of ganglia, man."

"I worked out exactly what happened. I had years to sort it through, to think it over. I know you dicked me in the eye. That much I'm certain about." Hands at his sides, he paddled closer to Dylan.

"How can you say a thing like that? If you feel that way, get out of my Jacuzzi."

"I'd like to strangle you," said Christopher, ingenuously. "But you're right. You're the closest thing to a friend I've got. I like your Jacuzzi, babe. A lot."

"You can't have it both ways, Christopher. You can't come over and live here and try to take me down. I'll throw you out."

"Tell me, Dylan," said Christopher, slipping off the float and back into the water at the deep end. "My friend," he said, "tell me that you weren't fucking Jenny behind my back."

"You imbecile," said Dylan. "Jenny's long gone. Jenny's been married for years. Understand? Jenny has three kids and a husband."

Gotcha.

"I thought," said Christopher, "that you weren't in touch with her. Dylan, pal."

A faint splash came from Dylan's end of the pool.

"Ah," said Christopher. "Ah, so." He smiled up at the night sky. The garden was atwitter with watchful life; he half-believed that the twinkling lights in the trees were fireflies with human eyes; that the remote control device was hooked up to microphones. Was he really free to do as he pleased, now, or had he entered into the wider, more comprehensive surveillance program, where he'd perennially be tracked and followed? He'd be dumped in a ditch by the side of a road like a sack of garbage. They'd put him in the electric chair if he did this thing, strangling his friend.

"Don't get all wound up," said Dylan. "Let's both let it go." He flourished his remote control. "Peace offering. I'm turning up the Jacuzzi for ya."

"Oh," said Christopher, as the hot jets whirred around his armpits and his lower back. He extended his legs and pushed off from the wall of the pool, letting his head sink down into the water. It felt nice and warm against his scalp. He reached around and massaged his bald spot. Fucker was getting bigger.

"I've been wanting to get out and be *here* all these years," said Christopher. "But there's no 'here' anymore, Dylan. You know? Here's not here," he said.

"Stop feeling sorry for yourself," said Dylan in his no-nonsense businessman's tone.

"At Triton I longed to see the things and the people that I missed. What I missed was all over twenty years ago. America's not the place I remember. I feel like Rip Van Winkle." Christopher, treading water, allowed himself to descend deeper into his sorrow. He'd never fit in: He was a relic, a loser, a bottom-feeder. As Christopher had discovered since his release, Blackwood Hills had no discernible counterculture. They didn't need a Pied Piper punk, the Christopher of old, in his beard-stubble and aviator sunglasses, his torn jeans and worn-down boot-heels. Blackwood Hills had no interest in the romantic figure that Christopher had once fancied for himself. The suburban town was dedicated only to affluence and commerce; it possessed no clear or comprehensible politics. How people dressed was no longer a guidepost of cool. The old landmarks that Christopher had relied upon were gone. The town was divided up, not along political lines, but by "lifestyle" categories, as if the town were itself a set of products arranged upon a rotating rack in a store's display. In Blackwood Hills, there were two zones. In the first, people lived in nondescript mansions nestled in the woods, each fronted by a row of hedges and a manicured green lawn. The second, on the outskirts of town, was populated by those who assisted the master race: the babysitters, the housecleaners, the waiters, the dishwashers, and the dog-walkers. Like it or not, these people were, at base, a species of servant. They lived in dreary apartment buildings that looked exactly like roadside motels, hopelessly drab gray structures with rudimentary outdoor stairs, made of rusted steel or weathered wood, leading up to narrow balconies. These teemed with laundry lines, but were devoid of niceties like flower pots or barbecue grills. Unlike the verandas outside his parents' apartment building, which had brimmed with urns and lush plants, these terraces were junkyards: repositories for broken appliances. As he'd strolled through the neighborhood on his first day in town, he'd noticed this, how the tenants placed their damaged blenders and lamps outside, as if they might be miraculously healed and repaired by exposure to the fresh air. Ambling in Blackwood Hills' "good" neighborhood, then back to the "bad side" of town, Christopher distinguished two opposing factions: those who did yoga but didn't do drugs, and those who didn't do yoga but did drugs. The moneyed meditated and took care of themselves, tending to their bodies with the high seriousness of botanists who cultivated delicate, exotic hybrid plants. The hired help got high. Women who were not on drugs, it seemed, found it imperative to exercise. Christopher had peered inside the Garden of Wellness, Dylan's health spa, and he'd seen all these beautiful, lean girls grunting and moaning, in intimate relationships with their exercise machines. If he could somehow infiltrate their gym class, he'd get laid. Maybe.

In the brave new world of Blackwood Hills, chicks paid no attention to Christopher. Not the young ones, not the ones his own age. The only females that had talked to Christopher since his release were old broads. They seemed charmed by his courtly manners when he offered them a seat on the bus or held a door open. His future, if he had one, lay with the seventy-and-over crowd. Women who hadn't hit retirement had no use for Christopher. He might as well have been holding a sign that said: "I have no job or money, I own no car or real estate. And by the way, I have a prison record."

Christopher was a leper. In the two weeks since he'd been released, he'd tried all his old tricks. He'd tried to smile his trademark smile at a waitress. He'd given compliments to a hip-looking café chick. Response: zip. No woman wanted to be noticed by Christopher. The young women turned away from him with mild distaste when they crossed his path, stepping over him daintily as they might avoid a hairy spider. A spider would have startled them, at least. Christopher didn't even warrant a gasp, or a sigh of annoyance, or a rolling of the eyes. Not a sex god anymore, as he'd been called (well, okay, only once, and by his housekeeper, whom he paid) in his youth, Christopher now didn't even possess enough charisma to rate as a public nuisance. Instead, women looked through him, their eyes focused on a fixed point in space.

Still, Christopher liked being around women, that Saturday he'd arrived in town. He'd liked watching them in the morning, with their rolled-up exercise mats tucked jauntily under their arms, and the thin cotton sweat suits that were their uniforms, the tight zippered hoodies and the butt-hugging yoga pants. He'd had his coffee at the cart near Dylan's spa on Duane Street, a spot that let him watch women as they walked up the hill by the dozen, somnambulant beauties with long uncombed hair, like the members of a cult drawn to the temple of health by a silent gong, their faces pale in the morning light, their lips bare of lipstick, their eyes full of sleepy zeal for their own superior physical fitness, single-minded in their pursuit, if not of individual happiness and liberty, than of health, hot bods, and sag-free tits.

Dylan's spa on Duane Street was a mecca for these yoga babes of Blackwood Hills. But as much as he'd tried to comprehend them, observing their behavior like an anthropologist visiting from a distant land, notebook in hand, they defied him. He no longer knew anything. For instance: The yogis weren't hippies, as he might have supposed. They were hedge fund managers. Meanwhile, the druggies weren't sensualists or rebels. They were assholes. They were glassy-eyed pathetic deadbeats no one would speak to, least of all Dylan, or his staff at the spa, or any of the yoga girls. As Dylan had explained to him on his first day in Blackwood Hills, people who used drugs were now uncool. They were just sad misfits who'd lost their teeth and their sanity, who'd die young and broke. (Insanity and self-inflicted poverty, both highly admirable goals in Christopher's day, were now anathema.) Meanwhile, however, Dylan kept two dozen prescription pill vials in his medicine cabinet, and he popped a blue tablet twice a day. So. Where did that leave matters? How could Christopher find out what the deal was now? Could he fit in to this new scheme of things? Doubtful.

Above Dylan's lawn, Christopher could see the stars, not just a patch of blackness and a few twinkling dots through barred windows. He perceived the round fullness of the hemisphere, the curvature of the earth, the constellations above, the Big and Little Dipper, two twinkling cups, and Venus, Mars, and Orion, the bright guiding lights. Christopher stretched one naked arm upwards. He reached out towards the galaxy, his hand grasping for the scattered white diamonds. He could almost touch Venus with his index finger. The entire sky was Christopher's. He was out. He was once again lost and anonymous in the world, just as a beetle or a snake wanders around the ground unobserved, as a hawk flies, or a rat crawls. He was free as a bird.

Moving Pictures

Dan's wife had turned forty, and the cold snap of spring had given way to a tropical summer of heat waves and cloudbursts. One humid Tuesday in July, Dan hung up his lab coat and slipped out of the hospital for a midday drive. He parked his Saab on a muddy road at the top of Rosewood Mountain. He sat down at a damp picnic table. Lifting a pair of binoculars to his eyes, he scanned the horizon. The fuzzy pink hill in the distance turned out to be a breast, hugely magnified. It belonged to a young mother, three tables away from his, suckling her infant beneath the shade of an elm. Spotting Dan, the woman shook her curls and covered up her chest with a checkered napkin. Her voice carried on the wind.

"Can you believe this?" she asked the woman across from her. "Look over there, Pamela. A Peeping Tom. You'd think no one had ever seen a mom before. Hey, you! Hello, this is what a tit is *for*."

Ignoring them, Dan refocused his binoculars on the tree line.

"He's just a birdwatcher," he heard the second woman say.

"Oh, right, sure he is," said the first.

Dan moved away, edging towards the precipice that overlooked the town below. The terrain was soft and rolling here, abundant with deciduous trees, ploughed fields, and farmland. It took him several minutes to locate his quarry with his binoculars. What he saw through the lenses was a movie theater, a short distance from where he stood. Vines swept down from the cinema's sagging roof to form a scraggly canopy of green. Black letters came into view: a sign on the door. He adjusted the knob to bring the words into sharper focus.

"We buy and sell films in all genres and formats," muttered Dan as he read the sign aloud. "Widest selection in the U.S.A. Hitchcock's *Vertigo* now playing. Polanski's *Frantic*. Classic cinema all night and day."

Dan squinted at the blocky lettering along the side of the building. "The Film Society," it said. A line came into frame now, followed by an explosion of color: a painting. It was a caricature of Groucho Marx and Mae West. They cavorted along the cinema's cracked limestone walls. Dan made out other famous faces—Boris Karloff and Bela Lugosi, Janet Leigh and Anthony Perkins, Humphrey Bogart and Peter Lorre. Someone had assembled this Noah's ark, a parade of Hollywood pairings in crimson and white, each figure outlined in smoky shades of charcoal.

He retrieved a crumpled sheet of paper from his pants pocket and consulted it. It was a letter which he'd taken from Nadia's purse, signed by Dylan, her "old friend." It referred to the time they'd spent, "when we were kids," at a "cult-like" film society at the foot of Rosewood Mountain. Dan grasped the note between his thumb and forefinger. Even on this humid day, a wind reeled around the mountain peak, tugging at the thin, creased sheet and tossing it against the ball of his hand.

Dan passed through the heavy glass doors of the film society. The funky little space appeared to be an amalgamation of a museum, a movie theater, and a store. Against the blistering heat outdoors, it felt cool and dry in the foyer, where densely patterned carpeting matched the wallpaper and the air smelled of cologne. Music and voices flowed into the entryway from the adjacent screening room. Movie posters from a bygone era were displayed behind an empty ticket booth. Rounding a corner, Dan came across dozens of locked glass cabinets, each shelf lit from beneath. Row upon row of objects had been labeled and sorted like rare specimens, but these cases just contained old movies, not precious Greek amphorae.

He tunneled on to the back of the theater. The ceiling grew lower and the surfaces began to glint like a pharaoh's tomb. Film directors' autographs caught his eye, winking and twinkling. The names, he saw, had been silk-screened to form a silver chain along one wall. Dan glimpsed the signatures of Antonioni, Bergman, Fellini, Ford, Godard, Hitchcock, Murnau, Rossellini, and Welles. Blue floodlights shone softy, recessed into the faux marble floor at the end of the corridor. Arrayed on a counter were apothecary jars, brimming with shiny wrapped candies, chocolate snowdrops, and multicolored gumdrops. The barstools had retained deep impressions in their cushioned leather seats: film fanatics must have glued themselves, like barflies, to the chairs. The soundtrack to *Vertigo* reverberated loudly through the plaster, with a gruff masculine voice bouncing off a fluting trill. A brass bell rested on the counter. Dan picked it up and rattled it.

A small, fine-boned person rose up from between two jars. "Yes," said the clerk, who had a shock of white hair and an orange tan.

"You're open for business?" Dan asked, surprised. "You sell… er, rarities?"

"I am. I do. What is it you're looking for? My shop specializes in lost film. For a small fee, we can find missing footage and restore it for you."

"I'm trying to find an experimental film," Dan said. "It was made twenty or thirty years ago."

"What type of film is it, specifically?" the clerk said in a cultured voice that held traces of a vaguely European accent. His hair, parted far to the side, fell boyishly over one eye. With a withered hand, he gesticulated towards the glass cabinets. "Foreign? Independent?" he said with a note of encouragement.

"It's an art film," said Dan, swallowing hard. His mouth was parched.

The clerk had begun turning the pages of a thick, bound reference book. "Ah, art," he said. "I see. Tell me the title. I'm sure I can help you. Thousands of feet of celluloid were burned to ash during the upheavals, of course, but I'm proud to say that I, myself, have recovered the master prints for many of them."

"This one was produced by an artists' cooperative called the Bond Street Aktionists, that's all I know," said Dan, who had spent the last three days plugging strange words into his laptop, running a string of crazy phrases through a half a dozen different search engines.

The clerk's hand, which had been moving down the page, came to a sudden stop. On the other side of the wall, inside the theater, a church bell pealed. "Oh, dear," said the clerk. "The film you're looking for isn't… it isn't *A Wanted Man*, I hope."

"It might be," said Dan.

"I don't stock that sort of thing here," said the clerk, gently. "I'd very much like to be able to. But naturally I can't." Leaning back, he gazed past Dan and into the middle distance.

Dan stood motionless. In the room next door, Jimmy Stewart's voice was drowned out by the crash of cymbals.

"What sort of thing *is* it?" Dan said, wrapping his arms around himself.

The old man took a toothpick from the dispenser on the counter and peeled away the paper wrapper. "Restricted material from the old days," he said. "You remember how it was back then."

"I was in medical school," Dan explained.

"The laws kept shifting," said the clerk. "After the justices resigned. Those were the hellish years." He shook his head. "Shootouts. Bank holdups. Secret political alliances between parties on the radical right and left. The awful, deadly Years of Lead."

"I was aware of what was happening," said Dan, who had little interest in politics.

The clerk removed the lid of an apothecary jar and stared into it, as if it were a deep portal to the past. He shot Dan a questioning glance. "No," he said, after a moment passed. "No, I can't. It's impossible for anyone to ascertain what the legal status of that film is, even now. *A Wanted Man* started a cultural firestorm. It isn't finished."

"My interest in the film is entirely personal," said Dan. "How could I get a hold of it?"

"That, I wouldn't know." The clerk pointed towards the apothecary jar. "May I offer you a gumdrop, though? Do help yourself. I'm afraid that's all I... that's all I can do for you. I was merely an operative," he said. "Now I just select old films for the screening room and put them on our schedule. Nothing more."

Dan reached into the jar and let his fingers close around the candy. He scooped up a handful of jelly beans and began segregating the reds and yellows, placing them in a line on his napkin.

The clerk came forward and clapped Dan on the arm. "If you know what's good for you, you must forget."

"Why is that?" asked Dan, fixing the old man with a stare.

The clerk's eyes flashed. "Those were bleak, black days," he said, lowering his voice. "Our screening room was under government surveillance for three years, and our telephones were tapped. We still don't know what our position is. That's all I can tell you. Where we stand now isn't up to you or me. I am so sorry."

When Dan got outside, the temperature had dropped, the sky grown mottled gray. He was sure he'd been in the Film Society for only a few minutes, but his wristwatch declared that half an hour had elapsed. The clouds, tinged with red, mimicked twilight. As Dan collected himself, the cool theater behind him seemed more congenial than the close, humid air that enveloped him. He walked away on wobbly legs. As he reached the corner, he threw the rest of the jelly beans in a trash can. They hit the bottom of the bin with a rat-a-tat-tat.

Halfway to Riverbend, he stopped at a traffic light and discovered that a mysterious item had been slipped into his pocket. He turned the car around with a screech of the brakes.

Down in the bowels of Mercy Medical Center, Dan parked the Saab in the space reserved for him. The clerk's gift sat on the passenger seat in an opaque plastic case. Its title was formed by a series of black thumbprints arranged to spell out *A Wanted Man,* with *A Film by the Bond Street Aktionists,* typed along the bottom edge of the cover.

When Dan opened the case, he saw a grainy photograph of a person of indeterminate gender, its face and nude shoulders marked by primitive scarifications—circles, dots, and crosses. It wore a transparent shawl draped over its head. Dan detected a pair of eyes, nostrils, and the hint of a mouth underneath. The figure reached out from under this mantle to hold its hands out towards the viewer, beseechingly. The dark, frightening smudges on its hands and torso might have been paint.

Dan slipped *A Wanted Man* into his briefcase and took the elevator upstairs. The doors opened to release a burst of hygienic odors—ammonia, floral air freshener, and rubbing alcohol. In the hallway, Dan stopped to stare at two empty hospital beds on wheels, left outside the elevator doors, as if a pair of patients had wheeled themselves there and had left. He glanced nervously into each of his patients' rooms, checking their vital signs on the scanners above the headboards, where blood pressure, pulse, and respiration were illuminated in three parallel yellow lines. As far as he could tell, no one was missing.

In the inner sanctum of his office, he sat down in the dark and switched on his computer. Responding like a cat being fed, it made a contented burbling noise as he inserted the clerk's secret disk. An electronic message began to form at the top of the monitor, one letter at a time.

"CAUTION: the following material may be offensive, indecent or illegal," said the screen. It went dark, and a new message began. "*A Wanted Man* is unsuitable for viewing in a professional setting."

The screen scrolled forward. "This material is not recommended for viewing in public or in private." After another few seconds it continued: "Though disturbing to witness in the presence of others, it is highly deleterious to watch *A Wanted Man* alone."

Now a new sentence formed in a looping black cursive. "This programming has been brought to you by the Bond Street Aktionists and by the artist known as 'Mr. X.'" A musical score began playing, at a remove, as if from far away. "Join the Aktionists," came a whispered voice over the speakers. "Just press play, babe." Two black rectangles appeared in a vertical line down the center of his screen. They were numbered "Door #1" and "Door #2." Dan manipulated the mouse and clicked on the first box. He propped his elbows on his desk and moved in close. The music was chipper and light as a pleasant male face appeared inside the frame. Dan recognized him as Joe Chaplin, a talk show host from the early years of the century, a man with sparse auburn hair and a cordial grin.

"Greetings from our studio in New York City," said the host. "I'm Joe Chaplin and I'm here tonight with 'the artist known as Mr. X,' a leading figure in the grassroots anti-war movement, members of a growing network of civil rights advocates, artists, actors, and musicians. Frustrated by the failure of traditional tactics, they have banded together to protest last month's controversial attempt by the House of Representatives to temporarily suspend the first, second, and fourth constitutional amendments."

The camera pulled back to show the guest on the other side of the table. Wearing a soldier's helmet, he was dressed in camouflage. His face was hidden, from hairline to throat, by a mask. As rigid and shiny as porcelain, the mask had no clearly defined features, only a blank rounded area to suggest a nose and, beneath that, a small circular mound, an abstracted pair of puckered lips. Eyes shone like two beams from the mask's eyeholes. He leaned forward and gesticulated with his hands. "I'm Mr. X, veteran of war," said the man in an accented voice that sounded like the clerk's. "Each of us has taken on that name. Our membership is, of necessity, anonymous. No one knows who we are, or how many we are. We are the sons and daughters of athletes and tailors, of postmen and secretaries. We are children of movie directors and road-workers, of waitresses and fortunetellers, accountants and entrepreneurs. We are a multitude." His hands were covered in a pair of gloves like those traditionally worn by mimes. Clad in white, the restless, fluid fingers were spellbinding.

"Tell us, just what *is* the group you represent, the Bond Street Aktionists," said Joe Chaplin.

"We don't wish to define ourselves by any of the existing categories, Mr. Chaplin," said the masked man. "We are a moving target. Some of us are powerful, some of us aren't, and together we respond to current events in a state of flux. We object to propaganda and demagoguery. We demand a full restoration of fundamental liberties. We vow to use any means available to stop the cycle of unwarranted attacks."

Joe Chaplin cupped his chin in his hand and frowned. "You're warning us that you'll use extremist tactics—bombs, armed uprisings. Is that it?"

The masked man raised his hand and crossed his fingers. "I can't divulge just what our game plan is, except to guarantee that it exists. The day that explosives and grenades start to detonate, right here, inside our own homes and gardens. Playgrounds. Classrooms. We..." Now a single, shrill, high note began to sound, drowning the discussion out. "Stay tuned for the Joe Chaplin Show," read the screen, but the program had been discontinued.

Dan clicked on the box designated "Door #2." A silent film showed a theater as it began to fill. Men and women pushed passed one another, walked down the aisle quickly or slowly, chewed gum, tapped messages into hand-held computers, folded up coats and umbrellas. When the lights dimmed and the audience grew still, the faces turned to stare directly at the camera, which must have been mounted behind stage. Every pair of eyes focused on something out of sight, riveted by it. Cringing, some people rose up, waving, pushing and shoving. Others threw their hands over their eyes. Spectators swept forward in a tightly knotted mass, stepping over one another in a disorderly rush for the exits. The camera recorded a man and a woman filling the screen. A pair of arms, hands in supplication. A field of gray as the camera was knocked out of focus and then, at a strange angle: a vacancy. It was a film of row upon row of abandoned seats. After ten minutes spent watching nothing, Dan pressed "fast-forward," only to find more of the same. An empty theater, aisles littered with the forgotten belongings of a distant summer: a bottle of mineral water, a pair of sunglasses, a sunhat, a parasol, a shopping bag, a fan, and a baby doll in bonnet and diapers. Handbags of every shape and color had been left out on the seats. Dan let the film run for thirty more minutes, until a mothlike movement flickered in the corner of the screen. A policewoman loomed at the edge of the scene. Patrolling the aisles, she stopped to collect each purse, hooking the straps onto her wrist, one by one, as if the owners had been aboard the *Titanic* and, at last, the ship had sunk.

Tyranny and Possession

In the scorching summer heat, Nadia rolled up the windows of the jeep and turned the air conditioning higher and higher until bursts of gelid air blew through the vent and ruffled the hem of her gauzy cotton skirt. She was driving back from the town dump, where she'd disposed of the packages she'd received from Christopher over the last eighteen months. He was out by now, or so his last letter had claimed. She hadn't heard from him since May, when she'd received a parcel bearing the U.S. penitentiary stamp, saying he'd be released from Triton that coming July. Here it was late August, and no further letters had arrived, no more telephone calls had been attempted. She had an idea he was nearby—footloose, or, at least, at liberty. Now that he'd fallen silent, she thought about him all the time.

As she drove down Maple Street—past the general store and the antiques shop with the canopied porch swings—she assured herself: How smart, how right she'd been to do what she'd done to him. She'd had no choice but to take flight, choosing Dan over Christopher, leaving him. She'd hardened her mind against Christopher, but thanks to his letters she was softening. In the end, she knew, she'd harmed him worse than he'd hurt her.

"You had to, you had to, you had to," she said aloud as she drove up to the entrance of the river walk. She sought shade beneath the pergola and stared through her dark lenses at the river. It lay draped across the landscape like a necklace, twinkling in the sun. Nadia told herself: I will not think about him. I will think about my daughter, my Simone.

In those first early years after Simone's birth, Nadia had become uncharacteristically serene. She'd walk from room to room of the Palace, as she called it, a spacious new house where she lived in a state of grace, having arrived by chance in a harbor of tranquility. How proud of herself she'd been that, at no small cost, she'd built a nest for her young. She'd milled around the Palace, basking in the sun as it flooded her cavernous kitchen, delighting in the breeze from the Big Eddy that stirred her new curtains. A novel sensation had come to her as she'd held her child close, standing on her back porch, watering her petunias in their hanging wicker baskets. The feeling was so aberrant, it brought tears to her eyes. This was unaccustomed, happiness.

For as long as she could remember, Jenny had been tense and angry, throwing herself around. Then Christopher had seized hold of her. He'd induced the bright internal mayhem of an intoxicant, a forced glee that threw her down to new lows after a high that didn't last. She'd liked the lustful delirium, but when he was gone, the tyranny of Christopher was over and she felt sensational.

It had been a sane, quiet sort of bliss to become Nadia, wife of Dan, Nadia, mother of Simone. To carry baby Simone into her garden and to see, instead of city sidewalks and dumpsters filled with plastic sacks of trash, a river burbling through the hills that rolled beyond the lawn. Cupping the solid weight of Simone's head in one hand, Nadia had gazed out at that sinuous body of water, winding and infinite in either direction. Her house looked out at the Delaware River at its deepest point, where it ran as black and smooth as liquid agate. Sturdy pines sheltered the banks; ospreys glided across the sky. Strolling through her new house—Nadia the Landowner—she'd cradled her baby in her arms, her warm, sweet-smelling, freshly powdered daughter resting heavily on her shoulder. This was a baby that no one could pry away. She'd caught a glimpse of herself in the mirror above the fireplace—not Jenny the sleaze, but Mrs. Nadia Orsini, a nice young mother whose husband was in medical school. She wasn't trashy. She had a ring on her hand.

She'd found herself saying one word over and over again. Mine. Clasping Simone's soft smooth, chubby legs in her hand, mine. She'd walk from room to room of the house—mine—from the kitchen into the formal dining room, with its polished table and ladder-back chairs, its cabinets full of fine china, mine. Into the living room, with lamps, rugs, and curtains that came from Sorrell's Fine Furnishings, at full retail price, not discounted, not from the Second Chance Society or the Salvation Army or Goodwill. Mine, my furniture, worth tens of thousands of bucks and I deserve it and I can afford it. Back out the porch door onto the deck: I own all this; I belong here and this belongs to me. And into the yard, my garden, my rosebushes, my begonias, my lilies, my delphinium, my basil and rosemary, mine. Everywhere, she saw herself reflected; she'd expanded across the water, she'd grown up into the tallest trees. No one would ever clap their hands for her again. No one would ever see the doctor's wife roll over and play dead, performing on cue like a trained seal, cooperating with a pervert's request. No one would ever hand *Mrs. Nadia Orsini* a twenty-dollar bill, with a condescending wink, knowing it was the first of the month and she was a hundred dollars short of rent. They couldn't get to her now because she had everything. She needed nothing.

The Blackmail Artist

After a hiatus, she received a new delivery. A small red envelope came in the September mail, a perfect square, with a big black question mark instead of a return address. Inside, she found a beaded valentine. On closer inspection, the beads were eyes—the replacements that toy stores sold for children's beloved, one-eyed teddy bears. The paper heart had been ripped into two uneven, jagged halves. The right half said, "I think of you." The left half said: "Outside." The postmark was Blackwood Hills.

She sat in the dark living room by herself, that night, while the boys were out at a party and Dan was at Mercy, tending to a post-operative emergency. In her long cotton nightgown, the fabric thin with wear, she lay on the couch, letting the ceiling fan blow her hair around, alone in her empty house, remembering. His words dragged her under, pulling her back to the other place.

At a private room in his club on Fifth Avenue, Senator Benedict had sat down beside Jenny, each of them in an armchair. The shades had been drawn while, on the screen, Jenny had watched herself being 'maimed' by a man in a rubber mask, wielding a broken bottle, slashing at the air around her, prodding and jabbing at the space just in front of Jenny while she screamed her practiced scream.

The senator had watched exactly fourteen seconds of the

film—Jenny was counting the seconds as they went by. His face had been red—burned, scalded, boiled. He walked up to the movie projector and turned it off.

"I can't stomach much more of that," said Senator Benedict, turning to her. He looked exactly like Christopher, except that his hair was white, his skin was wrinkled, and he was fatter. The resemblance was disconcerting. He wore a navy blue jacket, tan slacks, a pale blue shirt, and a bow tie. His shoes were polished. As he sat down, he crossed his legs, coy, self-possessed. He had on a pair of round rimless glasses, which he took off now to wipe his face with a monogrammed handkerchief. He had told Jenny that Washington was rampant with slime. He said he never should have gone into politics. He wished he'd remained as the president of a university.

"What is it that you want from me, young lady?" asked the senator.

"Just something to help me support my baby."

"What are we talking about here?" He cleaned the lenses of his glasses with elaborate care. "Money. Yes?"

"I need help to raise your grandchild," said Jenny. She had delivered a note to the senator within days of Christopher's arrest in California. It was Dylan, not she, who had snitched on him, providing the state police with the address of the safe house and telling them about the drug-running. Christopher had been charged with twenty-eight counts, possessing illegal firearms and selling a controlled substance.

Jenny had just come to collect what she was owed.

Senator Benedict cocked his head, as if hearing a rumbling under the floorboards. "Why not admit that you're an extortionist?" he asked. "I'm terribly sorry that my son got you mixed up in this indecency. But be careful. Is that a threat you just made?"

"Christopher mentioned," said Jenny, undeterred, "the amount in his trust fund."

"I see, I see. And did you plan all this?" asked Benedict. "Answer me."

She didn't respond to his question. "When your son made this film," Jenny said, "I'd just finished the tenth grade."

The senator rested his cheek against the chair, sighing. It was the long melancholy sigh of someone, demoralized and disillusioned, who had known many woes. Aging and sad, he sat in the posture of a much younger person, curled into a ball, his long thin legs folded under him like a pretzel. After a while, he took out his checkbook.

"Cash," said Jenny.

"Very well, but you'll have to wait here for me," said Senator Benedict.

"I'll go with you. We'll go to the bank together," said Jenny.

"Absolutely not," said the senator. "I will not be seen entering the bank with you, and clearing out an account for you. They know me. You understand?"

"How do I know you're coming back?" asked Jenny.

"You don't. You'll have to trust me. And here is why I'll do what I say. It's as much to teach my son a lesson as it to capitulate to you. Extortion is a significant crime, and if I chose to, I could report it. My word against yours. I have an excellent lawyer. Do you see?"

She only looked into his eyes.

"May I offer you a drink?" asked Senator Benedict. He poured himself a glass full of clear liquid from a crystal decanter.

"No thanks," said Jenny and patted her abdomen.

"Stupid of me, yes, of course," said the senator. He was unfailingly polite, and she found herself charmed by him, wishing she had fallen not for the son but for the father.

"It's Christopher's inheritance that I'm giving to you," said Senator Benedict. "You have no idea what it's like to try to raise a boy like that. Whatever I do, he despises me. He hated his school, so I took him out of it. I put him in another school. He hated that one, too. I found him an alternative program. He was thirteen years old when,

God knows how, he discovered cocaine. Imagine...?" He shook his head, closed his eyes. He pointed at the blank television screen. "He barely comprehends the harm he's doing. My son is absolutely without any sense of responsibility. He has no conscience." The senator stood up and with an awkward, formal bow prepared to leave. "Wait for me and I'll be back with your money," he said. "I'm sorry my son is an idiot."

Jenny waited for what felt like hours, sitting in the upholstered armchair, watching rich people walk up and down Fifth Avenue in their mink coats, their dachshunds wearing jeweled collars, their limousines pulling up outside the club while the doorman hurried over to open doors. She half hoped that the senator would return with a lawyer or a detective, to press charges against her. Having seen what a nice man he was, she was ashamed of herself.

But he came back, almost an hour later, with a gym bag embossed with the Parallel Club logo, a coat of arms, in red and white. Her money was in stacks inside.

"Thanks, Senator Benedict," she'd said quietly, dazed by her success. "Could I ask one more thing? A favor?"

"This is the end," said the senator, but kindly, nodding, like the professor of economics that he'd been. "Is that clear? If you come to me again, I'll press charges against you. This is Christopher's bank account, drained. For you. But I have to draw a line now, Miss."

"Jenny. Call me Jenny if you like. I mean, I'm having your grandchild."

"You're not under the impression, I hope, that there is anything unique about a grandchild. Due to my sons, I have two others of these bastards, already. I'm going broke because of all of you. I tell you, Jenny, I have reached my limit."

"It's not a fiduciary favor," Jenny said, pleased that she was able to articulate the five-syllable word.

"What favor is it, then?" asked the senator.

Jenny wondered if he might have had another drink at the bank, or on the way back to his club, because his face looked even redder, and his eyes seemed to be coated with a sheet of transparent plastic. He looked at her, blurrily, as if he didn't want to see.

"Could you write a letter to the library at Yale?" she asked him.

"A letter to the Yale library," Senator Benedict said in the tone of someone used to negotiating, to listening to others' points of view, to being reasonable. "But Christopher never showed up at Yale, he deferred his admission indefinitely. What would you want there? Why, in hell?" he asked, raising his eyebrows.

"When Christopher and I went to New Haven," she stammered. "A friend of ours in the art program. Some weekends, on the campus. When we—" None of these sentences could be brought to a conclusion. "I like to go there to read." This was the truth. Despite her difficulty spelling, Jenny had loved to read, and to paint and draw, from the beginning. Dylan and the library at Yale: They would be her refuge.

"You'll settle in New England, will you?" said the senator.

"I don't know. Just write a letter saying to whom it concerns, please let Jenny Rodriguez use the library."

"Carrying this around by yourself isn't wise," said Senator Benedict, tapping the bag. "What will you do?"

"I'm buying a house," said Jenny.

The bag full of money was heavy, as if she were transporting a dead body. She kept her hand on the handle and never let it go. Dylan accompanied her on the drive to Pennsylvania. It took a week before they found the house for sale by the river. Jenny paid in cash.

The Red Circle

Christopher shielded his eyes against the bright sunlight that filled Dylan's kitchen. "I wish," he said, sleepily, "that you had heavy fucking cream. Do you know what they put in our dishwater coffee at Triton, Dyl?"

Dylan had spread the newspaper out on the kitchen table. Whatever he was reading had fully absorbed him.

"They gave us the same milk that the Red Cross feeds to refugees in third world countries," Christopher said. It was the morning after their swimming pool confrontation. "Powdered milk, Dylan. Mixed with water."

"If you're trying to get me to feel sorry for you," said Dylan. "It isn't working."

Christopher poured the skim milk into his coffee and, with a sigh, began stirring honey into it. "This isn't what I want," he said. "I'm craving the real thing."

Dylan roused himself. "Hey, I'll pick up a pint of fresh heavy cream on my way home from the office," he said. "How's that, old buddy?" But instead of looking at Christopher, Dylan's head remained bowed to his new god, *The Wall Street Journal.* It had been delivered to the front door of Dylan's house early that morning.

"That'd be great," said Christopher, uneasily. He hated seeing his old friend poring over the stock pages, the way Christopher's father once had done. It revived in him a malaise he'd been battling ever since he'd arrived at Dylan's place. "Cream and sugar," he said, closing his eyes. "You have no idea how good it's going to taste. I've been waiting for a decent cup of java for years."

"You had some on Saturday," Dylan said, only half listening. "Have more. Take a stroll into town and buy yourself another latte from Flashcups Café if you like."

The body snatchers had invaded, replacing humans with vegetative pod people. Subtle, abhorrent little changes had taken place in his absence. Now he himself, Christopher-the-unrepentant, was gradually, insidiously transforming into one of Them. If he wasn't careful, even he would become the sort of supercilious fuckhead who peppered conversation with the words "dysfunctional" and "inappropriate."

It was weird. Here Christopher was, sitting at the breakfast table in pajamas, being ignored by Dylan, who was dressed for the office. The office! Dylan! Before his incarceration, they'd both agreed that offices were cesspools. Now Dylan's bank account was robust (late at night, while he tried to open locked doors, insomniac Christopher had riffled through Dylan's bank records in the file cabinet). Dylan's appearance was impeccable. His shirt was dazzling in its whiteness. Christopher's best friend had cleaned up his act so fastidiously, he might have been stand-in, a replacement, not the actual grungy sweaty Dylan, but an actor selling soap on a detergent commercial.

"I'm boycotting Flashcups Café," Christopher said.

"No," said Dylan, rustling his newspaper.

"No?"

"No, boycotts are over. We don't do that these days," Dylan explained.

It was Monday morning, and Dylan was in his corporate drag. He'd come down to the kitchen, from a room upstairs that Christopher had not seen—no "grand tour" of Dylan's house had been offered to him because, perhaps, Christopher the ex-convict wasn't welcome to tread upon the clean white carpeting, or to enter the mysterious east wing, a recently constructed extension to the house. The east wing was closed off, its French doors locked against him. Though Dylan hadn't come out and said so, Christopher was barred, too, from any of the rooms on the second floor, up the grand staircase. The staircase was a work of art in itself. Its wood was tawny and silken. It had been custom made of golden teak from Indonesia, designed to Dylan's precise specifications. This was what Dylan did with his money: had staircases installed in his castle.

Early that morning, not long after Christopher had quit snooping around the house and had finally fallen asleep, Dylan had appeared in the kitchen at the unholy hour of 6:00 A.M. He'd awoken Christopher from sound slumber with the clatter of his battalion of kitchen appliances, making fruit juice in a giant electric-juicer contraption. Today, Dylan had dressed in a dark blue suit, with sharply creased trousers and a well-tailored jacket, nipped in at the waist and wide at the shoulders. Dylan was doing four things at once—drinking his fresh fruit and yogurt shake, reading the newspaper, flipping through the pages of a novel titled *Quarterly Earnings Report*, and fidgeting with one of several gadgets that he carried around with him everywhere.

"So when do you want to start, old buddy?" said Dylan, his attention fixed on his portable computer.

"Start what?" said Christopher, anxiously.

"Your job. Working for me."

"I don't need the job. I think I told you that."

"Then what are you going to do, exactly? Rob a bank?"

"I'll figure something out," Christopher said. Who was he fooling? Any day now, he'd borrow a suit from Dylan and he'd succumb. Christopher took a sip of coffee. It was stronger and more acidic than the coffee he'd become accustomed to. Everything here was bold and rich—the juice full of flavor and pulp; the apples shiny red in their smooth wooden bowl.

A scrap of memory rolled across his mind, of Jenny at age fifteen, standing outside Tiffany's, acquisitive, greedy, looking in the store window at Christmas at pretty trinkets beyond her means—a crescent moon of platinum on a midnight-blue velvet backdrop. Now, in his daydream, he saw her going inside the door, smiling contentedly at the security guards and the clerks. She was carrying a briefcase full of greenbacks. She set it down on one of the glass cases and pulled out thousands of dollars in cash. She was drowning in diamonds, greedily pocketing them, draping herself in necklaces and bracelets.

"Excuse me a minute," said Christopher. He shuffled back to the guest room and sat down on the windowsill, pressing his forehead against the glass. He closed his eyes. "I was going to buy a small place on the beach," he said, when Dylan came into the room without knocking. "I was going to retire on that account. The Benedict account, my trust fund. I was going to move out to the coast and live by the sea."

Dylan handed Christopher a mug of hot coffee and a ceramic sugar bowl. He stood by the door, sipping from an espresso cup, watching Christopher intently. "Like I say, you're welcome to stay here as long as you like," Dylan said. "You can come work for me. Just, you know, don't harass my employees."

"What's that supposed to mean?" said Christopher, heaping sugar into his mug. Sixteen days ago, he'd stood in line to receive a cup of boiling water for instant coffee. The men in the unit at Triton had each been allowed one packet of sugar. This had been served to them, like a delicacy, in the center of a small paper plate.

"The world has changed, that's all I'm saying," said Dylan. "You did a lot of..." He raised an eyebrow. "With chicks you just sidled up to at the park, in the bars, on the street in East Harlem. With the women who worked for you. In your parents' apartment. It's not cool."

"Hey, fuck you, babe."

"I'm just telling you what you need to know. I'm the head of a fucking company. No pawing at the employees. It doesn't sit too well these days."

"You talk to me as if I were a simpleton."

"I'm explaining shit to you." Dylan eased himself down onto a chair by the colorless curtains. "Don't get all worked up over it. At my spa, you'll see a lot of class-A pussy. That pussy is paying my bills. It sounds sexy to you, maybe, but it isn't. That's business, see, and you don't touch it."

Christopher felt that dizzying sensation again, like seasickness. "You're remembering me from a long time ago," he said. "I mean, screw you, Dylan. You know? I was twenty. And so were you. You don't have to treat me like a sex offender."

"Impulse control. The Christopher I knew back then, let's be honest. You didn't have any."

"*Et tu, Brute*, babe," said Christopher, looking at him carefully. "I don't need your job."

"Calm down, man. Stop shouting."

"I'm not raising my voice. You just don't like what I'm telling you." Christopher had begun to pace the room. He marched towards the bookshelves, spun around, marched to the window. It looked out onto the driveway, bordered by a row of bushes. For all he knew, Jenny lived across the street. For all he knew, she had taken his money and squirreled it away right here under his nose, right here in Blackwood Hills, where she and Dylan could hold reunions to giggle about him.

"This is a difficult transition for you," said Dylan.

"Don't talk like that to me." Christopher wheeled on his heel and hurtled himself back to the other end of the room—towards the fucking Matisse print in its frame, the symmetrical oak bookshelves, the spines of the books lined up with a sterile precision, the covers of the volumes harmonizing with the wallpaper and décor. Beige on beige, tan on ivory, everywhere he turned. "I had that transition crap, that psychospeak," he muttered. "I had enough of that at Triton. What are you, Dyl? My parole officer? My guidance counselor?"

"Sit down, Christopher. You're making me nervous."

The robe Christopher was wearing had come untied. It ballooned around him as he walked. "I don't have to sit," he said. Away from the shelves, to the window again—the driveway, the bushes, the identical white houses past the stretch of manicured lawn, and another one past that, all down the hill, matching boxes of white and beige, repositories of wealth, up and down, as far as the eye could see.

"The way you look right now is scary to me," said Dylan.

"I know what you're going to tell me. You've got the doors locked. You want me out. If I don't play the game, if I don't act right—your kind of right." He took his hand out of his pocket and slapped it against his leg. "Slam, the gate gets shut. Say it. The invitation has been rescinded. Is that correct?"

"You need to slow down here," said Dylan, looking at his wristwatch nervously.

"Is that a Rolex? It is. You are in league with Satan, too. I knew it."

"I have to get to work, man, that's all it is. What's your problem?"

Christopher had tangled up his fishing line. It poked out of his hand. "You're the same as all the rest. You're a turncoat," said Christopher.

"I'm not a turncoat," said Dylan. "Get a handle on your paranoia, already. What the fuck is that in your hand?"

"I have a right. To bear arms," said Christopher.

"Let me see what you've got there. Is that thread?" said Dylan.

"Yup, just my thread," said Christopher. "I've been spooling it out. I follow the thread to find my way back. Out. I hate it here. I hate your house."

"You don't need to personalize this," said Dylan.

"Personalize!" said Christopher. "Inappropriate. Spa package. Issues."

"Uh, Christopher, is there somebody I should contact? Are you derailing?" said Dylan.

"Earth to Christopher. The pod is in the spa. Personalize the appropriate issues. Jenny is inviolate." He came to a standstill. "Hey, do you have any Valium? I looked around, but I couldn't find any. If you had a Valium or two or a few. Five or six, that'd do me. I tell you what. Give me some Valium. We could settle our differences."

"It wouldn't be a bad idea for you to chill out and lie down."

"Might as well," said Christopher.

Dylan had left the room and returned. He handed Christopher two pills and a half-liter of mineral water.

"Water in a bottle," said Christopher. "Makes me weep." He put the pills on the back of his tongue and drank. "Designer water, designer jeans."

"Time passed and I grew up," said Dylan. "You knew me when I was a young mule, a man with a van, transporting coke from Mexico." He was fluffing up the pillows. He was patting the bed, gesturing to Christopher to lie down. "Get some sleep, old friend. Give this some time."

"I'm going to New York City to have dinner with my parents," Christopher said. "Then I'm going to the West Coast. I'll buy a bungalow on the beach in Big Sur."

"Sure you will, Christo. Sure you will."

"Stop talking to me that way. Am I in a sanitarium? Am I in a Bardo state? Or purgatory."

"I'm not talking any way," said Dylan. "Shh, shh. It's me, man. Don't flip out on me. Go back and lie down. Come on, I'll get you settled."

"Don't treat me like I'm sick in the head." He closed his eyes. "Were you and Jenny sleeping together?"

"Um, well. When?" said Dylan.

"Bingo. That's all I need to know," said Christopher. "You're my only friend, and that's the kind of friend you've been."

"Jenny was a little loose, let's face it, kiddo," said Dylan.

"While I was seeing her? While you were acting like my best friend?"

"Honestly, truly, I don't remember. She's a married lady with her own photo studio," said Dylan.

"You said you didn't know what happened to Jenny," Christopher said. "Last night, I got you. You lied to me."

"Let's don't," said Dylan.

"She doesn't want to see me. Is that what it is? You're in touch with her, you know where she lives."

"Get some sleep," said Dylan. "Are you sure you're on the right dosage of that medication they prescribed at the clinic? And it's okay to mix and match that shit with Valium?"

"Yes, yes. So that's how it is," said Christopher, talking to himself. In the guest room, as generic as a room in a midpriced hotel, tears rolled down his cheeks.

The light had changed. It was glaring and penetrating when he awoke in the next life. Seconds passed, marked by a ticking clock. Christopher did not know where he was. The pillow beneath him was concave, the mattress thin, uneven, filled with hard lumps the size of golf balls. The odor of ammonia entered his nostrils. He heard the distant echo of a metal door slamming closed, the faint clang of keys jangling on a belt, low voices speaking in a room beside him. Maybe he was in the unit and never had been released from Triton. He'd remained in his prison cell all the while, lying in the upper bunk, with no one below him, in a supermax facility for violent felons, in solitary confinement. He'd been talking himself to sleep, whispering to himself as his old, wrinkled hand moved across the cinder block, writing invisible words on the wall, an endless saga, a confession. At night in his cell, he'd written on the cement ceiling in disappearing ink. By day, when he'd been permitted to have a tablet of paper, he'd written legibly, with a pen. For years he'd been writing to Jenny, a love letter she'd never read. An illusion.

***

He'd been dreaming. In his dreams, he could go where he liked and do as he pleased. Spectral, he'd walked into a 7-11 to buy a six-pack of beer and, standing on a line, he'd screamed. When he'd gotten to the cash register, he saw that the man behind the counter was Christopher. He was both the customer and the cashier. When he turned around, he saw four men, each holding a six-pack of beer, waiting his turn. Each face was his. Everyone in the 7-11 looked just like him.

When he opened his eyes, Christopher was on a single bed, looking at the window. There were no bars on that window. What he saw was wooden slatted shutters. He was inside Dylan's guest room, ensconced in beige. He listened to his own breathing. Outside the guest room, he heard footsteps.

Padding into the living room, Christopher was startled to see a redheaded woman in shorts and a tank top, standing at the console table behind the white sectional couch, fiddling with her cell phone. At long last, then, it had happened. Christopher's life had turned into a skin flick. From now on, babes would appear fantastically from out of nowhere and begin, immediately, to disrobe. He pictured this one, who had a muscular jogger's body, lying down on the kitchen table with her arms and legs stretched wide to accept him, her back curved, pelvis arching upwards, a neat triangle of pubic hair—that same inviting shade of copper as her strawberry tresses—undulating with her hips, extending its satiny invitation to Christopher. The fact was Christopher had forgotten what it felt like to fuck. Still, the pussy-vision fortified him for a few seconds until it disintegrated. The redhead, catching sight of him, opened her mouth and spoke lines a porn star would never speak.

"I left Dylan's toe fungus ointment in the master bathroom," she said. "We were able to clean up the entire big toenail in time for the dance recital. What a relief. Would you give Dylan that message? It's great stuff. Please thank him for me."

Christopher's happy skin flick dissolved. "Uh, sure. I'd be glad to." He thought about asking whose toenail they were talking about, but decided to skip it. He tried his grin out on her. "Hey, I'm an old friend of Dylan's. We were tight in high school."

She wasn't even looking at him. She was checking her cell phone messages.

"We were going to study art together at Yale, but I bailed," Christopher added. "What I do now is, uh, I'm a novelist."

"I know who you are," said the redhead, whose hair was straight and fine, and who might not have been wearing a bra. He watched her move, noting the way her shirt clung to her. "You're the senator's son. The ex-con." She smiled at him, confusingly, as if "ex-con" were a particularly bold and stylish career choice. He'd forgotten what great fakes people were, out here, deftly disguising their prejudices.

"The ex-con, that's me," said Christopher, feeling clobbered. "How nice of Dylan to be discreet about it."

"He's my husband," said Red. "He tells me things."

"I see. I didn't know he had a second wife."

"Well, we're separated."

"Pleased to meet you." Christopher extended his hand.

"Muriel," she said, but instead of offering him her hand to shake, she put both her hands in the front pockets of her shorts. "I'll be out of your way in just a second."

"No problem." Turning away, he hastened back to his lair at the other end of the house. Exiled. Like a child sent to his room without supper, Christopher sat stupidly on a chair, doing nothing, pretending to be busy there in the guest room with its beige paisley pillows; its anonymous beige décor. He stared at the wall, waiting until Red had left the house.

"Good-bye, Christopher!" she called out. "Nice meeting you!"

Like hell it was. He heard the door close behind her, and her footfalls on the road leading down the hill and out of the complex. Watching through the window, he saw her tall angular form, like a Giacometti sculpture, sprint past the willow tree. She vaulted over the footbridge towards the concentric stone circles that marked the herb garden. Herb garden, jeez. He'd walked around in there, looking at the hand-printed labels, the herbs so rare he'd never heard of half of them. It was a garden for the "community" alright. It was intended for the exclusive use of homeowners in the immediate vicinity, the pod people, who'd filled out application forms in triplicate.

When he left the guest room to take a shower, Christopher noticed that the assless jogger had forgotten something. In the hall, tumbled on a table, lay a heavy keychain like the one the prison guards had carried. Keys of every shape and size were spilled beneath the mirror in which Dylan, two hours earlier, had stopped to admire himself.

"I opened my home to you," Dylan had said. But that had been a lie. To Dylan, Christopher was an intruder. Out of prison, Christopher belonged to society's dregs.

In Dylan's library, thumbing through the Rolodex, Christopher had finished studying the U's and the V's. He flipped to the next card, and began with the W's. He soon came to an address and phone number that gave him pause. A "Nadia Tatiana Larina" lived on Bridge Street in Riverbend, Pennsylvania. He recognized the name, of course. It came straight out of an opera by Tchaikovsky, one that he'd taken Jenny to see at the Metropolitan Opera House that long-ago summer. Dylan had not filed this card under the letter "L," where it belonged. He'd filed it under "X."

As he reached for the phone, Christopher's hand shook as badly as it had when he'd had delirium tremens from the Triton moonshine made from mouthwash and paint thinner. He punched in the number with trembling fingers. On the other side of the line, the phone squawked. One, two, three, four, five, six, seven, please answer, please.

He heard her voice.

Christopher dropped the telephone. The doorbell was ringing, its high peal piercing the air. The receiver fell on a chair and bounced; the phone crashed to the floor. Slamming it down, Christopher hurried to the window and peered between the Venetian blinds. Dylan's ex-wife was standing on the doorstep.

"Just a sec!" Christopher yelled.

Tremulous, Christopher hurried out of the office and through the hall. This wretched house Dylan had bought was too large, room after room converged in the corridor and everything looked the same. He took a wrong turn, opened a wrong door that had been left unlocked and finally made it back to the front hall just as the doorbell began to ring repeatedly with new insistence.

"Hey," he said, swinging the door open and smiling at Dylan's ex-wife. "Forget something? Or was it that you missed me?"

Dylan's ex, walking up the two steps to the door, pushed past him. "I forgot my keys. You haven't seen them, have you?"

"Nope."

"That's odd. I set them right down on the counter here, I'm sure."

"I'll help you look for them."

"No, don't bother," she said. "I just thought..."

"I'll keep an eye out," said Christopher.

"You sure you haven't seen them?" She gave him a hard look.

"I just woke up, I'm afraid, and I'm out of it," said Christopher.

Her eyes scanned his face.

"Do you think *I* took them, Muriel?" he said.

She made a big show, pretending to be shocked by the suggestion. "Of course not, Christopher. No, no."

"Well let's take a look for them, then," said Christopher. "I'll make us a fresh pot of coffee."

Dylan's ex-wife crossed her arms, flushing slightly. "I'm in a hurry, actually. I ran back here for just a second assuming I'd find them on the counter. I'm almost certain that's where I left them."

Christopher stayed quiet.

"That's okay," she said. "It's not important. I can't be late."

Christopher trapped her eyes with his for an instant.

"I have a meeting," she said brusquely.

"You and Dylan seem to have quite a few of those. Do you work with him at the spa?"

"No, I don't, Christopher. I run an agency."

"I had an agency myself, of a sort, once. What kind of agency is it that *you* have?"

"I'm in advertising." Her lips had flattened into a frown. They'd turned into a thin straight line.

"Tell me more about the meeting," he demanded. He wrapped his arms around his waist and made it clear to her that he was checking her out, appraising her from her neck, down to her nonexistent tits, to her short-waisted torso, to her crotch, to her munchkin thighs. He made himself look directly in her eyes, to convey just what he thought of her, of all of her.

"No," said Red. "I don't have time. I need my keys. I have to go."

"I don't have your fucking keys," he said, contemptuously. It was apparent to him that never in a million years would he be able to woo a female. He was too inept to interact with women, with humans. He'd forgotten how to speak to them, how to behave in front of them. His manner, his belligerence, his disrespect: All this Red had noted. He was Christopher-with-a-prison-record.

"I'm meeting with an associate, if you must know," she said, coldly. "If you don't give me my keys, I'll have to call the police."

"Go ahead," said Christopher. "I don't give a shit. You think I want to live in your gated community? I preferred my prison cell. Fewer assholes."

"I doubt that, somehow."

"What time is your *meeting*, baby?" said Christopher. She had no meeting to go to. That was obvious.

"Um, it's. At noon," she said, faltering, staring out at the door like a cat as it plans to bolt, to climb a tree.

"You sure about that?"

She stole a darting worried glance at him.

He smiled. She was lying.

"Yes," she said. "I am." She wanted to flee, of course, but she couldn't admit it. This was how these people were, the hypocrites of Blackwood Hills who lived behind these gates. They'd make public speeches about poverty and crime, never venturing past the boundaries of their hermetic habitats.

"Plenty of time to look for your keys, then, Jenny," said Christopher. "It's only nine o'clock in the morning."

She twiddled with a lock of her hair. "Muriel's my name, and I have to get going," she insisted, weakened, flustered, turning her back to him, propelling herself forward. He stared at her ass in retaliation. It was an all-American ass of a certain stock, flat and asexual. He could see the outline of her skimpy buttocks clearly through the fabric of her jogging shorts, gray with a metallic silver sheen. Her sneakers, equipped with thick foamy white soles, seemed to be made of marshmallows.

Christopher stroked the fishing line inside his pocket. Any time he wanted.

"I've got to run now!" she called over her shoulder, hastening towards the door to escape from Christopher-the-criminal. "If you happen to see my keys, will you let me know?"

"I'll do that, Muriel," he said softly. "917-256-2972."

Muriel spun around, a frightened expression on her tight, dry, sun-damaged face. "How did you know my phone number?" she said.

"I was reading it," said Christopher, keeping his eyes on hers and tapping the list that was posted on the wall, where the name Muriel appeared under the number for the local police precinct and the fire department. "It's right here."

"Right," she said, raising her hand, waving good-bye, but already turned away from him. "Thank you so much," she said with the crisp courtesy of a businesswoman. With that one phrase, she had reduced Christopher to the status that he must have held all along: a little person, a blip on her screen, the taxi driver, the delivery boy, the plumber.

Just like that, the Big Red Stick had annihilated him.

The instant she shut the door behind her, Christopher crashed. Standing in the corner, he slid down to the floor. He made a cradle for himself with his knees and arms, retreating into the embrace of his own body, his face buried in his hands, his eyes covered by the curtain of his hair. Inside the shelter, his own place, he cried out.

When he lifted his head, the light in his corner of the floor had gone away, replaced by dancing shadows. Aimless, after swallowing a couple attractive pills he took from the upstairs medicine cabinet, Christopher began to wander. He weaved through Dylan's house, walking in and out of rooms, as if he were a prospective buyer of this mansion, testing out the couches, bouncing his butt up and down on the mattress in the master bedroom, turning on the television, sampling the aftershave on the shelf in the dressing room, sniffing at the blossoms on the potted hibiscus tree in the hall, breaking open the box of chocolates he found in a basket behind the bar, straddling two barstools at once, crunching handfuls of roasted almonds and sipping brandy that he discovered in the liquor cabinet. The brandy, he read from the label, had been bottled in 1891. He replaced what he drank with tap water. He felt immeasurably better.

On the third floor, in a room with a mirrored wall and a grand piano, Christopher discovered a gallery. Dylan had displayed a collection of paintings here. Christopher shuffled through the gallery in his borrowed bedroom slippers, the borrowed terrycloth robe sailing behind him. When he turned the corner, as the fading sunlight shone through the window, he came to a dead stop. He was standing in front of a portrait. It was showcased, here, alone, the only painting on a fifteen-foot expanse of wall. Christopher's hands fluttered as he approached this portrait, his fingers hovering around it. The thick, whirling strokes were agitated. The painting showed a narrow room, a monk's cell. The palette of grays and browns was permeated with jewel-like hints of violet, ruby, and gold. The composition of the objects inside the frame was off-kilter. The bright, violent colors contrasted against the darker shades, the buildup of paint taking on the depth of a sculpture. Whoever had painted this had been on a sustained rampage, splashing paint at the canvas for hours before slashing at it, hacking it up. The surface was covered with ruts, fissures and gashes. Holes gaped where the paint and even the canvas itself had been gouged out. His hands touched the pit that had been a nose, the scar that had been an eye. One figure in the painting wore pink pajamas and a fedora. The lean, handsome face belonged to Christopher. A second figure, female, stood beside Christopher's and in her arms, she held a child.

Yes Is the Answer

That night, Christopher kicked off his bedclothes, feverish and sweating. She had come to him, berating him. He switched on the weak lamp by his bedside and, there in that room without any character, he faced his last memories of Jenny, the ones that he'd been saving. He'd forbidden himself from thinking of them while he served his time out at Triton. These recollections were too precious to him, and too frightening.

"I could stay," Jenny had said, shyly, in a soft voice, eyes downcast, twisting the bouquet of daisies and irises in her hands.

"Stop. Hold that for me," said Christopher. "Don't move."

She'd posed for him on the windowsill of the warehouse on Bond Street, contained within the window frame, her face in profile. Like many an overweight girl, Jenny had a delicacy about her face. She had her attractions, yes, but she was full of defects. Christopher, oppressed by the Benedicts' worship of athleticism, had initially been drawn to her sickliness. Jenny had sunken, deep-set eyes, shadowed by purplish circles. Potato chips, soda, doughnuts, and French fries were her four essential food groups. In Christopher's family, no one was fat—fat people were looked down upon by his mother, who was unable to hide her aversion to them. That Jenny was overweight had recommended her to him. His lust for her pillowy belly and pendulous breasts commingled with a thrill of repulsion at the loose wobble of slack flesh.

Simply by standing by the window in her transparent dress, this buxom girl subverted all that generations of Benedicts had preached. Sloppy and cheap, she laid waste to the Benedicts' Calvinist *Weltanschauung*, their shit about decency, self-control, and perseverance. Her huge tits repudiated the puritan work ethic. Her puckered thighs denounced the allure of elite private colleges. Her soft hips spread out over the sill to question the benefits of good taste and advantageous social connections. She was a poor fat girl with dirty hair and torn underwear who fucked strangers on her rooftop and lived off government checks.

How Christopher's camera worshipped his muse! She'd been a bad girl turned good by the Second Chance Society—Mrs. Benedict's favorite charity for inner city girls. The Second Chance volunteers had Jenny studying hard and staying sober during her school semester, when Christopher and his camera came to Jenny's rescue. He'd seen her original sins that day and he'd restored them, turned wild Jenny loose, gave her back to herself. She was a slut from Spanish Harlem who'd been hired, by Mrs. Benedict, to feed the household parrot and water the plants. And he wanted her to remain like that. Savage Jenny, saved.

Christopher had been looking at Jenny through his viewfinder—he was never without it—and now he peered up at her with his naked eye instead. It had taken him all this time to hear what she'd said.

"Did you just ask me for my hand in marriage, doll, or am I losing my marbles?" asked Christopher.

I think I could marry you.

She'd said this, he was almost certain of it, but she'd spoken softly. Jenny now examined the peeling paint on the window casement.

Christopher, who had two cameras strapped around his neck, raised one of them, his Rolleiflex. He preferred that to the Pentax.

The Rolli's slower shutter speed would heighten textures and make each detail prominent: the pebbled surface of the wall, the wilting sateen petals, Jenny's skin.

Click. He captured her as she twisted daisies in her two red, work-roughened hands. It was the end of summer and Christopher was leaving. He had to drift away before finishing anything. He did this deliberately, in order to upset the extended family of Benedicts, who complained about him. "Where will you end up if you don't buckle down and apply yourself?" "We opened doors for you." "We invested in you, Christopher." And Senator Benedict's perpetual gripe: "To get you into that school, you realize, I paid a visit to the favor bank."

None of this meant anything to Christopher. He would become precisely what the Benedicts feared. He aspired to be a low-level drug dealer, a rake, an impregnator, a thief, a penniless heroin addict. A degenerate.

Well, they could go fuck themselves. He was leaving for California and British Columbia. Dropping out of art school for the second time, he'd be taking what his parents called an "extended academic leave." He planned to travel across the country on his motorcycle, from the East Coast to the West, arriving in Seattle by early October. From there, he'd take the ferry to Victoria and go on to Vancouver, where he and his fiancée would breed racehorses on her farm.

Christopher had told Jenny only that he was taking a trip and would be performing *A Wanted Man* at a playhouse on the West Coast. He'd suggested that he'd be back in the warehouse in Brooklyn in a few months and that he'd be returning to New York in time for Christmas. He expected to see her again.

"That's good," said Christopher, aiming the Rolli at Jenny.

"Excuse me," she said, crossing her arms. "Are you deaf? Did you hear what I just said?"

Across the room, amid the cameras, tripods, boxes of film, and piles of black-and-white contact sheets with the best shots marked up in grease pencil, Christopher sat draped over a leather club chair, one leg thrown across the arm. His fervent wish was to ignore whatever Jenny had said to him. He only wanted to keep on snapping, photographing her to the beat of Blondie, playing on the stereo.

Jumping down from the windowsill, Jenny landed on the floor with a heavy thud. "Christopher," she said, in a voice of displeasure.

"You know I do," said Christopher, in response to a question she had asked him.

What he'd said had been untrue. Christopher was ashamed to be seen with a fat, slatternly girl in public. Now she crossed the room and sat down, literally, at his feet, her hands on his knees, looking up at him.

"You mean it?" she said, earnestly. The expression on her face—open, needy—made him want to smack her. "Do you ever think," she said, glancing down, picking at the rubble between the rotting floorboards of his factory. "Ever think of getting married?"

"Not to you," said Christopher, in a voice that was taunting, cruelly playful. "Why would I marry you? You're a loser." She'd dropped out of summer school by the middle of July, after her grades had plummeted. She'd started sniffing glue again, on the roof, in June. She'd completed the two Aktionist films with him, produced and directed by Christopher, each twelve minutes long, by the first week of August.

"I thought we could get a marriage certificate in Las Vegas on the way," she said, angrily. "Since I'm sixteen now. If we… if we ever wanted to."

"On the way where?"

"Across the country," she said in a strident, high voice.

Where had she gotten the impression that she was coming *with* him when he departed for the Coast? He slid out of the armchair, stumbled to his feet, and strolled into the kitchen, where he leaned against the kitchen counter, knees buckling, hungover. The sense of foreboding didn't go away until he'd pried the cap off his bottle of beer. As he drank, he envisioned the course of his life as it would unfold without her. He would leave the city earlier than he'd intended, without mentioning the change in plans to Jenny. She'd become a royal pain in the ass.

"Here, take one," he said, when he returned to the central room of the warehouse, with a bottle of beer in either hand. She was approaching him, lips pursed, eyes wide. He felt himself recoil from a foul atmosphere she was generating. He thrust the beer at her to deflect her embrace.

"No, thanks," she said. "I stopped drinking." Her eyes telegraphed some new message.

"When did that happen?" said Christopher.

"I gave it up as of last week," she said in a determined voice. "I gave up drinking. For a while. I gave up alcohol when I got back from the health clinic." She opened her hands and examined a fingernail, painted black, which had broken.

"Suit yourself," said Christopher.

It would be easier to leave than to break up with her.

He pictured himself on his motorcycle, alone, driving through Arizona, the dry, flat landscape, with its dramatic rust and red hues and its molten sunrises. Nothing felt as good to Christopher as leaving. He loved to leave. He loved to leave without considering anyone else's feelings, without asking anyone else's permission. He loved to leave in a hurry, like a wanted man, throwing a change of clothes and a toothbrush into a bag and skipping out. He was terrific at leaving because he got a lot of practice at it. He'd been leaving for years. He'd been in first grade, six years old, the first time he'd left. He'd simply walked out the classroom door while his teacher's back was turned to the blackboard. He'd walked down the hallway to the fire exit, which no one was supposed to use, and he'd pushed open the door and he'd walked through it onto the sidewalk. He'd walked down the block to the candy store at the corner. He'd bought himself a Snickers bar and a water pistol. He had given no thought to any of this. After playing with a stranger's children in a courtyard, he had arrived home to Eighty-second Street. He had been perplexed to find his mother collapsed in a heap beneath the crucifix in his father's study. The housekeeper was tearfully putting his toys away, as if Christopher had been flattened by a passing truck.

Now it was time for leaving Jenny. Christopher had done it before—picking up a new girlfriend, getting carried away with it for a while, then running off without saying good-bye. Girls glommed on to Christopher and he was never entirely sure why. The less he needed a girl, the more she'd suck up, attaching herself to him. Jenny-the-blow-job-queen, Jenny-the-exhibitionist, Jenny-who-liked-to-fuck-in-doorways. He drank from his bottle of beer and smacked his lips. He considered himself the victim of false advertising. She just wanted to entrap him in a little ranch house in Oklahoma or someplace, out in the bland flat stretch of land that was Middle America. He'd be bored after a month. She wanted to cook for him and play house and be the mother to his... Well. He wasn't falling for it.

Now she turned away from him, picking up a paintbrush from out of the jar he kept them in. She squeezed tubes of acrylic onto the palette, dabbed the brush in, then painted a stroke on the wall, a work-in-progress, picking up the pattern from where she'd left off the last time. Neither of them said anything while Jenny painted a female figure shaped like an hourglass.

"Hey," he said, to change the subject. "I'm going over to Lenny's studio in a couple minutes." He didn't invite her, though he didn't explicitly exclude her, either. Christopher hadn't taken Jenny out with him in weeks. He'd been avoiding her, heeding an aversion he'd developed towards her.

But in the warehouse, she put her arms around his neck and began, too passionately, too intimately, to kiss his chest.

"Stop it," he said, and pushed her face away. "Stop."

Jenny's eyes shone with injured pride. She raised her hand, lashed out and, before he could make out what was happening, her sharp nails had scratched his neck.

It came out of nowhere, a thunderclap of desire, wanton, unstoppable. "Get off me, witch," he said. The feeling was unnervingly similar to arousal and, as he gave her a shove, his head swam with it.

She slapped him in the stomach.

"You stupid cunt." A hand collided with a cheek. A human head shielded itself from the blows which rained down upon it. No one had done this. It was being done. Incredibly, Christopher was the one beating her up. Again, he struck her, not quite where he'd aimed, decking her on the jaw. Her head was flung back from the force of his smack. She was turned away now, looking over her shoulder. She stayed like that, the round shoulders shaking, then becoming far too still, transformed into a statue.

The space between them had expanded, as if Jenny had sped away from him on a conveyer belt. There had been a fine line drawn—an unspoken agreement - and, just now, he'd broken it, he'd crossed it. He'd hit her before. She'd always hit him back. She'd growled like a big cat, snarled at him, and punched him out and, afterwards, neither of them was ever sure who the hell had started it. They'd just licked each other's wounds, they'd just laughed at it. They were being two untamed young animals.

This time, Jenny kept her back to him for a while. It was taking too long. Something was different. Nothing was okay, nothing was funny.

"You're good," she said, at length, each word brittle and distinct. "At ruining things." Still, she wouldn't look at him. She was standing up, she was stomping over to the door, carefully brushing off her dress. Her gestures said: I have worth. I have limits.

Too late, Christopher noticed the sweet pink rhinestone barrette in her hair. Now he saw the frilly dress, the care she'd taken to prepare herself for him that day, like a vestal virgin. Jenny's harder edges had been prettified and softened. Ordinarily bed-rumpled, her blonde hair had been neatly combed when she'd arrived today. It had formed ringlets that brushed her cheeks and curled upwards, like a duckling's tail, at her neck. And what the fuck had happened to her *face*? How had failed to see all this before? The smeared black-eyeliner was gone. Her skin was naked, except for a shimmer of pink lip gloss. She'd arrived here looking beautiful, on purpose. But a crimson line ran down the side of her mouth and bright red blotches spread over her nose and cheekbone where he'd struck her. A black eye threatened to appear; he'd messed up her daintily arranged hair. He studied all of this distantly, objectively, his eyes mechanical as cameras. He perceived the pitiable romantic hope she'd nursed. With a shudder of recognition, he saw that she'd fallen in love with him.

He wouldn't allow himself to acknowledge any of this, not to Jenny. "May I take your picture, now, like that, before you go?" he heard himself ask. His voice sounded artificial and coldly remote.

She put her hand on the brass knob and yanked the door open.

While she stood on the threshold, facing the Dada-inspired mural they'd painted in the hall, Christopher observed the two spots of perspiration on her lower back, noting how the fabric wrinkled, clinging to her sweaty skin.

"If you leave now, Jenny," he said, "you can't come back."

She slipped through the door and down the corridor. He saw her head bobbling up and down as she maneuvered down the staircase.

He listened for her response, even a "Fuck you!" But he only heard her footfalls, climbing down the steps, then the sound of the door as it creaked open on the first floor. He imagined the rest as if he were watching a movie. Slam (the first door had closed with a rattle of frosted glass). Thump (the second door had shut). He pictured her, still just a few feet away, on a doorstep in a lifeless Brooklyn street, a low-rent beauty on a summer's day, illuminated by the sun, gaining her freedom. She would march up the block with her angriest and most assured gait, barefoot, navigating the broken glass and the bottle caps, limping slightly because he'd stepped on her toes during their altercation. She'd left her sandals beneath his window. They were the same sandals that, a year earlier, he'd let her filch from the Benedicts of Fifth Avenue.

The Accident at Lucidora

Christopher cleared out of Brooklyn within a week after Jenny left. He filled two canvas rucksacks with the essentials for survival: a six-inch M19 and a .38 lightweight snubbie with a two-inch barrel; a box of 110-grain copper bullets and a box of 158-grain lead roundnose; his *Aktionist Manifesto*; a canteen for water; a flask for scotch; thirty film canisters marked "Do Not Expose to Light!" each concealing two grams of cocaine; a package of condoms; a bottle of body oil; a change of clothes; a sketchbook; 300 milligrams of Mexican Black Tar; a paperback edition of *Naked Lunch;* a collapsible pup tent; his vintage Rolli in the original leather case; a cigar box full of fifties rolled into cylindrical metal tubes.

He locked up the warehouse as dawn broke and threw the tarp off his vintage Yamaha model GTMX. With a roar, the bike catapulted Christopher and his baggage through the streets, taking him across the river. Dirt and bugs flung themselves at his visor while the motor purred beneath his thighs and the speedometer jumped, quivered, and jumped again. He took the I-80 to Chicago, switching to the I-94 to Milwaukee. Here, on the open road, Christopher and his metal steed formed an elegant unit, a mechanism built for clarity and speed. As he drove, he trained his thoughts on Lucidora, where the Pacific would churn against boulders and sun-bronzed boys could ride over water, half-naked, soaring thirty feet into the sky and sliding back down again with the agility of dolphins. Out West, Christopher would find private mountains where condors floated above the ocean. He'd never been to Lucidora before, but he knew it to be the free spirit's utopia. Its inhabitants were painters and sculptors, surfers, subversives, and seekers. After they'd attended Christopher's Aktion, they would bathe with him in freshwater streams heated by sulfur beds underneath the sand. A leader of the Bond Street Aktionists might walk along the beach for miles and meet no one but a sea lion. No one would ever find him.

Christopher's intention was to ride across the country in twelve days, stopping at flea markets to assemble the "ingredients," crashing on friends' couches, spending a few nights bunked down in a cheap motel or camped out in the hills. His fingers were loose and easy on the handlebars. His driving gloves shielded his hands inside a firm skein. In the small towns, women turned to stare at him—the rambler, the biker sheathed in rugged black leather. Admired by female eyes, he took off, without so much as a nod of acknowledgment. It was in transit that he felt himself to be a man.

For days, he moved on in a state of supreme contentment. He was at one with the scenery, becoming a part of everything he passed, absorbing trees, towns, highways, sunlight, rain. It wasn't until he got to Jonathan Wolff's house in Minneapolis, where Christopher lay in the hammock in the backyard, that Jenny's memory first caught up with him. Like a dybbuk, she began rebuking him. Christopher had intended to stay with Jonathan for a week; instead, to outrun that nasty gnome, he bid his friend a hasty goodbye. He broke away from Highway 94 to get lost among the back roads of Montana, ignoring the wisdom of his chosen route, neglecting to consult the bright green line he'd drawn earlier on his map. He sought now to delay his arrival by several days, pushing closer to the date of the *Wanted Man* Aktion. It was scheduled to take place on Saturday, September 9, far into the thick, unpopulated redwood forests of Lucidora, inside a hundred-year-old playhouse, now vacant and crumbling, high above the shoreline.

Christopher had been publicizing the event, sending out the password and secret location through the grapevine. *A Wanted Man* would be filmed this time, and performed for a selective, handpicked audience. But on the road, Christopher was twitchy, startled by any sudden noise, the trill of a nightingale or the rumble of a passing freight train. He drank too much at night, losing count of how many shots of bourbon he'd ordered, losing track of how many twenty dollar bills he'd paid out. Instead of selling the coke, he snorted most of it himself, inhaling so hard that, one morning in his tent, blood poured out of his nostrils and flowed copiously into his cupped hands. He spent most of one Sunday locked in an outhouse in a cornfield forty miles east of Boise, vomiting so often that he burst hundreds of blood vessels in his face.

In Salt Lake City, he put the finishing touches on the performance piece, adapting it for the short movie they'd make, and mailed the stage directions to his three conspirators. He wrote first to Badger, a counterfeiter who'd moved from Detroit to San Francisco to study acupuncture, and then to Cameragirl, who'd dropped out of UCLA film school.

Christopher rode for hours at a stretch, covered with grime, saddle-sore when he dismounted. Yet he reached Reno in good spirits. It was here that he maintained an accommodating, on-again-off-again girlfriend, a drummer nicknamed Cat. She was expecting him. He decided on the spur of the moment not to show. Instead, he rode past the city limits into a campground, paid the attendant fifteen bucks, set up his tent, and slept alone. He dropped two tabs of acid on an impulse. He was witless for the next eighteen hours, babbling to himself as he hiked up slippery rock formations in a pair of cowboy boots and his underpants. When he regained his rationality, he was dehydrated, caked from head to toe with sand, as if he'd buried himself alive. It took him most of the next day to find his way back to the campsite.

He bought one tablet of Ecstasy from a girl in a tuxedo in Vegas at a crowded club called Cave. He danced listlessly with a blank-eyed woman who said she was a bookkeeper on vacation from Fargo. He offered to take her back to her hotel. Seconds after they entered her room, still fully dressed, he pushed her hard against the wall and went down on her. She made a noise of surprise but did not object. He interrupted himself to get her a drink, promising to bring back a bottle of champagne from the hotel bar. "Call room service," she told him with a shrug, but he didn't want to do that. He walked the length of the lobby and never returned.

He left Nevada in a mean mood. Hunched over a table at the back of a truck-stop diner, Christopher sketched Volume 9 of the Aktionists' comic book. It came to him in bursts of thought; he scribbled dialogue and pictures in his notebook, letting the lines spill over onto the paper tablecloth. He tore the sketches into shreds and stuffed them into his empty glass. At a coffee shop in Sonoma County he ordered a plate of biscuits, eggs, and bacon, pushed it aside untouched, and began to draw again. This time he drew Jenny's face with a black eye and a split lip. He left it there for anyone to see.

At a flophouse in the Tenderloin, he considered turning around and driving back to New York to make amends. He was scared. During the year he and Jenny had chummed around, Jenny had learned all about the operation. She had access to secret codes and addresses: the safe house in Northern California; the headquarters in Brooklyn; the Lucidora performance space. She had figured out that Christopher ran the whole project, with help from a few friends. He'd manipulated the media to make himself look larger. The little man behind the curtain couldn't afford to make an enemy of Jenny. She knew exactly what he was, and how easy it would be for everyone who wanted to—the Man, the Law, the Ministry of Culture—to fuck him over.

A WANTED MAN

A Bond Street Aktion

(Recipe for an Uprising)

Ingredients: (1) dinner bell (20) votive candles arranged on the floor of the stage in a circle; (1) ostrich plume.

(1) fork (1) knife (1) spoon (2) gloves of satin (1) flacon of perfume (1) set of finger paints in yellow, red and blue (10) cans of spray paint, divided evenly between black paint and white (1) bowl of rose petals (1) M19, unloaded.

(1) handful multicolored confetti (1) handful dried white rice (1) horse whip (1) box of matches (1) draft card (1) loaded gun (1) water pistol, filled with red wine (1) keg of beer (1) jar of peanut butter (1) pair of scissors (1) bottle of Hershey's chocolate sauce (1) aerosol can of commercially prepared whipped cream.

(1) ball of string (1) roll of tissue paper, 40 feet long (1) bolt of silk.

(1) voodoo doll (24) sewing needles (12) safety pins (500) rubber balloons

(1) lipstick (100) jars Gerber's baby applesauce (1) straitjacket (1) burlap sack (1) feather boa (1) box Rice Krispies cereal (200) Gillette razor blades

Curtain.

Stage Director rings dinner bell.

Mr. X, in AKTION MASK and UNIFORM, enters from stage left, lies down on floor in center of circular arrangement of candles. Mr. X must wait in place, holding position, for sixty minutes.

Audience does whatever it wants with Mr. X.

After sixty minutes, Assistant Director rings dinner bell to signal that the Aktion is over.

Mr. X stands and bows to audience.

Audience claps or boos.

Mr. X gives the Aktionist salute.

Exit stage right.

Curtain.

A Wanted Man

The summer of Christopher's release, he spent hours floating around the swimming pool on his back. He tried collecting certain memories and sorting them out, but they only swayed like the leaves in the trees and, if he closed his eyes, the shadows trembled. He resolved, for a few hours one afternoon, to stop obsessing about Jenny. He began thinking about Private Emma. If he'd known more about her, he would have left the poor kid alone.

Christopher had met Private Emma on his way to Lucidora, while riding across the country. It was in North Beach, up on the Coit Tower observation deck, that he saw her first. Christopher had paid a quarter to look through a telescope at the aquamarine water, the russet-red bridge and the floating houseboats. Hills, the color of sage, appeared to undulate like waves. When he peered through the tower's arched windows with naked eyes, the height was dizzying. Forty stories below, dogs had been let off their leashes to chase one another around a statue of Columbus. The bouncing, leaping golden retrievers were as small, from up in the tower, as crickets. A puppet-like man and his two children stood to one side of the statue flying a kite over the rooftops, setting long streamers flowing up towards the clouds. As Christopher raised his Rolli to take a picture, he heard even, ringing footsteps. Ascending the spiral staircase to the top deck was a soldier girl. She carried a bulging plaid zippered suitcase in one hand. She threw it onto the metal floor of the observation deck, leaning over to catch her breath. Her lapels were loaded with medals. Christopher, sizing her up, guessed that she weighed 110 pounds; that her measurements were 34-24-34; that she was barely twenty-five years old; that she'd been born and raised in a small, conservative town. Private Emma had clear-skinned good looks and nice proportions. She had one attribute that most young women her age do not: a gaping hole in her right cheek.

Something had cut away a slice of her lip and mouth, exposing a three-inch chunk of gum and teeth. The effect was hard to take. Though the newspapers tabulated the number of soldiers being injured, it was rare to see one of the freshly maimed out in public. It took a concerted effort not to gawk at her. Like a boy with bad manners, he wanted to make a prolonged study of it. Her injury looked otherworldly, a ghoulish bit of makeup artistry from a big-budget horror movie. One jigsaw-puzzle piece gone from an otherwise comely girl, narrowing her options into a permanent night of trick-or-treat.

Christopher pretended to keep looking out the window, while stealing sidelong glances at the soldier. He flattered himself that he saw past her screwed-up face to her core. What he could not possibly have known that day was that, beneath her cool exterior, Private Emma Calhoun was mentally ill. She'd received an honorable discharge. This would come to light after the accident at Lucidora.

All Christopher saw was a decorated war hero with a missing piece of face. There was pathos to the way she stood at the window and lifted her hand, turning it outward, like the Phantom of the Opera, an imperious, damaged diva gesturing to patrons in their box seats. It did not occur to Christopher that day to ask why she was waving to the deep, frozen waters of San Francisco Bay, pressing her hand against the glass as if to test its strength. Nor had he stopped to marvel at the hundreds of braids she had woven into her hair, a hairstyle which no one on active military duty would sport. He didn't dwell upon the pointy-toed boots she wore, either, noting only that they were emerald green, like footwear for a leprechaun. He assumed she was on leave. Christopher read her wrong.

He walked slowly from one observation window to the next, seized by a glorious idea: an injured, decorated Army private would be an invaluable addition, a jewel in the crown of the Bond Street Aktionists' anti-war movement. The group had always claimed to be backed by war veterans, but that had been "artistic license." The fact was, no vets would give the Aktionists the time of day. Military men and women, from the South to the Midwest, remained suspicious of the product of Eastern boarding schools: wealthy, draft-dodging aesthetes.

Christopher took in the view and thought to himself: "I can turn her."

Even before she spoke to him, the private had a strong personality, a distinct presence. She stood very tall there in the tower, gazing out upon the bay like a ship's captain surveying the open sea. She had glossy chin-length light brown hair. Her demeanor was grand. She looked like she ought to be piloting airplanes. The private slipped her hand inside her jacket and, for an insane instant, Christopher pictured her withdrawing a Smith & Wesson Sigma SW9VE and blasting away the peaceable tourists below, taking them out from the top of Coit Tower, like a sniper. What it was in the stranger's bearing that had set off this fear, Christopher would wonder afterwards. All the private did was to take a flat brown paper bag from her breast pocket. She slid out a postcard, leaned it up against the window, and began to write on it.

It was only eleven o'clock in the morning, but when he got downstairs, Christopher ordered an Irish coffee from the outdoor café. He asked for an extra helping of whipped cream and a second shot of whiskey, to fortify himself. He drank the hot liquid down, his eyes never leaving the tower door. He was waiting for her.

"Can I take your photograph, Lieutenant?" said Christopher,

promoting her rank, when the Army girl strode down the stairs towards the café. It was a radically incorrect pickup line, a calculated risk. Christopher stood up and grasped the back of his chair. The metal felt smooth and solid against his palms. He leaned there, making prolonged eye contact with the young woman.

"I'm not a lieutenant. I'm a private," she said. Her gaze was cold and direct.

"I'm Christopher Benedict." He extended his hand. "Can I buy you a coffee?"

She glanced down. Christopher, not entirely sober, had offered the woman his left hand, the one with "666" tattooed across it. He took his hand away and put it in the back pocket of his jeans. "Don't mind me," he said. "I don't believe in anything."

"Private Calhoun," said the soldier. She added, after a slight hesitation, "Emma." Instead of hanging back, she seemed to brazenly show off her face, as if she were daring him to deal with it. "Pleasure to meet you, Mr. Benedict."

Christopher hovered, placing a hand on the back of the empty seat. "Would you mind if I joined you?" He expected to be turned away.

"I have to leave in a minute," the woman said, guardedly.

"For a minute, then," Christopher said, agreeably, and waited for her to gesture to the chair before he sat in it. She regarded him with an icy curiosity. Maybe the soldier thought he was a San Francisco street person, the kind that did odd jobs around Telegraph Hill, sleeping rough in the park beneath the trees. "I must look like shit," he said. He saw this was the worst thing to say to a woman irretrievably deformed. He could think of no conversational openers, except to ask about cosmetic surgery. He became flustered.

"You do look like hell," she told him, helping him to continue.

"I just traveled 3,000 miles across the country by motorcycle," he finally managed. He pointed at his bike, in the parking lot. The private turned to look at it.

"Out here on business?" she said.

"You might say that. I'm an artist."

"What kind of art do you do?" Without asking him, she was helping herself to his coffee. He tried not to watch the business with the cup, the raising of the lip, the hole inside her mouth, the slight spillage, the dabbing with the paper napkin.

"It'd take me all afternoon to tell you," Christopher said.

Private Emma looked at him blankly. Without any change in expression, she opened her hand, as if to show him something. But what she said was "Waiter, menus." She had eyes like pistol shots and a hard gaze designed, he thought, to scare onlookers away. The little boy with the kite was staring at her, as children do. It was so very hard not to.

He revered her because she embodied his complicated and contradictory aesthetic philosophy.

It was to be one of those encounters that Christopher lived for, where two people with nothing in common—people who should find each other odious—briefly, improbably, erotically, united. There was a setting aside of preconceived notions and assumptions. Christopher found himself behaving unpredictably, with a level of genuine interest and compassion that he'd been incapable of, or had held back. What happened was this: They went over to Christopher's room at the Nob Hill Motor Inn, watched the porn channel, drank a quart of rum and snorted the last of the heroin.

"What are you doing?" said Emma, in the middle of the night.

"Taking your photograph, babe. That all right?" Christopher was attaching the zoom lens to his Rolli, preparing for an extreme close-up. He was fascinated by Emma's decimation—not only the skull-face situation, but also a damaged left breast and a lumpy 18-inch gash that ran across her thigh and down along her right leg. He had summoned enough willpower to refrain from asking her about all this.

Emma gave a karate kick and the Rolli shot out of Christopher's hand. It landed on top of the mini-fridge with a sickening crack. "That's my camera, sweetheart, Emma." He wasn't angry, and already Emma had him in a headlock, down on the floor, before he had even fully registered what had happened.

"Fuck you, Emma, what are you? Catwoman?" asked Christopher, timidly.

"You're the trickster," said Emma, grabbing him by the hair and shaking him, hurting him. "Who are you working for?"

"Nobody, honey, get off. I told you. I'm a fucking two-bit performance artist."

Emma let go. "You'd better not be lying."

He played dead, going limp like a possum in her arms. After around an hour, during which he was convinced that he'd be strangled by this ninja-girl, he felt her muscles slacken. She kept him in her arms, but now he was just lying across her, his face in her warm, hard, flat stomach.

"You never know where photos like that would get to," she told him. "No one exploits the armed forces. Is that clear?"

"Forget it. I shouldn't have asked you," he said, sitting up.

"Hah. They thought I'd have trouble getting dates," she said, shaking her head. She made a cage out of her fingers and, briefly, held it against the hole in her face.

He was not sure what she meant by this. Maybe that she was relieved that Christopher liked her. They climbed back into bed, passed the bottle back and forth. Private Emma grabbed the remote and began to flick the channels much too fast, blinking dazedly at the cheap motel TV.

"What's it like? Being at war?" asked Christopher as T&A, infomercials, and creaky old television programs went past.

"It's not like anything."

"Do you feel that you were..." He stopped. He started again. "That you were risking your, you know, um, life. For a just cause?"

Emma lifted up the bedspread and, slowly, covered herself with it, draping the ivory polyester fabric over her head. "Are you a reporter?" she asked, from beneath her cloak. "Is this another motherfucking interview or is this a private conversation between two adults?"

"I'm a guy who picked you up at Coit Tower, Emma. I just went to bed with you. That's it."

"I'm a trained professional," she said. "It's a job, okay? I graduated from West Point. I do my work like anybody else. I try not to feel things." A certain amount of time passed and then Emma said, "I'm starting to think the good guys and the bad guys might be the same."

Early the next morning, Christopher invited Emma to Lucidora, never expecting her to accept. Dressed, showered, bandaged (a bandage had materialized), she said she'd try to come. Eight days later, on September 9, she walked into the Lucidora Playhouse on the afternoon of the performance. The woman who'd wrestled with him in a San Francisco motel room was not exactly as he'd wanted her to be. Christopher was embarrassed. He worried that he'd used her in a low-down way.

Later, he'd forget how it came to pass. Emma talked him into it, he thought. That night, at the Aktion, Christopher did not perform. Emma took his place. His instincts had told him this was unwise. He might have used various arguments: that she had never done it before, that she was wrong for the part, that the piece called for a male, that the title was *A Wanted Man*. But to dissuade her from appearing onstage would make it seem as if he found her disgusting to look at. Besides, he had already described the Aktion to her, in detail. He'd shown her the stage directions. She knew that it was the easiest role in the world. In every theater and gallery that he'd performed in, the audience did the work, not him. Christopher did nothing. All Emma had to do for the Aktion in Lucidora was walk out onto the stage, take a bow and lie there. That would have been simple. She didn't.

He cast himself back to the night of the production in Lucidora. He and Dylan had staged the Aktion the previous winter, performing at galleries, apartments, and alternative performance spaces in Rhode Island, Massachusetts, Chelsea, and South Brooklyn. *A Wanted Man* had been favorably reviewed by a few esoteric art critics, including one in the *Boston Sphinx*. The Aktion was conceived as a series of spontaneous, unpredictable events and its true, unstated purpose was to test the audience. Every time Christopher performed the Aktion, he lay down on the floor of the gallery or stage like a sacrificial lamb. In Brooklyn, the show was a crashing bore: Little else had happened. The audience just sat quietly for an hour. After sixty minutes, a buzzer went off as planned, and Christopher got up and left. The Massachusetts audience, on the other hand, had been made up entirely of college students. At least twenty of them came right up to the stage and helped themselves to "the ingredients." One woman unbuttoned Christopher's pants and pulled them off his legs, while another painted an olive branch on his stomach with a can of spray paint. In Manhattan, a giggling couple tickled him with a feather. A hundred boisterous people ran up on stage and joined in, pinching him, groping him, covering him with chocolate syrup and throwing handfuls of rice over his prone body. He never moved.

He was unprepared for Lucidora. The audience looked friendly as can be: a bunch of easygoing, suntanned surfers. Private Emma walked out, naked, onto the stage, carrying an empty bottle of rum. She smashed it against the wall and proceeded to crawl across the floor on her hands and knees, over the broken glass. She stuck her tongue out at the audience and cursed them, tore at her hair. She did not lie down. She crawled over to the prop table and grasped the six-inch M19 that Christopher had placed there. Its only purpose had been to add an element of excitement, of danger. The gun, naturally, was unloaded. But no one knew that. The crazy girl took aim, shockingly, at the audience, pointed the gun into the dead center of the sleepy Lucidora Playhouse.

A kindly-looking California hippie woman in her forties sat in that doomed seat. Her lips compressed and her thin, sun-burnished hand reached to her left to grasp a child's shoulder. He was a long-haired little boy of perhaps ten or eleven, dressed in engineer's overalls and clutching the stub of an orange Popsicle, which had smeared his chin with blotches. Every head in the theater turned to watch Private Emma's target.

The woman jumped from her seat but the child continued sitting. She grabbed his forearm and yanked, pulling him up. The Popsicle fell onto the bib of his overalls. Against the striped fabric, the color orange looked bright as a flashing streetlamp.

Up on the stage, the spotlights cast deep ruts on Emma's cheeks.

A mob streamed backwards, shoving, scrambling towards the exits, while others separated themselves, bolted upstairs and made a run for it. Voices called out, "Don't shoot. Stop, please."

Private Emma seemed not to notice the two Good Samaritans who were moving in unison towards her. An older man, with sandy hair and a mustache, took the lead. A graying woman, dressed in a knee-length skirt and fitted blouse, drew up at the back. She looked preternaturally composed, as if she were adept at disarming lunatics.

Private Emma turned to her, eyes aflame. She now aimed the gun at herself.

"There's no need. You don't have to do this," the woman said, with the assurance of someone who might simply have been declining an expensive gift. "Why don't we sit down and talk it over?"

"Yes, I do," said Private Emma, and pressed the muzzle to her temple. The blast was followed by a queer hiatus. Private Emma gave her head a series of twitching shakes, like a diver bothered by water inside her ear. The gun hit the boards and fired again, blasting a hunk of plaster out of the wall. Emma must have loaded it when Christopher wasn't looking. She fell into a scarf of red that wound itself around her neck.

"Shut the operation down. The party's over."

That was Dylan's voice. Christopher, panting, stood shaking inside a phone booth in a gas station on Route 1, in the dark of night, somewhere between Monterey and Los Angeles, many hours away from either place. He'd tried to clean it up, but his shirt stank of vomit. His Yamaha was behind him and the motor was idling.

"Shut the Aktionists down?" he shouted into the telephone, looking wildly around at the over-bright windows of the all-night convenience store.

"You got someone killed, Christopher. Your bullshit's finished," said Dylan.

"My bull…?" Christopher's immediate response to the accident had been to snort soothing quantities of Black Tar on a deserted beach. This was highly inadvisable, due to the junk's chunky consistency. He hadn't had time to smoke it, so he'd choked. Plus, at least fifty priceless milligrams had blown into the ocean, thanks to Lucidora's infamous high-velocity winds. Now he listened to Dylan's perfidy in disbelief.

"You're fucked," said Dylan, from the protection of his off-campus house in New Haven, over the telephone. "It's already network news. They've blown it up into a drug syndicate. The senator's son implicated in a suspicious death, shadowy political conspiracy, arsenal of weapons. You know the drill. You're in deep shit, my friend. Head to the safe house, pronto. Oh, wow! Your *dad* is on channel five, right now, talking about having you indicted on racketeering charges. Under RICO. He had some undercover narcotics agent trailing you, I guess. Listen to this!"

Christopher heard a blathering, out of range, through the receiver that Dylan was holding up to his television set on the other coast.

"Did you hear that?" said Dylan. "No one is immune and so on. Wants to make an example of you."

"What the fuck did *I* do?" said Christopher. "Man, an Army chick blew her brains out in Lucidora!"

"Looks like someone's out to get you."

Christopher dropped the phone and let the receiver swing from its cord. Off into the cliffs he rode, channeling Jesse James, Bonnie and Clyde, James Dean—except he kept hearing heaving little yelps coming from his own vocal chords. "I've been screwed, God, they went against me," he hiccupped out loud, on the road, to the roar of the tide against the rocks. Christopher and his bike raced along the hairpin turns of Route 1 and up into the dirt roads, precipitous shortcuts through lonely mountain passages. Heading south, he could smell the redwoods above and the salt air of the Pacific below, but the sea and shore bled into one another, both the shade of ink. No one but Dylan and Jenny knew the location of the Aktionist safe house, and he had told nobody else where he was going.

He made it to the safe house by morning. The sea lions barked from their boulders on the beach as he bolted the locks and sat down on a futon mattress, breathing evenly, carefully filling his pipe and smoking chiva, beginning to regain control. It was not until the middle of the next night that Christopher heard the sound of car wheels right outside. It was followed by a great pounding on his door.

"Open up here, please. Police."

He should have tried to return the last delivery of the Tar, the bag he'd picked up in Lucidora, but he hadn't. A brick of muck, potent black heroin, was just sitting in his open rucksack, in plain sight, as if it were a sack of planting soil. He should have emptied fistfuls of the costly mud-colored granules into the toilet bowl. He should have felt a rush of adrenaline that sent him spinning into motion, but his instinct for self-preservation failed to kick in. His terror had subsided; now he felt nothing. Yawning, stretching, he clambered out of his bed, opened the window and leaned out of it. How surreal to see six men in helmets, each holding bulletproof shields. One of them was aiming a machine gun at the door of the old beach house. He stamped his boots on the sandy ground. The wind blew around his trouser legs and puffed them up like parachutes.

"Hello there," he called down to them, waving gaily.

Six faces, hardly older than his, looked up at him. The gun tilted upwards and trained itself on Christopher.

He blew the rifleman a kiss. "You fucking goon," he said, raising his arms over his head. "Go right ahead and shoot me, killer."

News for You

At Dylan's house, Christopher spent a part of each morning contemplating Jenny's painting in the gallery. Looking at her portrait depleted him of energy. One Wednesday in September, while he was mired in a soap opera—having fallen to daytime television—the telephone began to ring. Christopher shuffled into the kitchen. He lifted the receiver and answered with a tense "Yes?"

The voice that responded was a man's, resonant and self-possessed. "Hello," it said. "Who am I speaking with?"

Christopher reached out to the window and untied the braided cord which held the curtain back. The lustrous fabric, unbound, fell across the pane of glass. "This is the Dickerson residence," Christopher said, warily.

"Is Christopher Benedict available?"

"Who's looking for this Christopher Benedict person and why?" said Christopher, sinking into a silk upholstered love seat and tugging at a covered button. The thread was coming loose.

"It's *you*," said the caller. "Am I mistaken?" The voice became demanding, tenacious. "Hello, hello! This is Christopher Benedict I'm speaking to right now. Isn't it?"

Christopher put his feet up on the table, crossing his legs at the ankles. "Who's this?" he asked, evasively.

"My name is Dan Orsini," said the man.

Christopher waited.

"*Doctor* Orsini," the caller repeated. "Does that ring a bell for you?"

"I'm afraid it doesn't. What can I do for you, mister? Do I know you?"

"You ought to. We have something in common."

"Oh?" Christopher took a raw peanut from a bowlful and crushed the straw-colored casing with his thumb.

"Let me make this easy for you," said the caller. "I'm talking about a woman."

"I see," said Christopher, gnawing on the peanut. His own voice sounded formal and composed.

"If you *are* Christopher Benedict, I have news for you," the caller said. "I married your girl. She was three months pregnant, by my estimate. I was pre-med. The symptoms of pregnancy are as obvious as signposts. I never asked what made her run, but it was me she came to, not you. Are you hearing me?"

Christopher let out his breath. "Why exactly are you calling?"

"You've been sending parcels to my wife," said the caller. "You knew her as Jenny Rodriguez, from East Harlem. Is that correct?"

Christopher opened his hand and let the crumbled remains of his mid-morning snack fall onto the woven off-white carpet. "Yes, sir," he said, softly.

"Jenny is not the same," said the caller. "She's not the person she was when the two of you were..." He seemed to search for the accurate term to describe what Jenny and Christopher had been. "Sleeping together."

"Of course she is," said Christopher. Padding into the kitchen, he opened the refrigerator and took a swig of milk.

"You need to know," said Jenny's husband, "that she never received anything you sent her. Understand? I set your weaseling letters on fire. I see right through you, Benedict. I destroyed all your stupid opportunistic crap."

"Ah, destroyed," said Christopher.

"I hope we understand one another, you ball of slime," said Dan. "Just in case there's any confusion in your mind, listen to this. The woman is my lawful wife. I will not let any harm be done by a bottom-feeder, a reptile. Am I getting my message across?"

"Perfectly," said Christopher.

"If you interfere with my family in any way," said Dan. "If you come over here… If you ever… even… brush your hand against… my wife's *studio*. If you put your big fat toe across the state line into our town. If you so much as inhale the exhaust from one of our cars. Do you know what will happen to you?"

"I can make an educated guess."

"I will get rid of you," said the caller.

"Yes?" Christopher asked. He uncorked a chilled bottle of sauvignon blanc left over from dinner last night. He raised it to his nostrils and sniffed.

"I will put you back where you belong, with your fellow criminals."

"I got it," said Christopher.

"I thought you might. Take a tip from me," Dan said. "Don't come anywhere near my patch of earth. Go to hell. Go farther than hell. Go to Africa, Australia, South America. Far, far away from my wife and my children. On a separate continent."

"That's interesting advice," said Christopher, who had entirely lost his backbone. "Start over, clean and fresh."

"That's right."

Neither of them spoke for a time. Christopher kept expecting Jenny's husband to issue further commands: Lock the door. Stuff a towel in the crack. Turn the oven on. Insert head.

Dan cleared his throat. "Tell me, Benedict," he said. "Do you need money?"

"Hah!" said Christopher, not really laughing, just making noise. "Heh-heh. I thought you were going to tell me to stick my head in the oven."

"Look, I'll pay you to leave my wife alone," said Dan.

A formless emotion welled up in Christopher. As he raised the bottle, he saw his own arm shake. "How much?"

"Name your price, maggot."

Christopher swished the wine around. "Two hundred and fifty," he said. "Thousand."

"You're leaving North America for that price tag. You're relocating. Correct?"

"Correct."

As they spoke, as Christopher imbibed, he ambled crookedly along the corridors of Dylan's house, until he arrived at the last gallery, with its single framed painting and its mullioned picture window.

"You will put that in writing," Dan was saying. "This is a legal document, an agreement, contractually binding."

Christopher stood gazing into his own painted face, rendered in two dimensions. He turned away from the oil painting. The landscape through the window, two soft-edged horizontal stripes—blue sky, green lawn—resembled a Diebenkorn. "That won't be necessary," said Christopher. "I thank you for the generous offer, Doctor, but I can't accept."

"You ought to. Remember," said Dan. "If I see your face, I'll remove it for you."

"That's all right," said Christopher. "Bye, bye."

Under the quilted blanket, he slept hard, sunk into a malarial fever of the soul, drained of his strength, waking briefly with his eyeballs glued to his lids and his tongue blistered. He came to early one Sunday and sensed a change in the weather: clean, brisk. The fall.

Christopher contemplated the phenomenon of Dr. Dan Orsini

while he paddled back and forth in the pool, his arms growing bigger, firm and ropey, swimming two hundred laps a day, doing the backstroke, the butterfly, the crawl. Christopher speculated about Dan while he raked the weeds for Dylan and watered the lawn, and on until the branches lost their leaves and the first frost descended one night, turning the backyard outside Dylan's window into a white-coated world, the ice ages. From the little kernel he'd perceived—a taste of Dan—a husband with a direct, even, commanding voice on the telephone, he began to build a guy, a snowman. He tried to hate him but by the time he had fully imagined Dr. Dan Orsini, he could see perfectly well why Jenny had preferred him. By late October, Christopher had come to admire Dan, looking up to him as one respects an older brother.

Thanksgiving approached. Christopher packed a bag with the clothing he'd worn the day he'd been sent to Triton, the only possessions that belonged to him. He let himself out the front door on a Wednesday after lunch and, with little more than a bus schedule, a pocketful of peanut-butter sandwiches and an empty jam jar, he walked away. It took him five weeks to get to Riverbend by public transportation. He took forty different local buses through one town into the next, waiting for hours beneath bus shelters in the cold, waiting on the open road, exposed. In the towns, he sat in doorways with his jam jar, holding a sign that said: "Out of jail. I NEED HELP." People walked past him without looking. A heavyset man in Scranton, Pennsylvania tramped by with only a quick glance. But he returned, wordlessly, ten minutes later, to stuff five twenties in his jar. Christopher splurged on a cheap motel room and a pizza. By the time he arrived in Riverbend, it was December, and the people who felt sorry for Christopher had given him $146.

Congratulations, It's a Girl

Standing inside Dylan's grubby bathroom in New Haven, Jenny tugged at the waistband of her skirt. In these four weeks following Christopher's arrest, it had grown tighter, the cotton gradually restricting her legs, the elastic cutting into her skin. She turned right, appraising her profile in a chipped mirror on the tiled wall. A diabolical swelling had begun to take shape above her hipbones, where a mound of gut protruded, audacious, bullet-shaped. At the women's health clinic on 103rd Street and Lexington, a nurse had shown Jenny how to decipher the sonogram screen. Inside an empty gray cone, a curled blot rested, shaped like a tadpole. Jenny would never have noticed it unless the nurse had pointed it out: "Look closely, Jenny. See it? See it now?" It was hard to believe that this black dot had any connection to her, or that the field of gray was her womb. Her innards were projected there on the nurse's console, two feet away from Jenny's head. The uterus with an embryo growing inside it was just one blurry little feather caught in the beam of a television monitor.

But there were portents. Jenny felt anesthetized. She grew nauseated and threw up sometimes. Her brain stopped working at inconvenient moments. When Sister Anna had described the Gettysburg Address at school one afternoon, Jenny had lost the lecture's thread. When Sister had asked a question, Jenny had started to speak, then found she had nothing to say. She'd nearly burst out with the words: "Help me, Sister, I have sinned again."

Within a week of the pregnancy test, she'd mobilized with the crisp efficiency of an automaton. Like a mercenary, she'd acted decisively and pragmatically, first, separating the senator from his money, second, hitching a ride to New Haven with Dylan. Now, here she was, stuck, and she didn't know what to do. She spent hours in the bathroom, needing time away from *them*, Dylan and his pretentious friends—several of whom had been Christopher's allies, tagging themselves as Aktionists. They'd all known Christopher as the Bond Street Aktionist leader, while he'd been dropping in and out of undergraduate visual arts programs at Pratt and Cooper Union. Jenny's plight—as the girl Christopher Benedict had knocked up before his sensational bust—went unmentioned. They gave her a wide berth.

"Where's Jenny?" Dylan would say, and Dexter Murphy answered, "She's in her office." They let her have the basement bathroom all to herself. It seemed to Jenny that she'd grown up inside lavatories, from the Bronx to Connecticut, never having had a room of her own, like a gypsy tramp. In the pigsty that was Dylan's group house in New Haven, she sat on the rim of the tub or she stood, mutely, eyes closed, trying to think. She'd come to hate the grating sound of the music they blared from the other side of that nicked, scuffed bathroom door. Dylan and his brethren lived an easy life, out there, reading Brecht and arguing over Hegel and playing pool.

They were full of talk about radical new art forms they were concocting, but they never made any paintings or installations, and they seemed to have forgotten who their common enemy was. They conspired lackadaisically against one thing and another—the Yale administration, the state, their parents, the art world, commercialism. They huddled over the pool table and drew on a huge sheet of paper, tracing maps and timetables, charting out subversive activities, plotting infiltrations of major corporations, developing lists of future Aktions to carry on what Bond Street had stood for. They would release *A Wanted Man* for distribution: It was, they claimed, the ultimate in protest art. But without Christopher's charisma, the group lost its sense of purpose.

Jenny concentrated on one thing only, repeating it to herself, trying to make sense of it. "Am I expecting? What am I expecting? I am expecting." She required long stretches of time to gather her thoughts, but her thoughts dispersed and wouldn't be collected properly. For hours, she obsessed over her predicament, planning how to extricate herself painlessly. The blot on the screen was nothing to her, after all. It had been a clump of undifferentiated organic matter, along the lines of, say, mold. In her neutral way, without taking sides, the nurse at the clinic had confirmed this. But when she lay down on the cool tiles of the bathroom floor, Jenny imagined her belly contained a consciousness. She named it Thing.

She'd pictured Thing as a humanoid weed, like an android hatching out of a pod in that old sci-fi thriller she and Christopher had watched. She'd regarded poor Thing as a monster, a carnivorous juvenile reptile, like the baby alligator she'd been paid to feed at 1010 Fifth Avenue, up on the second floor. Jenny repeatedly consulted the biology textbooks in the library at Yale, where she was not matriculated, of course, but was permitted, with the senator's letter, to request books for reference only. She'd examined the chapters on sexual reproduction. The dry scientific information refused to be linked with human babies, with their wide-eyed alertness and their twitching arms, their inexplicable red-faced tantrums and their gurgling attempts to communicate. She reminisced about the sturdy bundle which, two years earlier, had been her newborn son—the small head, no bigger than a fist but harder than a motorcycle helmet, the tenacious grip when he'd clutched at Jenny's shirtfront with the hands of a doll, extravagantly beautiful. Thanks to some minor bureaucratic error, she'd been allowed to hold him for almost half an hour before the physician's aide had come to trundle him out of her hospital room. When she thought about him, the nameless baby that she'd let go of one morning in the maternity ward at Mount Sinai, Jenny's arms wrapped themselves around her stomach. Robbed of her little boy, she'd been grief-stricken, though it was Jenny who'd signed the papers, waiving her rights, abandoning her first child. She'd missed most of the seventh grade.

"I want to keep you, Thing," she whispered in New Haven, rubbing her belly in a circular motion as she'd seen expectant mothers do. "What the fuck do we do now?" She felt an acute awareness of herself, the softness and heat of her own skin, not alone, replicating, pulsing, heart beating double-time, a twinning.

That night, when Dylan and his housemates drove to Rhode Island to see the Professor, who manufactured crystal, Jenny stayed in New Haven on her own. Mixing dye in the bathroom sink, she colored her hair, which had grown down to her shoulders, painting the goop on with a paintbrush, like shellac. An hour later, she became a brunette. She bundled her old clothes into her knapsack and pulled out a black dress, carefully folded, and a pair of pumps and stockings. This would be Nadia Larina's costume. A visual arts student, a Yalie who spoke of Beuys and Duchamp, Nadia was her alter ego. She was a chaste and conservative young lady. She was spoiled, self-possessed, and from a family that had once been extremely rich. She was the anti-Jenny.

It exhilarated her to don this outfit, like Superwoman, there in the basement of a squalid student house. She'd get herself out.

She arranged her hair into a tight, high ponytail and pulled on a black velvet headband—an accessory that her true, actual self would never wear. She smiled a prim, demure smile at herself, clipped on a pair of pearl earrings that she kept concealed in a zippered compartment of her knapsack, and encircled her neck with a strand of pearls. She'd stolen the pearls from Apartment 16A at 1010 Fifth Avenue, in Christopher's parents' building, the first week she'd begun to date him, along with an enormously valuable small painting. They'd raced back up the six floors to the Benedicts' penthouse, breathless, suppressing the squeals of laughter that later erupted in Christopher's old bedroom. They'd worn scarves tied around their faces, covering their noses and mouths, like a pair of bandits.

Donning the pearl earrings and necklace, she shucked off Jenny, the girl who needed food stamps at the grocery store. Nadia Tatiana Larina had never done anything degrading. She moved with haughty grandeur. Off Nadia went, across town, to the Yale campus, to the library.

Doc Orsin was the bartender in the yuppie pub on the other side of town. Nadia Tatiana Larina, bored of her myriad rich suitors, had her eye on him.

A guy like Doc, with his rolled-up shirtsleeves, his clean-shaven cheeks, his crew cut, and his rimless glasses, had a reassuringly masculine quality. He wasn't like Dylan's roommates. Doc was far removed from, say, Tad-the-Rad, a snide young rebel from M.I.T who hung around cadging cigarettes and vodka, with his condescending attitude, his sideburns, and his stovepipe hat. Doc wasn't cut from that cloth. Doc's father owned a fruit and vegetable stand on Staten Island. Doc was the first person in his family to attend college. Doc studied all day and tended bar all night, and through the weekend. He was trying to accomplish something.

"What can I get you?" said Doc, one night at the bar.

"Just an orange juice, thanks, Doc. I don't drink at all anymore," said Nadia.

A split second of silence took place. Nadia feared any further questions.

"Good for you," Doc said, his eyes gently releasing hers. "There's a study I'm reading which makes some connection between alcohol intake and mortality. It's not there in the data, but if you extrapolate. Want your orange juice on the rocks?"

"Yes, please."

"You got it, Nadia."

She let out a breath. She had every right to stop drinking, anyone could. Let him think she was a reformed alcoholic or a health nut. Nadia had been coming to the yuppie pub nightly for the last three weeks. When she wore her black sleeveless dress and her stolen pearls, she introduced herself as Nadia Tatiana Larina from an old Russian family that lived in Cornwall. Her last two names came from Tchaikovsky's opera, the one Christopher had brought her to on their first date. She'd been dressed in a twenty-dollar gown from the designer discount store; the Benedicts had left their unused season tickets at the box office. That had been just before they'd begun an Aktionist project: Robinhood, their game of stealing treasures from the Benedicts' building.

"What's your name?" she said to the bartender, boldly, setting her bare arms down on the bar counter and clasping her hands. Her fingers flashed with stolen rings. She felt pretty.

"You know my name, Nadia," Doc said, catching her eye for an instant while he scooped ice cubes with a metal utensil he kept behind the bar. It was shaped like a small shovel. "You just said it: 'Doc get me a drink. Doc, get me a juice.' And you said it last night, when you came by, and yesterday, too. 'Hamburger, Doc, medium rare.' Everyone calls me that around here."

"But Doc's a nickname, isn't it? That can't be your given name, the name you were born with." She tucked a stray strand of hair behind her ear. By then, she'd had her hair waved as part of her Nadia disguise. It felt thick and resilient, as if accruing energy, coiled to spring.

"I don't use the name my parents gave me when I was born," he said. "I hate it." He poured juice into a daiquiri glass for her and stirred it with a pink mixing stick. Doc stored hundreds of these novelty items in bins behind the bar. This one was shaped like a mermaid, with a naked torso, long hair, and a fish tail. Her figure was round at the bottom and the top, like a guitar. Nadia wondered if he'd selected the pink mermaid especially for her.

"You hate your name?" she said, taking the glass from him. The mermaid shifted in her bower of ice, clinking against the rim. Its machine-made, molded face looked a little like Nadia's, but she might have imagined it.

"Can I offer you further decoration?" said Doc, coquettishly, sorting through a bag of party favors. He picked out a tiny Japanese umbrella made of paper. He opened it and balanced it on the lip of her glass, his forehead moving close to Nadia's. They stayed like that, with his curls tickling Nadia's hairline.

"I can tell you what it is," he said, resting his elbows on the counter. He cupped his chin in his hands. His gaze had nothing in common with Christopher's. It was more intelligent and softer. "You have to promise, though. Not to laugh."

"Promise," she said. She drank her juice.

His cheeks colored as he produced a paper flower. "This is an Oriental snowdrop," he said. "You put it inside a cup of water, see, and it opens. Watch what it does." He let the paper flower fall into her water glass. "It takes just about fifteen seconds," he said. The purple paper in the bowl of water was expanding.

"So, tell me," said Nadia, reaching out to touch the flower with her fingertip.

"It's Dante. Dante Orsini," he said, glancing at her nervously.

"Why would I laugh at that?"

"It's a touch self-aggrandizing, don'tcha think? I registered at the university as Dan Orsin."

"Why? I think Dante Orsini suits you," said Nadia. An urge rose in her to reveal her true name, too. Her hand reached towards him and her mouth opened. No. She could not tell him, not now, not ever.

"To get ahead in the world," said Doc. "I'd rather not stick out. I'd rather fit in."

"But you're already ahead," said Nadia, heart racing. "You said you're going to medical school, aren't you?"

"People make assumptions. They think you're fresh off the boat," said Doc. "I'm an American citizen. I'd rather not remind everyone—my professors, lab technicians—that my mom and dad are illiterate, that they grew up on top of a mountain in Sardinia, herding goats. You know?"

"Sure."

"How about you?" asked Doc.

Opening and shutting her miniature paper umbrella, Nadia gave her practiced recitation. "My name is Nadia Tatiana Larina. I came to this country when I was five years old. My grandparents were White Russians who left everything behind and moved to England after the Revolution. My mother and father lived in... in, um, Cornwall, in a very... close-knit community... of Russian émigrés."

Again, Dan was quiet for a second, as if thinking. "Are they still around? Where are your folks these days?"

"We're estranged," Nadia said. "Look, I'm sorry, but I don't like to talk about it."

"I can respect that," said Doc.

"Thanks," said Nadia, curtly, and she felt as if he'd given her something more, just then, an offering.

Birth of Venus

Jenny was the chubby girl who'd posed nude for a line of coke.

Jenny danced around the Lava Lounge topless underneath her suspenders, a fat girl wearing someone's necktie and someone else's tinfoil tiara.

Jenny, laughing, charged into a stranger's stall in the men's room and climbed into the backseat of some idiot's hired limo.

Jenny sailed. She'd belonged, in her own eyes, to a higher rank, a weightless goddess with many arms, floating above the rest. But, in the minds of others, Jenny had been a bimbo.

The girl Christopher wanted had glossy dark sleek hair, the color of the black sable coat that hung about her like a cape, its silk-lined hem brushing the marble floor of the Metropolitan Museum.

The girl Christopher wanted looked petite inside her big coat. She had long fingers and suntanned hands.

Her feline face commanded adoration. She was the Other Woman, Jenny's nemesis. Jenny was no match for this gorgeous brunette rich girl and, even from across the room, before a single word was spoken, Jenny knew it.

"Christopher? Is that you?" the Other Woman asked, as she entered the fourth floor gallery of the museum.

Jenny and Christopher were standing in front of Botticelli's *Venus*, on loan from the Uffizi Gallery, at an exhibition preview for museum trustees and their families. Christopher at age twenty: sexy, disheveled, in a too-tight smock that he'd found in a thrift store and wore as an overcoat. He had, in the last few weeks, grown a Fu Manchu mustache. He wore rectangular glasses with bright blue lenses. He had shaved his head.

"Nadia, baby doll!" he'd called to the beautiful dark girl at the other end of the gallery. He walked towards her, comporting himself in a manner Jenny didn't often associate with Christopher—unctuous, obsequious, with both hands extended towards this attractive newcomer. "I thought you were in Lisbon, my darling!" he crowed. "When did you get back home?"

She took his hands in hers but stared with displeasure at his face. "Look at you," she said. "Did you forget to bathe or what?"

"I'm in art school, sweetheart," he explained. "Without you around, I've let myself go."

"Of course you did." Her head turned a fraction of an inch towards Jenny. The shapely dark eyebrows lifted, silently posing a question.

"This is Jenny," Christopher said, drawing her forward. Reaching towards Jenny to pat her on the back, as one might pat a pony, he said, "Jenny is a dog-walker. She takes care of my mother's birds, waters the plants. Jenny comes to us from the Second Chance Society, my mom's pet cause."

When they'd run into other friends of his, Christopher only said, "This is Jenny Rodriguez."

"You won't see *my* photograph in the society pages," Jenny said, awkwardly. It was intended to be humorous, but as she said this, Jenny regretted it.

"I expect I can see it someplace else, though?" asked Nadia.

Not sure what Nadia knew, what Nadia meant, Jenny saw she'd made a bad joke at her own expense.

The Rival looked hostile. "I thought I recognized you from an... art exhibition."

Horrified, Jenny burbled on: "I live in a housing project on 109th Street. Christopher thinks he's going on safari when he comes uptown to see me. We go out shooting rats with illegal handguns. That's been amusing for him."

"My name is Nadia, by the way," said the Rival, giving Jenny her hand, grandly, as if Jenny ought to kiss the back of it.

Later, in the park, Jenny stole Nadia's sunglasses and slipped them into her schoolbag. When Jenny put the glasses on, she'd become Nadia, Nadia who Christopher wanted, Nadia who had come to look at paintings, in a special private showing, in the middle of a Thursday afternoon, dressed in a floor-length sable coat.

"What fun to meet one of the girls you go slumming with," the Rival said, as Jenny, still within earshot, walked away from Christopher and Nadia.

The Secret Agent in the Attic

With a squeak of his brakes, Dan pulled into the driveway too fast, nearly colliding with a barrel of petunias. The freak snowstorm of early April already seemed far away. The meadow was abuzz with yellow-jackets and honeybees hovering over an abundance of June wildflowers. A hornet floated in lazy circles around a new nest in the eaves of the front porch. It would have to be destroyed. He didn't want one of the children getting stung.

Protecting them from Nadia would be harder. A full two months had passed since Dan had lost faith in her on her birthday. He'd read hundreds of pages of her correspondence, by now, having cracked her code and opened her safe. He'd been practicing what to say to her, alone in their hotel room, when he took her away for the Mercy gala weekend. Before taking any irreversible step, he needed proof; the convict's letters hinted at how to find it.

As he stood in his driveway staring up at Nadia's attic tower, he was reluctant to break her, shattering the charming con woman he'd made his wife. He breathed in the scent of his land and savored it—that sense, however false, of cozy domesticity, the pretty house, the sun-bleached wooden barrels where she'd planted her pansies and her marigolds. He could see things clearly, past and future, inter-cut, juxtaposed, Then and Now, just like in a movie: His two boys, waist-high, threw open the door and ran outside, shouting "Daddy,

Daddy!" as if Dan were not merely a father and a doctor, but the prime minister of a country. He saw Nadia and the kids surround him, as the tribe greets its cherished leader, patting him, kissing him while he ran his hands through their hair. But, for too long, Dan had entered the house hours after sunset. If they were home at all, his grown-up boys were upstairs in their rooms, finishing their homework in seclusion. Nadia stayed in the attic with Blondie, flipping through her fancy picture books.

Dan stood in the hallway. The house was cold and dark. Not even Blondie rushed over to woof at him. He was more houseguest than owner as he approached his home. He mounted the stairs to the attic. Unlike the rest of the house, it had never been renovated. The door didn't quite meet the floor. Drafts crept in from under the windowsills; the temperature was ten degrees lower here. Dan stood at the window and pulled back the curtains. Rough against his soft, dexterous surgeon's hands, these curtains bore no resemblance to anything else in the house, which Nadia had decorated in the style of an English country manor. They were ragged and cheap, like the room itself. They bore a garish pattern of zigzags in hot pink, black, and yellow. To complement her vulgar color scheme, Nadia had picked up a set of used furniture in a junk shop and had painted it to match, in magenta and black. A temporary refuge for a starving artist, it had the atmosphere of a student's first apartment.

As he glanced around the attic, Dan thought it odd that Nadia would choose to spend so much of her time here. Here in the crooked attic, the warped plank floors had never been sanded or refinished. Their uneven surface was covered by a worn carpet woven from rags. Instead of tasseled and embroidered pillows, only a simple crocheted afghan lay on a lumpy couch. There was no coffee table here, just an old steamer trunk made of a thin black metal, dented and scarred.

It was spare and cramped, without any of the decorative knickknacks that Nadia had inherited from her family and had arranged in groupings, on the other floors, on end tables and next to vases of dried flowers. Nadia had set up just one triptych of family photographs in the attic, on an embroidered runner she'd laid out on top of the bureau that she'd inherited from her great-grandmother, her namesake, Tatiana Larina, a prima ballerina in Diaghilev's company. Dan leaned down and studied the sepia-toned photographs of the Larina family, dating back to their glory days in the early 1900s. A young and beautiful Tatiana, her hair gathered in a sleek bun, her shoulders bare, was posed in profile. She had a long straight nose, a proud bearing, and a swanlike neck. A lace collar swooped down her chest to reveal a hint of cleavage. Her hands, folded in her lap, were covered with rings. Dan lifted the heavy heirloom silver frame and ran his thumb over the glass. He turned the frame over and tinkered with the closure. The back of the frame had been sealed over, covered with a square of navy blue velvet.

Inside the attic, Dan used Nadia's exacto blade to remove the velvet backing. He peeled it off, slowly, separating the fabric from the strip of wood, which clutched to the velvet with strands of sticky, yellowing old glue. He opened the mechanism which secured the photograph inside the frame and pulled it out. He looked, once more, at the portrait before examining the other side of the black-and-white photograph. Something was written here, in pencil. It had been erased. Dan held a magnifying glass over the paper. Now he could read the pencil marks.

In the upper right corner, on the back of the photograph, someone had written: "Moscow, 1906. Photos $5./set of twelve. 50 cents/ea."

The damning photograph shook in his hands. Just then, a light went on in Red Barn. Dan dropped the photo, which fluttered like a kite before landing on the carpet. He ran to the lamp and snapped it off. If she'd seen him in the attic window, anything might happen. He ducked to the floor. Crouching beside the steamer trunk, Dan stole a peek at Red Barn. Light emanated from the round window on the upper level, in the hayloft. The studio was her prison tower and her sanctuary. She had been, for him, a princess, descended from Russian nobility, sheltered by a trust fund. He'd been so focused on medical school that, despite a certain flickering suspicion, he had never seriously doubted her family history. She'd introduced herself as an aristocratic young artist who was estranged from a noble family. She had money in the bank and a few Larina heirlooms—a set of silver in a velvet-lined box; a small, exquisite still life in oil; and a string of pearls. All of it from a junk shop, or stolen loot.

From the inner pocket of his jacket Dan withdrew his medical flashlight, the one he shined inside his patients' mouths to check for signs of cancer spreading to the throat. He directed its beam towards the floor and kept the bulb covered with his hand, so its ray wouldn't be visible from outside. The bright light was blocked by his fingers, which glowed red from his blood. He pounced upon the steamer trunk and opened it on an impulse. The lid flew back on its hinges; she'd left the key inside the lock. Inside, beneath a stack of film canisters, he found two small glass bottles. Each was half-filled with a clear liquid. He uncapped one of the transparent rubber stoppers, touched the liquid with his finger, and put it in his mouth. It tasted salty. When he tipped it over, he saw a label on the bottom. In miniscule print, it said: "Baum & Geld Lenscrafters. Store at room temperature in sterile saline solution. 'Brown Eyed Girl' extended wear soft colored contact lenses in dark brown."

He had not known her to wear contact lenses. She had changed the color of her irises. Nothing was real, not even Nadia's eyes.

PART THREE:

Simone

Return of the Prodigal

“Shit,” said Christopher, when the front door of a house sprang open early one morning in the town of Riverbend. Christopher, who stood on a hill across the road, bent down now, scuttling backwards, rustling through the dry dead leaves, hiding himself further in the brush. He watched a woman emerge from the Victorian house and stand on the veranda in a long white bathrobe. She was a brunette, not a blonde. She was tall and slim, not fleshy and curvaceous as he remembered her. Squatting down on his haunches, stiff with the cold, Christopher wondered if he'd made a mistake. Despite the shiny brass number on the door which identified it as number 24, she might not be the right woman. Had she passed by him in the street, he would not have known her. Her dark hair was gathered up high in a topknot on her small, delicate head. Her movements were clipped as she walked across the front porch to examine the fronds of a potted tree. But despite all of this he sensed that the stranger on the porch was his Jenny. He couldn't say why it had to be Jenny and still it did. Her posture as she stood holding the watering can, the attitude, the hand on the hip, the line of her cheek, the long neck, the way his breathing fluttered as she approached the front steps, as she looked up and down the road in each direction—he recognized her in his nerve endings.

What the hell was she doing, anyway? She stared down at the

lawn, tilted her head this way and that, as if she had misplaced something. She hopped down the stairway, stooped, and retrieved an object from the stubbly brown winter grass. It was a newspaper. That was all. She'd come out here to get the Sunday paper, and now she was turning, rubbing her arms in the cold, and running back up the stairs with the bundle clutched against her chest.

Christopher perceived each of her movements, snap snap snap, with the lightning speed of a lens and an aperture, though he had no camera, now. He caught her only with his mind, and it was only his eyes that recorded her, capturing in a fraction of a second who she'd become. She was the woman with the biggest house in Riverbend, the house on the corner of Bridge Street; the woman who had a satiny white robe and black pajamas with pink piping at the seams. She wore narrow slippers and no socks. He'd seen a glimpse of her skin: her wrists, her ankles, her face. He'd seen her as she was, without makeup, in her nightclothes; he'd seen parts of her that had once belonged to him.

When the door closed, Christopher turned from the woman who'd wanted to marry him, wending his way back where he'd come from, through the muddy leaves and the exposed roots with their craggy gray bark, among the fir trees and the mossy boulders, carefully stepping over the rocks, in a pair of sneakers he'd purchased at the dollar store for ninety-nine cents. Following the stream, he hiked up one hill and down another. Snow and ice dotted either side of the streambed. A broken tree branch lay in the middle of the water, upturned. It looked to Christopher like a ladder to the sky. But the sky was not as he remembered it, and he was no longer clear on his purpose. The sky now dwarfed him, shrank him to the size of a black ant. It looked down upon him, vast and unforgiving.

Christopher was a stranger here, with no place to go. The wind cut into his thin coat and gnawed at his hands, which he clenched tightly inside his pockets. His sneakers, as if of their own volition, took the easiest route, following a footpath that had been made by some other boots there in the snow. He walked for a long time, bothered by the orange and black posters that said: PRIVATE PROPERTY. NO CAMPING. What shitheads people were; this land was plentiful and wide, wilderness, without any houses or signs of human habitation, and yet some prick had to hang his little sign on the trunks of the trees: KEEP OFF. THIS IS MINE.

A half-hour passed before he found a refuge. In the wooded countryside, he spotted a lopsided vacant shack, its roof moldering. He rammed the door with his shoulder. The rusty chain held, but the door gave way, the soft, decaying wood splitting apart. The chain gave him half a foot of space to squeeze through. The shed was empty, except for a couple of metal toolboxes, a bundle of yellow newspapers, a hoe, and a shovel. It was only marginally warmer, but out of the wind. It seemed entirely possible that he might die there, freezing, as he slept. His face was raw from windburn and the spattered snow. With two uncoordinated hands, swollen into numb mitts, he arranged the crumbling newspapers to make himself a nest. He curled on his side, shivering, and covered his legs and shoulders with newspaper sheets. Christopher drew his knees up to his chest and thrust his arms between his thighs, where he felt his own warmth, an inadequate but steady-burning furnace. His eyes focused on the wall of the shed and the leaf-strewn dirt floor near his head. He thought continually of Jenny, her face imploring him to do something that he couldn't yet comprehend. She wasn't the way he'd expected her to be—the sheepskin coat, hanging open; the white robe under the coat; the black pajamas; the pointy slippers on her feet—all of it wrong for her, as if she had decked herself out in someone else's clothes.

He held on to her image as his thoughts screamed: It's too fucken cold. "Fuck shit, fuck shit, fuck shit," he whispered, his teeth chattering. Lying under the newspapers wasn't helping. The ground was frozen solid. He sat up again, scattering the papers, looking frantically around the shed for something, anything—wood to start a fire, a knife to plunge in his chest.

"Jenny fuck fuck Jenny," he muttered. She'd both honored him and disappointed him. Had he expected her, these twenty-five years later, to be dressed in those torn, tight jeans that showed her fishnet stockings poking through the holes in the seat of her pants? Had he expected her, after a quarter century, to be the obese urchin with the hungry eyes? Had he hoped she'd remain forever young for him?

Some hours later, he had lost sensation in his fingers, nose, and feet. He clutched his fishing line in his fist, but he couldn't feel it.

Here was the thing that was bugging him. He'd been compelled to come all this way to Riverbend, certain that if he found Jenny again, his destiny would be fulfilled. And here he was in her town, on her private fucking property, in her shed. And he knew beyond doubt that Jenny didn't exist. Jenny was his fiction, his creation, his protagonist. He'd invented her in his imagination while the years passed in solitude at Triton. Jenny was the girl with the broken front tooth and the crazy grin… the girl who never wore underwear… the girl who'd do anything with anybody, anywhere… the only person who'd ever loved him. She'd flourished in his dreams but out here, in life, she'd ceased to be.

A Stranger at the Door

Slicing scallions on a wooden cutting board in the kitchen, Nadia set down her knife at the sound of the doorbell. She stood motionless for a moment, chin raised, listening. She'd detected some other reverberation—a rustling in the air, a rumor. She'd been on edge for weeks, ever since she'd heard the news from Dylan. A dozen times she'd run breathlessly—for a ringing telephone, a pealing bell. Old half-buried pathways in her brain circuitry had arisen like excavated ruins. But this time, as Nadia walked down the hallway and peered out the window, she knew.

She recognized him right away. His eyes. Time had transformed the man who stood on her stoop, wrapping him in a middle-aged disguise. The long-haired rascal, in faded jeans and shredded T-shirt, languid, slinky, seductive, high on everything in the senator's medicine cabinet, had vanished. Here was a weathered version of the young man she'd once adored beyond reason. Now, he was stoop-shouldered, with crow's-feet and a receding hairline. It didn't matter. He had come to her. Her heart, her most treacherous enemy, leapt in her breast to go to him.

Stepping out of sight, into the corner, Nadia studied Christopher through the pebbled-glass window. He had remained a handsome man. He had his hands in his pockets. She could see the tears in his trousers, no longer an affectation. His clothing was ragged.

His thin-soled navy-blue sneakers offered no protection against the snow. A chaotic feeling rose up in her throat as she examined him through the glass. She was like a hatchling that had imprinted onto its first love. He belonged to her. She'd step outside and let an attractive drifter, her Christopher, take her by the hand. No decisions had to be made; no arguments; no words exchanged. Quickly, like two fugitives, they'd steal away together, gliding across the snow to the garage. Into the jeep, down the driveway, to the interstate: They'd be gone. Alone together, back where they'd left off.

He would mistreat her, of course he would, as he'd done before.

Nadia opened the door.

His eyes did what they'd always done, they caught at hers. It was here that Christopher was utterly unaltered. These eyes were keen and shining. It unsettled her to see these eyes of the young man left behind, in this older, wider, careworn face.

"Hey, Jenny," he said, inclining his chin to nod at her.

Nervous, Nadia spoke almost automatically. "I'm sorry, but you must have the wrong address. There's no one here by that name."

"Very funny," said Christopher.

"Who is it," she said, quaking in the cold, "that you're looking for?"

"I guess I caught you at a bad time," said Christopher, turning towards the hallway and squinting at the din of a distant detonation. Her sons were playing a computer game, exploding spaceships, in the family room. "When can I really talk to you?" he asked, pinning her with his direct gaze. "Come on. It's me."

She clutched at the lapel of her coat. "Okay," she relented. "So, how are you?"

"Me? Oh, I'm real terrific," he said. Looking past the house towards the riverbank, he screened his eyes with one hand. "I was just in the neighborhood, and I thought I'd stop by to say hi."

"Well. Hi," she said.

"I came over here to ask you. Would you ever want to have a

cup of coffee with me sometime?" He laughed hoarsely, as if at the preposterousness of it.

"I...," she began.

"Who's at the door, Dear?" Dan's voice rang out from the top of the stairs. "Is it a delivery from Mercy?"

Nadia wrung her hands as Dan turned towards the hallway. "I've got it, Dan!" she cried. "It's for me!" She listened for Dan's footsteps as he walked away towards his study. No, she explained to herself, no, no, she couldn't go. She was grabbing for her handbag now. Rummaging through it ineffectually, butterfingered, she handed Christopher something she had never meant to give.

He took it, his eyes on hers, without looking at it.

"Maybe," he said, "I could see my kid?"

"I'm sorry, no," she said, lowering her voice. "You have to understand, not now. It's too late, Christopher. I can't."

"I am *not* trying to fuck things up for you," he said, softly but emphatically. "Please believe that."

"You can't be standing here. You have to go," she said in an undertone.

"Why can't I, though?" He caught her by the sleeve. They both glanced down at the place where his fist grasped the cuff of her robe. "Can't I just take one look at my own son or daughter?" he asked. "It's what I want." Letting go of her, he crossed his arms over his chest.

Nadia bit the insides of her cheeks. She swung the door open wide. "She's right there," she whispered, leaning into him, speaking into his ear, for only Christopher to hear.

"Okay," he whispered back. She felt his breath on her neck. He tipped his head to the side, looking down the hallway into her house. They were standing so close together now that a lock of his hair fell against her shoulder.

"That's our daughter," she told him. "Simone."

The night before, Simone had come over to borrow the good china dinner service for a catering job, and she had stayed the night in her girlhood bedroom on the third floor. She'd recruited her brothers to help her earlier that morning, but they'd retired to the couch by now, and Simone was tramping up and down the hallway in her army boots, carting trays and pitchers up from the basement.

Nadia gripped the table by the coat rack, rattling a vase with her jittery movements. Simone, her back to them, plodded along, unaware that she was being looked at. She might have been Jenny's sister, from behind, with her solid, guitar-shaped figure, spiked hair, studded belt, falling-down jeans baggy at the knees. She set a crateful of china down on the floor, stood up, and pushed the hair off her face. She saw Christopher by the door. Wordlessly, she acknowledged his entrance into the house, looking at him with fierce, momentary curiosity.

"Ma!" she bellowed, hands on hips. "What the fuck is this? Can you close the door already, please, here? Do you *mind*? It's colder than a witch's tit!"

Nadia could have sworn that Simone was showing off for the visitor.

"Hello," said Christopher, humbly. His prominent Adam's apple leapt up and down, as if he were swallowing repeatedly.

"Who is this?" demanded Simone, surly.

"He's here to collect donations for the…," Nadia began.

"Salvation Army," Christopher finished, almost inaudibly.

Christopher stood in the foyer with his hands clasped in front of him, watching their daughter clomping along, her thick soles thumping on the Turkish runner. She entered the basement vestibule, gave one last inquisitive look at him, and disappeared.

"Who came to the door before?" asked Dan, as Jeremy passed him the bowl of salad.

"Oh," said Nadia, carefully, "It was a guy collecting old coats and blankets for… for the homeless… for charity. I'd asked him to come and then I'd forgotten. I haven't even cleaned out the closets." She was certain everyone at the table was staring at her; she felt her limbs trembling; her face felt warm. But her family was focused on their dinners. Will was grabbing the breadbasket. Jeremy was spearing a sweet potato with his fork from halfway down the table. Simone had gone.

"Jeremy," said Nadia, "do not reach for food like an ape, please. I will pass the potatoes to you."

Jeremy sat down.

The conversations continued, the voices murmured, the glasses were refilled with mineral water, and the silver clinked against the china.

Pardon Me, Miss

Christopher stepped away from her door.

"Wait," she said, following him out into the cold. Her hand jerked upwards to touch his face. She gave his chin a clumsy stroking. He did not dare breathe. He watched her slow undoing. So then, he'd been right. Nothing had changed between them. He caught her in his arms and pulled her to him. He felt all of her go over to him, just like that, out on her front porch, with her family in earshot, yielding to him. Christopher the pariah in his dirty blue parka. She was his for the taking. She turned him into a demigod. He held her close, the embrace telling her what he'd never speak aloud.

He didn't even try to kiss her. When they pulled apart, he saw her try to organize herself.

"Well, good seeing you," he heard himself saying.

She made a murmur of agreement. She reached behind her, into the hall, and thrust a woolen bundle at him. "It's eighteen degrees out," she said, eyes welling up. "Do you have someplace warm to go?"

"Jenny," he said, stirred, "I do. I'm fine. I want to thank you." He watched her struggle to regain composure.

"Until next time, then," she said, turning her palm upwards to the ceiling, her hand stretching out to bridge the space between them.

He brought her hand to his lips and kissed the back of it. Then the door was closed again and he scarcely knew what had happened. Whatever it was, it had puffed him up with pride. She had bestowed blessings upon him: her cheek against his, her heat, a trace of her old style.

The silky woolen things she'd given him must have been her own mittens. They had a band of fur trim around the wrists. The ladies' mittens were a size seven, according to the tag sewn into the hem. They were, the label said, 100 percent angora. They should have been too small, but they were woven loosely, and when he slipped the right mitten over his hand, it fit him snugly. As he walked down Jenny's front steps and into Jenny's yard, Christopher dug into his pocket and pulled out the envelope she'd handed him. His breath came fast. He squinted down at the envelope he held in his pink downy mitt. His name was there, in her handwriting, black letters spelling out "Christopher Benedict," and the address of the penitentiary. It was stamped, ready to be mailed. But the envelope was creased and its edges were blunted, worn soft by repeated rubbings against other objects inside her bag. How long had she been carrying the damn envelope around?

He took great thirsty gulps of frozen air. She had filled him up; he felt no sorrow now, no cold. He hurried away from Jenny's house with a swelling, soaring sense of gladness—and he ran so fast that he skidded on the sheet of ice that covered the driveway, nearly falling to the ground, catching himself on a tree branch and steadying himself against the trunk. Sliding, lurching, sinking into the ice-crusted snowdrifts, he retired to his burrow, the shack in the woods.

He tore the envelope open with his teeth. He stared at the paper, knowing what it would say before he had even finished reading her love letter.

In years past, words like these would have had a different effect on him, he thought. Seeing her confusion, he would have stepped in to confuse her further. This time, though, he would be merciful and leave her in peace. He had what he'd wanted: her declaration. He felt holy and neuter, like a Trappist monk. He felt pure and old, a tribal elder on the verge of a breakthrough, enlightenment. A great calm settled over him with the knowledge that he had found his sunken treasure in one girl's heedless passion for him. Crouching on the ground outside the shack, he began to poke a hole in the snow with his thumb. Inside the hole, he placed the coil of fishing line. Even if he never saw her again, he had won.

He murmured a silent prayer of atonement as he gave the fishing line a burial, covering it up with pebbles, twigs, frozen clots of dead leaves. He stood up, stomped his feet and, grinning wide, ran crazily outside like a child again, down the hill, seeing the beauty of the place, its glittering sparkles of ice and icicles on the bare white branches, enchanted, dazzling. He felt lighter, more fluid, stronger. He made his way to the road. He walked along with a sense of purpose and direction, full of hope because Jenny had given him his absolution.

Tender Mercies

Returning to Riverbend from the Mercy gala in Manhattan, Dan sat on the train with Nadia beside him. He listened to the muted roar of the steel wheels beneath their business-class car, while the train rocked him from side to side. Nadia, who had taken the window seat, was terribly quiet. She hadn't answered any of his questions about the letters addressed to Jenny X. During the Auction for Mercy the night before, she'd ordered glass after glass of cognac until, on a drunken whim, she'd placed a bid of $800 for a hideous ceramic umbrella stand. Dan hadn't intervened.

This morning over breakfast at the hotel, she'd been wan and penitential, ladling the fresh fruit salad onto her plate with a glazed expression, somnambulant. Now, on the train, all Dan could see of her was her back and shoulders, clad in a jacket the color of dark chocolate. From behind the current issue of *American Oncology,* Dan watched her out of the corner of his eye, as if she were a rare specimen and he were bird-watching. He registered the details of her appearance and behavior. He saw she continued to wear her wedding ring. She hadn't, he noted, put her hair up today. Stringy and un-brushed, it covered her face as she leaned forward to take ginger sips from her paper cup. It was the third coffee she'd ordered from the café car in the past half an hour. She looked ill. She had to be hungover.

She jolted up when the train screeched, switching tracks uptown, and suddenly became intent, focused on the passing scenery. Now and then, she gave her head a fierce toss, as if she'd been talking to herself. She seemed to have traveled far away from Dan. Her chest heaved, inhaling.

"Look, don't misunderstand. I don't want a divorce," he heard himself say softly.

Nadia set down her paper cup with care. She placed both hands on the plastic tray in front of her, splaying her fingers. Her hands were naked today, bare except for the one gold band. Dan wondered what had become of all her jewelry.

"Don't you know that?" Dan asked, drawing nearer. He sniffed the air for her scent, the commingled odors of his wife, her soaps, her creams, her skin, her powders, her perfumes.

She gave one sharp nod of agreement, her small pointed chin moving from side to side: Yes.

Dan heard a noise. It was his respiration. Relieved, resolved, he had let out a sigh. Dan placed his thumb on the vein inside his own wrist; he could feel his pulse beating at a steady rate. It was decided then. She could keep her secrets. She had come to him with her secrets intact. As an aspiring physician, he'd recognized her condition, soon after they met, almost immediately. She'd flinched, in evident discomfort, the night he'd first caressed her breasts. He'd heard her regurgitate in the dormitory bathroom in the mornings. He'd intuited her dilemma. She had been with someone else before him and Dan accepted her, in flight, pregnant with another man's child. Her romantic history, her scar tissue, the in-laws he'd never been introduced to, the beautiful Dutch still life with no provenance. He had trained his eye on other things, accepting what she'd given to him while leaving the rest alone. Now he would hold on to his mystery, his Nadia.

The package from Christopher Benedict was like a third person who traveled with them. It sat inside her bag, at her feet, tucked halfway underneath the seat in front of her. The yellow envelope, fat with Christopher's jottings, poked up between the leather handles. Dan could read the first half of the return address "U.S. Correctional."

"Dan," Nadia said as the train groaned to a standstill above a blighted stretch of streets. Broken windows glittered from vacant, discolored buildings. A single white window grille of ornamental wrought iron led onto a wall of cement; the houses here had been bricked up. Detached wooden doors were stacked on the rubble in a heap. An old staircase sat by itself on the asphalt, leading to empty space.

"Yes, baby," said Dan, who had never called Nadia "baby" before. Incrementally, as a plant seeks light through phototropism, Nadia inched over towards him. Her arm reached back, her hand grazing his tweed jacket. She sniffled. The tip of her nose was red, like that of someone suffering from allergies.

"We're here," she said.

"Um, no," Dan corrected her. He looked down at his wristwatch. "We only got on the train thirty minutes ago. We won't get to Riverbend until about two." Nadia didn't quite seem to know where they were. She must have had a lot to drink last night, he thought.

But she wasn't listening. She leaned forward and tapped on the window excitedly. "Right there," she told him, pointing. "Quick, quick! Before we pass it."

He looked out the window as instructed.

"See that red brick building?" Nadia asked. "See it? The one on the corner. Dan, look! The third window, counting down from the roof! There's a dead sort of a spider plant in a jar on the windowsill!"

"Yes," Dan said, but there were hundreds of buildings, and he didn't have the slightest idea which one Nadia meant.

Agitated, she hit the glass with the heel of her hand. "There, there!" she said, as the train passed by through the slums—a basketball court with faded graffiti on the walls, a threadbare baseball diamond, a row of pockmarked houses.

"What is it?" Dan asked.

"That's the block," Nadia said. "That's the building." The train seemed to wait, stalled near this desolate corner for an instant, before gathering steam and bulleting past it. They passed a billboard and an expanse of grass, strewn with litter, by the highway.

"You lived there," Dan said. "That was where you lived."

"Yes, that's right," she said, "Jenny did." He heard her exhale. "I did, Dante."

Hand in hand, in a serene silence, they rode back home to Riverbend—to begin.

The Homecoming

Six hundred years ago, in the Santa Maria del Carmine Church, Masaccio frescoed *The Expulsion of Adam and Eve from the Garden* in radiant pastels. Christopher first saw the fresco cycle during his junior year of high school, walking through the cloisters with his classmates to reach the tiny chapel. Adam and Eve appeared to stand behind a heavy dark gray veil. While the faithful came to pray, gazing up at the serpent with a human head wound around the trunk of the Tree of Knowledge, candles' smoke had been accumulating on the church walls since the fifteenth century.

As Christopher trudged along the side of the road in Riverbend, his breath forming white puffs in the air in front of him, he held the gemlike Masaccio in his mind. It had been decades since he'd visited the fresco, but the face of Eve remained with him. Her face had been rendered by the twenty-seven-year-old painter with strikingly modern starkness. He'd distilled her expression into three brushstrokes, three circles, two round eyes, a mouth. The remorse on that face had been unforgettable. Looking at it, back then, Christopher had almost heard a distant wail.

He'd hoped that the doors to paradise—an Eden of his own invention—would be reopened for him. He had formulated no other plan than to get his sorry ass to Jenny's house. He'd nursed a mystical hope that once he'd arrived at his destination, a miracle would occur. He'd no longer be a cipher.

He had received signs and wonders. Jenny's gloves. Jenny's love letter. He tried to turn his attention to the immediate crisis: his need for shelter and nourishment. The road remained right there, just ahead, black asphalt and white lines, hills in the distance, the lights of a town, the shapes of houses, all spread out before him. Like some mountaineer who had become separated from his tour guide in the Himalayas, all he could do was keep on going, hoping he'd live long enough to reach a destination.

He turned at the sound of a car approaching to his left. It was a small white van with the words THE SWEET SYNDICATE painted on the door above an illustration of cookies, pies, and cakes. Remarkably, this van slowed down to a creep. Leaning out the window across the driver's seat was a face he recognized with a start. It began to speak.

"Can I give you a lift?" she asked.

The door to the van was opening to him and his sore feet were rushing him toward the vehicle. Enveloped by the scent of butter and honey, Christopher was climbing in.

"I don't know how to thank you, Miss," he said. "It's dangerous to pick up hitchhikers. I hope you don't usually do this."

"I thought I could make an exception for you," said Simone, accelerating, focusing her attention intently on the road. "After all, you're my father, aren't you?"

A piercing sensation sent Christopher far back into his seat, with his fist pressed against his chest.

"Don't have a fucking heart attack on me," said Simone.

He gasped for breath for a little while and then the storm passed. "Don't worry about me," he said. "I'm like a cockroach. Indestructible."

"It would suck to meet your dad for the first time and in, like, two seconds, have him die. To be the one who killed your dad by freaking him out."

"That would suck," Christopher agreed.

"I've been waiting for you to show up," she said, taking a hard left and pulling on the steering wheel. An armload of silvery gypsy bangles jangled musically, like chimes.

"Have you?" he said, stealthily swatting the moisture away from his eyes. He looked out the window at a ranch, where a flock of sheep were waddling over a meadow. A slow whining electronic music played over Simone's radio.

"My mom kept a diary back when she was dating you and everything," she said to him.

"Oh?"

"I found it one night in, like, the seventh grade. I wasn't exactly surprised. I never fit in anyplace. To have someone like you as my biological father, it explained a lot of things."

"A guy with a criminal record, you mean?"

"Yeah, basically."

He stared at the steering wheel where his child's pale white hand was marked by a tattoo. "Some tattoo you got there," he said, disconsolate that she'd bought into the new hypocrisy racket. He made a fist. "Check this one out." He showed her the "666" on his knuckles. "I made it myself, with the point of a jackknife. In those days, see, that's what we'd do."

"See what mine says, though?" asked Simone.

He leaned down to take a closer look. "Um, it looks like a bloodshot eyeball," he ventured, examining the squiggle on her skin.

"It's a globe with an 'A' inside," she said. "I read about your art projects. The Bond Street Aktionists? Way cool. I agree with you."

"You *do*?"

"Aktion rules," said Simone, lifting her hand from the wheel and crossing her fingers in the old Aktionist salute.

"Simone?" he began.

"Yeah?"

"Simone Benedict," he marveled, "It's really something else to see you, kiddo." Reaching out to the steering wheel, he covered Simone's tattooed hand with his own, pressing it once, gingerly, before releasing her.

Acknowledgments

I became a writer with some idea that it would allow me to be utterly and gloriously independent. How wrong I was. Happily, I have been buoyed and guided by others. No words are adequate to describe my thanks to Vito J. Racanelli. His dedication to the project of literature is unshakable and his instincts are unerring. I am grateful to mentors, allies, editors and co-conspirators: Janet Dierbeck, Anne Edgar, Nora Eisenberg, Elizabeth England, Joshua Furst, D.W. Gibson, Ena Heller, Pagan Kennedy, Dale Peck, David Rakoff, Choire Sicha, Irene Skolnick, Pat Towers, Margo Viscusi and Jaime Wolf.

Special thanks to the Brooklyn Writers' Space, and particularly to its five indispensible, gifted muses: Heather Chaplin, Marian Fontana, Susan Gregory Thomas, Becky Mode and Martha Schwendener.

It's been an honor and a pleasure to work with two visionary publishers, John Oakes and Colin Robinson.

And thank you, especially, to Bingham Bryant and the ferociously talented forces of Mischief + Mayhem.

MISCHIEF + MAYHEM

Mischief + Mayhem is an editorial collective affiliated with OR Books. The group came together in response to the increasingly homogenized books that corporate publishers and chain retailers have determined will sell the most copies. Recognizing that there are readers who want to be challenged instead of placated, Mischief + Mayhem promulgates writing unconcerned with having to please conservative editorial boards or corporate bookstore executives. The Mischief + Mayhem collective comprises Lisa Dierbeck, Joshua Furst, D.W. Gibson, Dale Peck and Choire Sicha.

www.MischiefandMayhemBooks.com.